SILHOUETTE AND THE SHADOW

DELANEY ANDREWS

SILHOUETTE
AND THE
SHADOW

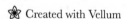 Created with Vellum

For my dad, Flip. Thank you for helping me discover my love of stories!
I miss you every day.

CHAPTER
ONE

I DIDN'T INTEND TO START MY DAY HALF-CONSCIOUS AND ON fire.

The miserable, icy breeze clawed at the line of exposed skin at my neck and wormed beneath my clothes. It threatened one last *snow* before spring fully arrived in Upstate City. I loathed the cold with every cubic inch of my short frame. Winters? No thanks, hard pass. Send me to Aruba. See you never.

Pale fingers going purple at the tips, I pulled my flannel tight over my sweatshirt and huddled closer to the small bonfire burning in the middle of the stone table. The flames jutted toward the sky, sinking their claws into the city's trademark shades of murky taupe.

The everlasting flame set in the middle of Terrace Park was a monument to the local vigilante. I sat on one of the benches circling the table, meant for viewers to use while reflecting in gratitude for all the hero had done. I snorted. He disappeared soon after the monument was completed.

People called him the Slip—slight, sneaky, and able to evade cops and criminals alike. Witnesses claimed he could lift a car, bulldoze a concrete barricade, and even leap to building roofs from the ground. His primary skill was evasiveness, so much so that many of the rumors surrounding the Slip were uncorroborated.

Superheroes and vigilantes weren't uncommon. Most cities had at least one—whether it was a justice enthusiast in a homemade suit or a bona fide mutant.

I didn't care about the Slip or his abilities. This was the only place I could feel close to my mother. This was the first time I visited since she died.

She'd been gone for almost a year, and grief always accompanied me. Sometimes as a small, sharp ache, and others a yawning chasm of misery in my chest. She'd helped build this monument not long before he died. Her name was etched into one of the donor tiles along the side.

Adelaide Alloway-Leo

My mom supported the Slip's work, among many other local community betterment initiatives. I supposed I should be grateful to have somewhere to connect with her. Mom didn't have a grave site. Just ashes, and Sam wouldn't tell me where he kept the gray tin from the funeral home.

"I miss you every day," I said, brushing my frozen fingers over the curves of her name. I suppressed the urge to carve my name beneath hers with a key: Melbourne Alloway. So people would know we belonged together. Pressure behind my eyes warned of frustrated tears on the way. I blinked furiously until they receded.

The wind howled in response, whipping the flames and the skeletal tree branches arcing overhead. My shivers doubled as a fluttering sensation jarred my stomach, a telltale sign every time I collapsed. I hadn't expected it to be this cold so early in the morning, but I wanted to make my visit without anyone else around.

"Come on," I growled at my body, "Keep it together."

The cold bench bit through my jeans, but the fire danced, beckoning me with a promise of warmth. I leaned forward and rested my head on my hand at the table's edge, mesmerized by the flames.

I squeezed my eyes closed, sure I could fend off one of the fainting spells that constantly lurked at the back of my head, prepared to pounce.

Please not today, I begged.

My body denied the request. The rustling of the trees muted out. The darkness behind my eyelids solidified like ice across a deep winter lake.

I felt my forehead connect with the cement table as if from a distance. Pain cracked the ice in my head, jolting me from near-unconsciousness.

Cracking open my bleary eyes, I saw my arm splayed toward the fire. A streak of beautiful flames ate up my sleeve.

I flailed with a yelp, slipping off the bench to land in an unceremonious pile of twenty-something on the frigid sidewalk.

My collision with the ground subdued the flames a little. I batted the rest in a panic with my free hand. They went out with a sour hiss, like I had ruined their fun.

The scent of burning chemicals bit through the air as I pushed aside my sleeve's cheap, melted fibers, hot and sticky against my fingers. My arm was bright pink and warm to the touch, but otherwise unmarked. I'd come to before any real damage could be done.

I rolled onto my back and stared at the sky, gasping. Crisis averted, mostly.

I hauled myself to my feet and attempted to roll my sleeve to hide the damage as I began the trudge home, smoke trailing in my wake.

Sam was right. I brought destruction everywhere I went.

🔥🔥🔥

LIKE A PRISON, SAM'S HOUSE WAS UTILITARIAN IN ITS grayness. Even the patchy lawn looked sickly. It definitely wasn't the type of house where a child's height was measured on a door frame each year, but I wasn't very tall anyway.

There were decent parts, like the rumbling old iron radiators, but thinking of it as home would make it harder to leave, which was the plan.

I climbed the crooked front steps, stopping only to grab a package that had been left on the tiny porch.

My eyes narrowed. It was a pristine, white, padded envelope, addressed to me.

I didn't get mail. Ever.

My breath quickened. Maybe it was from a college. I'd sent a few applications, but it was late in the season to guarantee admission. I was several years removed from high school and my grades had been average, but higher education was the best plan I'd come up with to escape Sam. And like all of my goals, this was one he tried to deter me from. Still, I kept up my argument, hoping he'd eventually relent and cosign a loan. Then, after a semester or two, I would transfer and never see him again.

I glanced at the package again. The return address was smudged. Tucking it beneath my arm and pulling my flannel tight over my torso, I shoved through the front door.

Thatcher gave her usual greeting from the kitchen table, a quick flick of her brown eyes up from her laptop screen to me and back, then the question: "How are you feeling?"

She started as Sam's research assistant, but turned more into a babysitter after my mom died. Thatcher spent most days here, fielding phone calls, scowling, and ensuring I didn't escape Sam's clutches.

"Fine," I called as I ducked through the opposite doorway and headed straight for the radiator in the cramped living room. The sun finally peered with promise over the trees outside the window. I shot a resentful glower its way.

I pressed my fingers directly to the radiator's indents, savoring the heat as it nuzzled my palms. Unconsciousness left its usual calling card, a cloudy headache tinged with the feeling that my brain and body weren't connected properly.

Thatcher came up behind me. "You look paler than usual."

I snorted, turning toward her and pressing against the radiator for more warmth. "It was just a walk. I needed some air. I didn't think to grab a coat."

She crossed her arms, the dark brown skin tight across her knuckles. Including her goddess braids, Kaye Thatcher was six feet of zero nonsense.

"You're bleeding," she said with a pointed stare at my forehead.

I swore, one hand flying up to feel the tacky blood where my head had met concrete. "I fainted in the park."

Thatcher looked unsurprised. "Of course you did. Now I need to—"

"Yeah, yeah. Let me clean up first."

She turned away and I bolted for my room, stashing the package beneath the quilt on my small bed before ducking into the bathroom for a clean towel to hold to my head.

When I returned, a needle and tubes were already spread on the dinged-up table. Thatcher snapped her laptop shut and looked me up and down.

"You smell like smoke." Her eyes narrowed. "Did you do something that will land me in trouble with your dad?"

I winced, having been too distracted by my mysterious package to change out of my singed shirt, though the damage was hidden in my rolled cuff. As Thatcher waited for an explanation, her fingers traced her sweater's knit pattern. Her eyes followed, like it was the most interesting puzzle in the world.

I offered a sweet smile. "I didn't do anything Sam wouldn't approve of. Promise."

Until the past year, Sam was never in my life regularly. He loved my mom more than anything, but had little interest in me. His job kept him traveling most of the time. As host and star of *Samson Alloway's Pet Project* on Chanimal, that environment-themed streaming service, his chiseled face and sky-blue eyes framed by crow's feet graced the televisions of most households across the country. Who wouldn't be endeared by a scruffy man determining if wildlife rehab facilities are up to snuff?

Me. His neglected only child. That's who.

After Mom died, Sam bought the house in a panic and moved me in with him. My part-time job at Upstate City's sole coffee shop, Sip the Bean, wouldn't cover my own rent somewhere else, so I didn't mind. He remained distant, like usual, but then my fainting started.

The first time was at home. The second was behind the wheel of my car, and that's when Sam lost it. As my fainting spells became more frequent, Sam became more of a jailer, attempting to control and reduce my movements as much as possible.

"Your irresponsibility could get someone killed!" he'd screamed after the incident with the car, when I'd simply driven it into a ditch and totaled it.

"Someone *else*," he'd huffed under his breath. He wasn't home the day Mom died, but I was.

He got my driver's license suspended, and Thatcher started coming around, applying her work as a vet to try and diagnose me while serving as Sam's assistant from afar. A "frail constitution" was the only explanation she'd come up with so far. I wanted to see a real doctor, but Sam wouldn't hear it. He was determined to keep me sequestered, to spare the citizens of Upstate City from my path of destruction.

I tried to eat well, sleep enough, and drink lots of water, but I still collapsed under the slightest insistence from a strong breeze.

Thatcher drew my blood with practiced ease while I stared at the dirt embedded between the laminated faux wood floorboards, a calcified knot of nasty feelings twinging in my chest while I thought about my mom. I barely felt the needle's sting.

Our old house had been all glorious, dense mahogany. On summer afternoons, I would rest my cheek on the banister because the sun streaming through the skylights made it feel like velvet.

The new house was always dusty. Sam certainly didn't clean.

Thatcher withdrew the needle and unbound the rubber around my bicep with a snap, drawing me back to the present.

She handed me a bandage and I trudged to my room without either of us saying a word.

My outdated TV was still paused on the movie I'd put in an hour before dawn broke, when I'd woken up shivering and struggled to fall back asleep. It was frozen on a grainy image of a man covered in mud staring at a mountain fortress. Goosebumps raced up my neck the second I bent to unpause it. There was definitely a draft.

I turned to the base of my window, where I had layered strips of duct tape because it never closed properly. Clingy winter drafts weaseled their way through every ill-fitted door in the house.

Grumbling, I sat on the bed and pulled the battered quilt tight around me. The package slipped from where I'd stashed it, and I eyed it distrustfully. I tugged my sweatshirt's hood forward, batting my hair out of its determined path to cling to my face.

A small flame of hope kindled in my chest.

The package was surprisingly solid for its size. I fumbled

with the flap, eyeing my name on the front. The handwriting was hectic, as if written by someone with bad penmanship and a worse attention span.

My fingers met a solid, cool surface. Withdrawing it, I eyed the smooth sheet the size of both my hands, one side was brushed metal, the other dark unblemished glass. Along the metal side, a logo was etched, barely visible unless it caught the light: a hollow, thin diamond bisected by a curved line, like a pupil, followed by two words.

LEO OPTICS

It was a tablet. Feeling foolish, I poked it.

Almost immediately, a ring of white light glowed beneath my finger then rippled away like I had bothered a still pond. As it reached the screen's edge, the entire thing lit softly.

A single application rested on the screen, designed like a small envelope to signify email.

I clicked it open. Then, as if drifting up from deep water, text appeared on the screen.

My heart stuttered as I read.

Melbourne!

My name is Bane. Brisbane. Dumb names run in the family. I'm your uncle!

Let me back up. Your mom is my older sister. I hadn't heard from her in forever. Until . . . I learned about her passing, and about you. I'm so sorry.

My parents, your grandparents, died a few years back, too. I won't claim to know how you feel, but I have felt similar, I bet.

Anyway, I've spent the last handful of years thinking I don't have any family. I never tried to track down your mom. I remember when she left. She made it clear she didn't want anyone to follow. I don't know if you feel the same way . . . But I'm so happy that you exist. I'd love to meet you.

I guess what I'm saying is, if you need anything . . . What's mine is yours.

I've attached scans of the documents that were sent to me anony-mously. It's only us left in the Leo family. I know it sounds crazy, but I can't live with myself another day without doing something. You are my niece, and the only family I have.

Crown City is a quick plane ride away, and it would be an honor to meet you. I hope to earn the right to be considered your family.

Your Uncle,

Bane Leo

PS: This tablet is a gift! It's Leo Optics' newest model.

My heart thudded violently. A dull roar echoed through my head. I read it twice more, trying to make sense of the words and the impossible order in which they were laid.

My mom had a brother. I had an uncle.

I knew Mom had a family she didn't talk to. I never pressed it. She was all I needed, and now she was gone.

I read one line over and over.

If you need anything . . .

Anything.

He was too good to be true. There was no way I wouldn't screw this up. I should have stayed on fire.

The floorboards creaked outside my room, the sound raking claws up my back and leaving goosebumps in their wake. Was Sam home early? One glimpse of the tablet and I'd be done for.

My fingers flew across the tablet, typing and hitting the send button before I chucked the entire thing beneath the covers.

A shadowy figure filled the narrow opening of my half-closed door. The light from my lamp caught on brown skin and matching eyes narrowed in concern, not Sam's gray-flecked gold hair and beard. It was Thatcher, likely making sure my head hadn't started bleeding again. She walked away without a word, and I released a breath.

Gasping around the lump in my throat, I pulled out the tablet and stared at the message I'd sent, wondering if I'd just made a massive mistake.

I need somewhere to go.

CHAPTER
TWO

"WHAT THE HELL DID I DO?" I WHISPERED.

An icy spike of dread shoved its way between my ribs. I might have floundered my first chance at a family by being rash. I probably sounded desperate. I was going to ruin my chance to know my uncle before I could even meet him.

The tablet pinged.

Okay! Why don't you come stay for the summer?

Then, a list of questions. The information he'd need to book me a plane ticket.

Just like that, I had a ticket out of Upstate City. I spent the week leading up to my flight laying low, making plans, and avoiding Thatcher's attention. Sam was scheduled a short break between shoots for *Pet Project*, but my flight left early enough that I wouldn't run into him before my escape. The irony of my dad's job nearly choked me, at times. He only visited me, his only child, a few times a year, but he could design ergonomic beds for koala bears or whatever for a day job.

I think Mom gave me his last name to try and make us feel close, like she knew he wasn't going to be a stellar parent.

I'd never cared before she died, because she was wonderful. On so many summer nights I'd lean against her on our little tufted sofa, watching her lithe fingers write in her journal while we talked, her voice melodic.

When she died, it was like the level of my soul where joy lived was closed off, bricked up with cement and sorrow. I didn't notice for a long time, between the crying and the hollow motions of bathing, eating, working shifts at the coffee shop. Watching dozens of movies and remembering none of the plots in my tiny new bedroom as Sam stomped through the kitchen, cursing the number of utensils a household needed to function. I figured any degree of joy was unavailable to me indefinitely.

But in the span of a moment, Bane's message punched through that barrier and rocketed past excitement and all the way up into hope, a feeling I'd forgotten existed.

But hope always held hands with risk.

Though . . . If Bane was anything like her, I wanted to meet him. After he'd agreed to help me, I'd rubbed my hands together, trying to will warmth into my fingertips to stop their shaking, and typed back again. We emailed sporadically throughout the week, neither of us ever offering to make a phone call. I gave him sparse details about my situation. He asked about what kind of food I liked, any amenities or accommodations I'd need.

Bane didn't specify which dates constituted "for the summer," but there was no way I'd let myself be dragged back to Upstate City and Sam's suffocating perimeter. I looked up colleges in Crown City. Camden College was the only university in the city, and they offered a summer term.

That's all it could be, I told myself. It could be purely transactional. He'd provide lodging. I'd be polite and grateful. Eventually, I would leave. I could transfer to another college's campus as soon as the fall and Sam would never know where I went.

If Bane meant what he said about his resources, maybe he

would help with tuition. A college education someone else would pay for was significantly more ideal than one I'd have to mostly fund myself.

I sent Bane back my information and spent the rest of the day on an application to Camden College's summer semester.

Only after did I do an internet search of my uncle, late that night the first time he contacted me.

I swiped the screen awake, typing "Brisbane Leo" so fast I misspelled it twice.

Headlines populated, as well as a photo of a handsome man in his early thirties who looked like he very much didn't want his picture taken.

Sadly, my uncle was brunette. My mom had been, too, but I'd hoped my flaxy hair wasn't solely a testament to Sam's strong genes. In the photo, Bane wore a tuxedo and a smile that curled higher on one side. He had a slightly crooked nose and two deep lines between his well-groomed eyebrows. He was listed as the Chief Innovation Officer of Leo Optics.

I scanned the most recent headlines.

They were not a positive endorsement for my immediate future.

CROWN'S RESIDENT RECLUSE FLIES TO MALDIVES, BAILS ON BUSINESS MEETING

FURTIVE LEO SKIPS THIRD TECH EXPO PLANNING MEETING

SCROOGE MUCH? LEO GHOSTS HOLIDAY CHARITY GALA

Rumors raged around Bane like wildfire. His love for privacy was legendary. Only a few people reported seeing the inside of his house since his parents, Sydney and Elizabeth Leo, had died. Folks speculated he had many fleeting flings with girlfriends, boyfriends. Travis Keep, Crown City's mayor, seemed to hate him with exceptional fervor, criticizing him in every other article. The Leo Optics CEO was one of few to defend him in these articles, citing his "capriciousness" as a side effect of his brilliant mind.

I forced myself to stop scrolling and tucked the tablet carefully between the clothes and sparse toiletries that stuffed my old backpack. I spared a baleful glance at my dusty DVD player and collection of movies. They were my steadfast companions, but weren't worth tracking down a real suitcase for.

I traced the faded seams of my quilt, doubt worming through my resolve.

If my mom stayed away from Bane, maybe it was for good reasons.

I hardly slept. Usually, I would put in a movie, watching it on repeat until I dozed off. I would have picked the heist one where the small, candy-colored cars raced across the Italian countryside. Instead, I replayed my favorite scenes in my head until I fell into a fitful sleep.

🔥🔥🔥

The morning I was to leave for Crown City, I woke up far too early and stared unseeingly at my dark TV screen, blinking heavily.

A horn honked out front, startling me so hard I nearly fell off the bed.

It was the cab I'd called for with shaky hands a half hour earlier.

I didn't survey my room to see if I had left anything or try to commit any parts of the house to memory. I was glad to never come back. I shouldered my bag. With a grimace, I wadded the quilt into a ball to carry with me and left.

My feet halted of their own accord before the front door. I'd lost track of my breath somewhere.

I shook myself. This was the right choice.

I reached, but the door pushed open before I could touch it.

My dad stood there, broad shoulders silhouetted against the sunrise. It made his cornsilk hair glow. Thatcher stood behind him, wearing a tight frown and holding a thermos of coffee bigger than my head. Sam was home from shooting a day early. He had one hand on the door, the other braced against the side of the house, as if he could physically stop me.

I hated how much we looked alike. At least my eyes were my own. His hazel ones searched my face.

"He found you, didn't he?"

My stomach plummeted as all the air rushed from my lungs, my mouth gaping soundlessly.

Sam had *known* about Mom's family.

I wanted to scream. I wanted to strike him. But I did nothing but shrink back, petrified.

"I'm leaving," I managed.

A breath hissed in through his nose. Dirt peppered his pale cheeks, smeared across his scruff, and he smelled the same as always, like hay and fur. His eyes sparked. "You'll ruin his life, you know," he said in his low, rock-tumble voice.

The accusation squeezed around my windpipe. Any response died in my throat.

A single word echoed through my mind.

Probably.

But anything was better than this.

I ducked beneath his arm and ran into the colorless morning.

It didn't matter what kind of person my uncle was. Crown City would be a better life. I'd make sure of it.

CHAPTER
THREE

THE MORNING TOOK TOO LITTLE TIME. UPSTATE CITY'S TINY airport was little changed from my handful of previous visits for spring break getaways with my mom to sleepy towns in the Pacific Northwest.

I stared out the window in the first-class seat Bane had graciously provided, watching the sky. It remained so constant in appearance, like we hardly moved, like I wasn't traversing hundreds of miles away from all I'd ever known. White married blue along the horizon, as if someone had simply smudged their thumb along where the sky and clouds met.

Upon landing, anxiety bubbled through my limbs, threatening to vibrate me to pieces. I was sure the fluorescent glow of the airport's lights coupled with my yellow sweater only highlighted the sleepless smudges beneath my eyes. Sam's parting words rebounded through my mind on an endless loop, tugging the corners of my mouth down.

I breezed past newsstands and souvenir shops lining the terminal, glancing at the displays. A "local flavor" section spilled out into the walkway with a strange array of collectibles, pulling me up short when I nearly toppled over a table in my frenzy.

You bring destruction wherever you go.

I bit my lip and gripped the table, righting the merchandise I'd disturbed. Stuffed toys of Bigfoot-esque creatures towered over documentaries on Crown's apparent mob scene and curious dark-helmeted action figures, all paired with matching slim paperbacks claiming to KNOW THE TRUTH. I picked up an action figure, captivated by its shiny face shield and sharp blue emblem. A quick glance at the signs told me he was apparently the Shadow, a local vigilante.

At least there would be something familiar in my new home. I set it back and my eyes caught on a tabloid's brazen red headline.

CROWN'S MOST UNRELIABLE BACHELOR BAILS ON BABY
FUNDRAISER!

A photo of Bane adorned the cover.

Wonderful.

I turned and stomped toward the pickup area, sincerely hoping Bane drove a car big enough to stow all the emotional baggage that brought us together.

A thin crowd milled at the bottom of the escalator. My gaze swept across the faces, searching for an uneven smile and disheveled brown hair. Bane wasn't here.

Stepping off the escalator two thirds into a mild panic attack, I nearly bowled over a lanky young man in an ill-fitting suit, glasses askew, who made me look positively serene in comparison. He didn't even glance my way as he walked off, though we had nearly concussed each other.

I pulled to the side, away from the crowd and the noise, to breathe for a moment. I resettled my backpack on my shoulders and tucked my quilt beneath my arm. This was the time he'd agreed to pick me up.

A supremely unhelpful thought flitted through my head.

I am going to screw this up.

I didn't think this through. I should have planned better. It didn't help that I hadn't turned my phone on since I left Upstate City, afraid of manic messages from Sam.

Twisting my bag's strap back and forth, I looked again, forcing myself to pause and spend a second studying the face of every dark-haired man in baggage claim. No crooked smile in sight. My heart sank to somewhere beneath my intestines.

Panic threatened to make itself known on my face through hot, hot tears. I gulped them back and made a plan to wait twenty minutes before and I'd call and coolly tell Bane not to worry, I could call a cab.

Then I'd take that cab as far as my checking account would allow, find a job at a coffee shop, change my name, and never have the opportunity to mess anything up ever again.

"Dramatic," I breathed, torquing myself upright. I strangled one backpack strap between my fists, taking out my frustration on the tired nylon.

The weight across my shoulders shifted suddenly, and my backpack careened toward the ground. Before it could smash against the floor, I swore and swung it into my arms, the strap I'd strangled flapping in dismay, torn and useless.

"Son of a—"

"Bit early to be throwing things."

My head snapped up.

Standing before me with light brown skin, all sinewy and slightly slouched, was the coolest-looking woman I'd ever seen.

"Um," I said brilliantly.

She gave the barest hint of a smile and picked my dropped quilt from the ground, folding it neatly into her arms. "Hi, I'm Chezza. Bane couldn't make it, so I'll be taking you home."

I knew what all her words meant individually, and it sounded like they were in the right order, but I couldn't make sense of them or her as a person. She ran a hand through her straight black hair, revealing a layer underneath dyed the color of the last watered-down sips of a watermelon slushie. She looked a few years older than me.

"Your uncle's stuck in a meeting," she said slowly. "He should have made a bigger sign."

She waved a tablet in front of my face. It was a twin to my own, and read "MELBOURNE!!!" across the screen in scribbled letters, surrounded by a field of animated balloons that sporadically changed colors.

"Nice to meet you." I stuck out a hand, nearly dropping my bag.

Chezza stood there, staring, and after a moment of taking in my ripped pack and harried expression, she laughed, throwing her head back. "So it's genetic," she said, giving my hand a gentle shake. "Ready to go?"

I clamped a hand over my bag's traitorous zipper and lied. "Yeah."

"Is that all you have?"

"Yes." I refused to sound ashamed.

Chezza lifted her brows and chin, pointing with her lips toward the exit so I'd follow.

As we walked, she flipped open her phone. "Clare, can you send over some seasonal basics in a size eight? Vennie's home. He can take care of them."

"You don't have to—" I started.

Chezza's face softened. "Bane insists. You need clothes." She swung around, her moto jacket and artfully ripped jeans swishing. I tried to keep up with her long strides that were extended by black heeled sneakers. Looking over her shoulder, she said, "It's nice to meet you, too, Mel. Welcome to chaos unlike any you've ever known."

THE SILVER SUV SPED TOWARD A RIDGE OF MOUNTAINS growing in the distance. I was dwarfed in the wide leather seat with my backpack settled carefully between my feet.

"How long to . . . the house?" I asked.

She glanced out the window. "Half an hour. The airport is technically outside Crown's limits. Once we pass through the mountains, we'll formally be inside Crown City, and you'll see what all the fuss is about." Chezza was nice enough. My shoulders loosened a fraction.

It was easy to see how the city got its name. The ring of mountains sprawled in either direction, encrusted in trees glowing like emeralds when the sun hit the leaves. Their peaks shot into the sky like the tips of a grand diadem.

Chezza narrated as we approached a tunnel. "The mountains keep us all contained in there. We're kind of in the middle of nowhere. It's a beautiful city with everything you could want in the valley . . . lakes, rivers, hiking trails, malls, a small city feel with big city resources. New neighborhoods. Old neighborhoods. But the seclusion is what starts all the rumors. The inventors and investors that come here are usually the ones on the fringe, wanting to try out crazy ideas on a small group and avoiding criticism from a bigger tech city with a bigger presence in national media." She sighed and turned her gaze back down the road. "Here, people can pretend the rules from the rest of the world don't apply."

My thoughts skipped to the airport kiosk. A place full of urban legends, but Chezza made it sound like it was even more than that.

Chezza tossed her hair, and I desperately wanted her to show me how to make mine as shiny as hers. "Of course, don't mind me. I didn't expect to end up in Crown City, so I'm bitter. The weirdness is what makes it good, too. We have a decent food scene, a few good concert venues. *Lots* of festivals. Give it a few weeks. You'll see what I mean."

My stomach slowly edged back to its correct placement. She spoke like she expected me to stay.

Her vote of confidence reignited my urge to ask about Bane, to find any paltry hint of what he might be like. Intimidated, I instead let us lapse into amicable silence as we were swallowed through a tunnel at the base of one of the mountains.

We emerged into blinding daylight on the other side, and Chezza spread a hand over the dash, palm out to a green-faceted paradise, endless leaves glinting in the spotty sunshine.

"Welcome to Crown City," Chezza said.

The tunnel gradually sloped upwards, so we exited midway up the mountain's other side, providing the perfect vantage point to view the city that would hopefully be my safe haven.

The mountains curved around a broad, flat valley, the peaks at the far end blurred and mysterious. Shafts of sunlight darted through the clouds, illuminating different neighborhoods. Just off-center of the valley's middle stood a regiment of silvery buildings jutting up in varying heights. A vast pewter lake curled around the cluster's western side, occupying the true center of the valley. The land became less and less populated with buildings as the ground sloped toward the mountains. In any space between buildings, the area was covered in dense woods, shifting in the breeze.

"How exactly do you know Bane?" I asked finally.

Chezza smiled wide, effusing that look of ease, but it didn't distract me from her dark eyes flashing back and forth, the look of someone thinking on their feet. "My brother and Bane are old friends. We rent rooms from him. You wouldn't believe real estate prices in the city. Bane cut us a generous deal. The house is too big for him all alone, really . . . You'll see."

We descended toward the valley's floor, and somewhere amidst the trees and shiny buildings, my uncle.

CHAPTER
FOUR

CHEZZA DROVE DEEP INTO THE WOODS AT THE OUTSKIRTS OF Crown City, passing the grand subdivisions until we were on a winding road where gravel side streets crisscrossed the path.

She finally slowed, and the sun rebounded in strange ways from among the trees we passed. Squinting, it took a moment for me to make sense of the scene. A sprawling, pale stone wall stood severe and glowering behind the first few rows of ancient tree trunks.

Chezza turned off the road toward a stoic cedar gate. The arched behemoth, drained of color by time, swept back as though expecting us. A neatly paved drive extended beyond it, the house set back too far to see. I swallowed quietly. In movies, estates like this usually featured a hero that ended up extremely murdered.

Elm trees sprawled around us, gradually thinning. My emotions nearly drowned me when they cleared enough that the house came into view.

Two tall stories of soft red brick nestled neat rows of pristine, white-trimmed windows and dark shutters. A matching, massive brick garage connected off the left side, nearly as large as the house itself. It was big, but the kind of big I could handle without having a meltdown.

It was harder to comprehend the colossal statue of a lion that towered in front of the house. It sat in the middle of the round drive, encircled by a dense, neat ring of purple tulips.

Carved from whirled white marble and at least twice as tall as me, the beast was frozen mid-roar, mane splayed, one tire-sized paw poised in midair. I turned nearly all the way around in my seat to stare as we circled it to park neatly before the front door.

Chezza stared at the closed garage doors, her brow furrowed, then followed my gaze to the lion.

She sighed. "It's something, isn't it? Your grandfather was full of . . . pride."

"He built that?" I asked in awe as Chezza turned off the car. She grabbed my backpack and left me to handle my quilt as she briskly led the way toward the house while I was still scrambling from my seat. She explained over her shoulder along the way.

"Not with his own hands, of course. He commissioned it. Sydney loved his last name nearly as much as he loved himself." She gestured at the front door, a burgundy behemoth with a lion-shaped knocker.

Chezza punched numbers on the shiny keypad next to the antique gold handle and ushered me inside. We stood in a tall, cold foyer. The floor was an ornate mosaic of dark stone. The face of yet another lion, ringed by laurel. A banner depicted in tiles beneath it featured the words "For Glory."

I tore my gaze away. The upper level displayed a neat landing beneath a sprawling ceiling, which topped a staircase that swept down the one side of the room, the banister topped with another lion's head. A motorized chair lift was situated at the base of the stairs. A table graced the foyer directly across from us, littered with car keys, sticky notes, and a tall vase held up by rearing, carved wooden lions inlaid with gold, dainty white flowers overflowing its brim.

Chezza set my backpack at the base of the stairs, and I plopped my quilt on top. I stepped to the table, drawn by the small picture frame in the corner. It featured a younger Bane, my grandparents, and my mother. She looked younger than I did in the photo, her brown hair long, her face stoic.

Footsteps echoed from somewhere in the house, drawing my attention. I forced deep breaths as quietly as I could while the sound neared, one footfall slightly sharper than the other.

I steeled myself.

A man that was not my uncle entered the room from a doorway on our left, his face angled down, focused solely on a tablet much like my own. He had the same brown skin and hooded umber eyes as Chezza, and his black hair was gelled back meticulously. He tottered through the room without glancing our way, his gait slightly uneven because in place of one foot was a curved plastic blade.

He was halfway across the emblem depicted in the middle of the floor when Chezza cleared her throat.

"Hey brainless, this is our new . . ." She struggled for a word. "Pal."

I pretended to not notice her fumble. I shared her senti-ment, unsure of how I fit with this strange family. My scuffed red sneakers glared a reflection in the perfect floor.

The man looked up, bewildered, his fingers flying over the screen's keyboard. "Oh, hey. Clare dropped off some stuff for you a few minutes ago. I put it in the guest room," he said, and disappeared into the hall behind the stairs.

Chezza gave an even longer sigh and rubbed her forehead. "That genius of social navigation is my brother, Vennie. He's friendlier when he's not consumed with a project, I promise. Are you hungry?"

Nodding dumbly, I shadowed her through the doorway Vennie had just vacated.

It opened into a kitchen much less grand than the foyer. The wood floor was worn soft and the dining set was a decade out of style. Chezza tugged out a high stool for me as she swept around the other side of the counter. "Now, Mel, we haven't known each other long, but I feel confident in assuming you're of sound mind and therefore like sandwiches?"

More dumb nodding from me. My brain was still processing the security wall and the lions.

"Lucky for you, you'll get your fill of Filipino cooking. Bane can only bake. Vennie and I are the chefs."

She clicked on the TV at the end of the counter. Another wide, thin screen, this one with the Leo Optics logo laser engraved in the bottom corner.

Chezza was clearly at ease in the house. Her house, and evidently her brother's too, as well as my uncle's. She layered turkey, cheese, and leafy greens while I stared around the room.

CULT! my inner movie critic screamed as I rubbed my arms. The house was chilly.

The telltale metallic shifting of a doorknob echoed from the foyer, and I froze.

My heartbeat pounded in my temples. Chezza minded the pan on the stove, looking expectantly at the doorway we had come through.

The moment had come. I had hoped Chezza would give me a heads-up when Bane was on his way, or I'd at least hear the garage door heralding his arrival. I had no time to compose myself. No time for a pep talk in the bathroom or a quiet freak out alone.

"Hello?" a pleasant voice called, followed by the struggle and thud of a shoe being kicked off.

The sound of his voice made my chest squeeze in an unfamiliar way.

"In the kitchen!" Chezza yelled back. My heart beat faster

than I could have imagined, faster than when Thatcher called, or when Sam showed up at the door. Blinking Sam's image from my mind, I eased from the stool.

Everything was happening too fast. My mouth was too dry and I could distinctly feel my *ankles* sweating.

He burst into the room amid a gust of cold air. Bane's hair was thicker than mine and tousled wildly around his head. His face was brushed with scruff, as if he couldn't decide whether he wanted a beard or not. Best of all, he was several inches shy of six feet tall. Apparently my short stature was genetic on the Leo side. Bane's pale complexion was similar to mine, though it was evident he spent more time outside than I did. His cheeks were flushed from the cool spring air and he was slightly breathless. He wore a blue sweater and jeans and only one shoe, like he couldn't waste time properly removing it to delay seeing me a second longer.

My breath disappeared. He looked like my mom. Her pixie-length hair was always neat, compared to his wildness, but his was the same shade. His face curved exactly like hers had, with a matching hint of a dimple in the middle of his chin that I'd forgotten she had.

When he finally looked me in the eyes, I jolted and saw what the tabloid photos on my Leo Optics tablet couldn't show me.

We had the same eyes. A noncommittal blue-gray that made me think of the wastewater in an artist's cup after they finished painting the sky. His were slightly downturned at the corners, giving the impression he was always slightly sad, and they had more lines at the corners than I expected to see on someone thirty years old.

"Melbourne?" he asked.

I managed a nod. My brain could hardly process him. "Mel's fine," I said.

He didn't move, smiling broadly as if in a daze.

The silence extended a few seconds, and Chezza coughed.

His head snapped to the side. "Can I have one of those?"

Chezza rolled her eyes. "Way ahead of you." She tipped a fourth completed sandwich onto a plate with its twin and exited in the direction of her brother.

Bane pulled one of the remaining plates toward him, and I followed suit. He scarfed down the sandwich, mumbling "sorry" around a mouthful. My nerves had me sated, but I ate it all anyway, wanting to be a good guest. Plus, it was delicious.

As soon as his last bite was gone, Bane leapt up as fast as he had sat down. "Do you like chocolate milk? . . . Wait, do you have any food allergies?"

I was only halfway through my sandwich. "Yes," I mumbled. "Yes to chocolate milk. No to allergies."

Before my sentence was done, he zipped to the fridge and dug around.

His head snapped back from behind the door, "*Lions*, Mel. I'm so sorry. For not picking you up at the airport."

I swallowed and picked at my sleeve. "Really, it's okay. Chezza said you had a work thing?"

Bane nodded absently as he searched for cups. He gestured toward the Leo Optics TV, sloshing milk over the open lip of the gallon. "That happens a lot. I mean, getting called into work last minute. The town gossip magazines like to call me a . . . What was it? Oh, a 'perpetually tardy, apathetic weirdo.' Only the first half is true."

He shut himself up by taking a long drink and set the other glass in front of me.

Realization struck me like lightning. He was *nervous.*

It was a relief to not be the awkward person in the room. "I hope it wasn't too stressful, whatever you had to take care of," I offered lamely.

Bane shrugged. "Just a . . . synergy issue. All good now." Quick as a flash, his smile was there and gone. "Crown City is hosting a massive Tech Expo in a few weeks. A lot of prep work is involved."

He halted again, glass in hand, fridge hanging open, staring at me in awe while I ate.

I finished my sandwich and was halfway through a sip of milk when he smacked himself in the forehead, making me jump. "Oh! We have a lot to talk about. You can bring that with you."

He spun and ducked out of the room, and I hopped from my stool to follow. He led us across the foyer in the opposite direction. As we walked, I craned my neck to see more of the house. A living room branched off of one end of the kitchen, and a wide doorway opened into a broad, bright space, almost like a ballroom, with sprawling wood floors and floor-to-ceiling windows lit so bright from the sun outside that I couldn't make out the backyard. That room was entirely empty.

Looking away, I followed Bane's sharp left turn into his office.

A sleek black desk commanded one side of the space, with an antique bookcase staring it down. A smudged, glass-topped coffee table sat in the middle, piled with unopened mail and pristine issues of business magazines.

Bane frowned over his shoulder. "Sorry, I'm a bit disorganized . . . all of the time."

"That's perfectly fine," I snorted, stepping to the bookshelf. It was lined with titles on management and company culture. There wasn't a single photo anywhere.

Bane shoved a heap of papers off his desk and sat in his chair. Half a pot of coffee sat forgotten on an oven mitt at his elbow. He scrunched down and kicked at the plain wooden chair across from him, attempting to make room for me to sit.

Instead, it slid backward three feet and toppled onto the rug.

"Nice," he muttered, kneading his forehead.

I righted the chair and sat.

Bane plunked a thick manila folder, nearly bursting along

its fold, before me, almost catching me on the tip of my nose with his downswing. The folder was smudged gray in places and heavily wrinkled. A burst of dust puffed out its open end as it settled its bulk.

I twisted my head to peer at the label, but the handwriting had faded.

"What are these?"

Bane tapped the folder. "These were sent to my office. It's files—information that you exist. No evidence of who sent it."

He riffled through another stack of paper, finding one he deemed unnecessary, and flipped it over to scribble on the back.

Another sheet slid free and landed near his elbow. Discreetly, I peered at it. It looked to be a half-finished shopping list. I could make out "grapes," "eggs," and "hydrogen peroxide" before he slid his paper beneath my nose.

He had written "SYDNEY LEO" in his hasty scribble.

"This mess," he began, gesturing between the two of us, and then in a wide circle, as if taking in the entire house, "was started when your grandpa came to Crown City in his youth, carrying nothing but a few dollars and a massive chip on his shoulder. Bitter toward his own humble beginnings, he started the business that he determined would have the most need in the coming decades, and therefore would turn the most profit." He tapped the *Leo Optics* logo emblazoned across the sheet in green block letters. "He met Elizabeth—my mom, your grandma—here in Crown." He wrote her name next to Sydney's and drew a line connecting them, then dropped it down between them. He then scribbled his name, and my mom's, then dropped a line beneath hers and added my name. My heart squeezed. Our little family tree.

"When did they pass away?" I asked.

"They died in a car crash six years ago." He glanced up. "And your mom?"

I swallowed. "It's been ten months." I didn't expand. The

flames rose up in my mind's eye, swallowing her as she begged me to run.

The look passed between us then. The mute conjoined solace of those who had suffered the loss of a parent, and felt that specific, hastily ripped hole in the world.

"I'm so sorry you lost your mom . . ." Bane started. "I knew—I knew her. For a while. There's a big age difference between us, so she wasn't around a lot by the time I was in school. Eventually she stopped visiting. I've always wondered why."

"She never talked about her family," I said quietly, hoping a note of apology entered my voice.

Bane's mouth twisted. "I'm hoping we can figure it out together."

Together. Can I handle "together"?

Bane broke my reverie. "Wanna see your room?"

I had hardly begun to nod when he sprang to his feet again. Exiting the office, he pointed to a room across from us, and then further down the hall. "The sunroom, and my room."

He lifted my bag from where I'd left it, frowning at the busted strap, and balanced the quilt easily on top. We started up the cushy, carpeted stairs.

At the landing, Bane turned right to a wide hallway with an open door to the left. He handed me my bag and waited in the hallway while I stepped into the room.

A small step down led into an airy space with massive windows draped with wispy curtains. It was furnished with a large desk and simple end tables on either side of the bed. The bedspread was the same yellow as my sweater.

I was awestruck as I crossed to kneel on the padded bench before the windows and peered at the back lawn. There was a sleek cement patio and a covered pool, and so much *space*. I couldn't make out the foreboding wall through the tree-spotted lawn, couldn't tell how far back my family's property went. A small mountain peak stood maybe a half mile back. The sun glared through the windows. It was amazing.

When I emerged, Bane offered, "We have another guest room if you don't like this one. This one has the best light."

"It's perfect," I insisted. "Thank you for letting me come here."

I won't be a burden, I almost added, but I didn't want to make a promise I wasn't sure I could keep.

Bane held out a hand as if to lay it on my shoulder, then paused and thought better, drawing it back. "Of course. That's what family does." His smile was the best gift I'd ever been given. Bane gestured his hands wildly, like he'd forgotten their function. "What would you like to do?"

He really was the man with no plan.

"I could use a few minutes to rest . . . unpack," I said.

Bane's face fell, just a little. "Of course. I was thinking pizza for dinner. Does that sound okay?" I nodded, and he shifted awkwardly. He began to back down the hall. "Shout if you need anything!"

The last syllable was punctuated by his own shout as his foot slipped over the first step and he nearly toppled down the stairs.

Shaking my head, I entered my new room and shut the door. I tossed my bag on the bed. The zipper gave up entirely, splitting to spill my belongings across the bedspread. My phone slid out among them. With a sigh, I turned it on. There was an informational session at Camden College tomorrow morning about the summer program, and I needed to double-check the time.

After the screen flared to life, the phone vibrated angrily as text messages loaded. Three of them, all from Sam.

You're making a mistake. Come back now.

You'll make things worse for yourself with him. You don't know him.

See if that uncle of yours is so charitable once he learns about your condition. Does he know he signed up to front medical bills?

I turned the phone off and chucked it in the back of a nightstand. Collapsing on the bed, I swallowed several times until I was sure I wouldn't ruin the dreamily soft pillowcases with my tears.

CHAPTER
FIVE

PERSISTENT, UNEVEN THUMPING SHOULDERED ME FROM SLEEP.

After a lot of greasy pizza and bad reality shows with Bane, Chezza, and Vennie, I'd fallen asleep instantly when I crashed into my new bed. Cracking my eyes to the steady glow from the moon through the windows, I felt frozen solid. I shivered so hard the headboard rattled lightly against the wall, enough to wake me, though I hoped not the rest of the house.

Dragging myself upright, I pulled the comforter tight around me. Even with my mom's quilt overtop, I was freezing. I wondered what she'd make of my situation, if she'd be happy I was free of Sam. Shaking away that thought, dread seized me. It was the groggy grossness that usually came before I fainted, like my thoughts were clawing through pudding to reach each other.

Sam was right. Not even a full day in the Leo house and I was close to passing out already.

I searched for a vent and found one along the wall beneath the open curtains. Hanging off the bed, I stretched a hand to feel not a whiff of heat blowing out. With a scowl, I went in search of a linen closet and more blankets.

Draping the quilt around my head and shoulders, I slipped

from my room. There was a single door at the end of the hall. I carefully turned the knob on the closet door and pulled.

Instead of shelves full of linens, it opened to a narrow stairwell. Even more odd, a tangible, gentle, warm draft of air wafted from it. My thoughts numb, instinct drew me up the stairs. Flickering light spilled across a small landing. I poked my head slowly above the final stair.

A small study perched at the top of the stairs, dark save for a cheerful blaze burning in the fireplace against the wall. I froze, listening.

The fire beckoned me closer. The rest of the small room held a tidy oak desk, a brown leather chair, and a decorative wood carving stretching to the ceiling behind it, depicting a pack of sunbathing lions. Before the fireplace sat a large wing-back chair upholstered in crimson velvet. It was clean perfection compared to the chaos of Bane's office.

Entranced by the fire and longing to feel the tips of my toes again, I circled around the armchair, offering a quiet apology to whoever was still up.

The chair was empty.

I collapsed into it, confused. A fire burning on its own was dangerous, but there was a layer of dust on every surface in the room. I peered at the flames, leaning close, and saw the source seemed to be from metal tubing underneath logs that were too gray to be real.

I settled back, trying to make sense of the space as the warmth seeped through my entire body, untwining the hunch in my shoulders. Thoughts of my mom swirled in and out, too. I let a little of the ache of how much I missed her through, floating in the pain. My brain went from frozen to fluid, slow in the exact opposite way of how I had awoken. I couldn't remember ever feeling so relaxed. Against my best intentions, I fell asleep.

🔥🔥🔥

I WOKE EARLY IN THE STRANGE STUDY, THE SANGUINE FIRE still crackling, and crept back to my room. My grogginess was chased away by the thrill of fully exploring my luxurious new bathroom.

Just off the bedroom and swathed in creamy tile with soft gold accents, a clawfoot tub overhung with rows of thick towels dominated one wall. Flakes of glittery stone dotted the tiled floor, and two small vases of lily of the valley sat neatly on either side of the sink, venting gentle sweetness into the air.

A huge glass shower stall stood in a second room, alongside a toilet featuring lots of buttons accompanying intimidating illustrations. A glorious cache of products in milky bottles stood in a neat row on a built-in shelf. I cranked the shower's left knob as far as it would go.

I took my time basking in the spray, letting it ease the tightness from my muscles. Pink from the steaming water, I wound myself in a thick towel and pawed through the drawers beneath the sink. They were full of everything a person could need—from floss to tampons, acne cream to exfoliants. Among a treasure trove of cosmetic samples I was thrilled to try, I found a new toothbrush. I reached to turn on the faucet, which of course had a handle shaped like a lion's head.

With one gentle twist, it broke off in my hand.

Sam's voice was immediately in my head, sending me backing against the wall.

You ruin everything you touch.

Mortified, I stared at the handle in my palm, the screw under its neck mangled. Under my thumb, the side of the lion's proud face had been pressed in, as if melted. I dropped it to the floor, where it clanged loudly in the morning-quiet house. Horrified panic rose thick and sour in my throat. Not even a full day in my new home and I'd already broken something.

Was this a new problem with me, too? Now I had to worry

about fainting and also somehow breaking things if I wasn't careful?

I tamped the thoughts down. There had to be a reasonable explanation. The screws were probably rusty from misuse. I had to get to Camden's campus—there was no time for this. I hadn't even unpacked.

Snorting at how comical my few outfits would look hanging in the walk-in closet, I stepped in to find it already half full.

A dozen sweaters in dark shades waited expectantly, alongside three pairs of jeans, a rain jacket, and a sturdy pair of boots. These were the clothes Chezza had called for, that Bane had insisted on providing, that Vennie had been at home to situate. One of the drawers even housed a pair of pajamas printed with the Leo Optics logo. Most glorious of all, a large basket occupied one shelf, stuffed with thick socks. A sky-blue skater dress hung shyly at the back of the closet, pretty and flowy and not exactly my style.

Overwhelmed tears pricked behind my eyes. I swallowed repeatedly until they receded.

I paired one of the new sweaters with my favorite old jeans and sneakers, and left my room. As I traversed the stairs, noise came from the kitchen. Bane was *loud*, even in the morning.

"I have to cancel on the cute barista guy to handle this mess?"

I turned the corner to find Bane and Vennie huddled over Vennie's tablet, staring at something intently. The glowing green lines looked like a map. Bane ran a hand through his wild hair, pulling a chaotic swoop over his forehead, and threw his hands up.

"Lions help me, I need a massage and an ice cream sundae in a five-gallon bucket—"

I cleared my throat. "Good morning."

Bane started. "Hi."

"Thank you for the clothes, and all the stuff in the bathroom," I stammered, rubbing my elbow. "You didn't have to do that."

Bane blurred to my side, and I noticed he'd buttoned his denim shirt wrong. I wondered if I'd ever adjust to his frenetic pinballing.

"When you said you wouldn't check a bag, I figured you might need some things. I hope that wasn't presumptuous. I want to help you have whatever kind of life it is you want, so if you need anything at all, just say so. What do you like for breakfast? We have cereal, fruit, yogurt . . . eggs, probably." He looked to Vennie, who shrugged.

"Cereal's fine," I assured them.

Vennie tucked his tablet away and returned to his oatmeal, sharing the counter with me.

I didn't know much about Chezza's quiet, stony-faced brother. "So, what do you do for work?"

"Tech consulting," he said, brown eyes flicking to his tablet, the screen now dark. That cleared up nothing.

He focused intently on the news playing on the TV, which recounted the actions from last night's episode of a reality show called "*Date Wars.*" The Leo house residents' dumpster fire show of choice followed beautiful people trying to fall in love during bizarre situations like naked bungee jumping followed by champagne and a hot tub in the middle of the desert. Vennie caught me staring and shrugged. "It's delightful trash."

Bane plugged his ears. "I wasn't paying close attention last night. I need to rewatch! No spoilers."

He was saved by a blaring alarm and red stripe overtaking the screen.

It was immediately followed by a digital video game–style jingle from Vennie's watch. Bane's phone emitted a screech that sounded like a velociraptor.

I jumped in my seat. "What the hell is that?" Bane scrambled at his pockets and a bright red text bar slid down across the top few inches of the TV screen.

SHADOW APPEARANCE LINKED TO SAYTO SCIENCES FIRE

A grainy photo of a dark figure dominated the screen. I recognized him from the airport display. It was the Shadow. The alarm stopped and allowed the anchor to speak.

"Breaking news in the development of last month's fire at Sayto Sciences. While the fire's source has still not been determined, a witness has confirmed local vigilante the Shadow was present the night of the fire."

The broadcast cut to a blurry photo of the Shadow, cited as from a previous date. It was taken from a low angle, like a bystander had been beneath the buildings the Shadow traversed. Glare bounced off his helmet, obscuring his face shield and shoulders. One powerful leg arced toward the next rooftop, the other behind him. His gloved hands were balled into fists. "Mayor Keep was unavailable for immediate comment, but representatives from his office reminded us their stance on vigilantism—"

"Sorry about that, Mel," Bane said as he cut the volume. "We have alerts set for major Crown City news. You know, stuff for the business. Sometimes it's not related though." He swiped the screen and the headline disappeared, allowing the *Date Wars* recap to return and share a conversation between the two self-proclaimed models drinking tequila in a restored barn.

"So that Shadow guy is for real?" I asked.

"You heard about him, huh?" Bane replied, having procured sour fruit gummies from somewhere. He absent-mindedly popped some into his mouth while watching a camel interrupt the candlelit dinner on screen, then he held the bag my way.

I shook my head and his hand retreated. "Yeah, he's all over. There was a display at the airport, and he was on the news . . . I know vigilantes exist and all, but he's got like, a *following*. Merchandise. The whole deal."

Bane raised an eyebrow. "Is that bad?"

I considered for a moment. "No. People seem to love him so much because he keeps the citizens of Crown City safe, right? That's pretty cool."

Bane opened his mouth to comment, but Vennie cut him off, cranking the volume.

"Shh! They're rehashing live confrontation from the aftershow."

I returned to my breakfast. As I ate, and opened a rideshare app on my phone, Bane made himself coffee that was at least half cream and tossed a handful of ice into his cup, sending spare cubes skittering across the counter. Vennie focused solely on his project.

Bane peered over my shoulder. "I didn't forget!" he insisted, far too loud for 9:00 a.m.

"Forget what?" I asked.

"You need to go to Camden today! I'm heading into town, too. I can give you a ride."

"Oh," I started, "I'll call a cab. It's not a big deal—"

He popped an ice cube into his mouth, grabbed his cup, and gestured toward the foyer, spilling a splash of coffee over his hand. "Good luck finding someone to pick you up this far out from town this early."

"Thanks, then," I said. "Lead the way."

Camden College was two square miles of neat limestone buildings and crisp green lawns bound by meticulous rows of wave petunias. I couldn't reign in my imaginings of what it would be like to learn and live there. My throat went tight. All of my actions for the last few years had been for a chance to set foot on a college campus, so that I could springboard from it into a life that was fully my own.

Bane dropped me at one end of campus, eyeing the school's seal embossed into a brick wall. "Did you ever attend here?" I asked.

Bane pursed his lips and spoke slowly. "For a semester, before they kicked me out."

I raised an eyebrow.

Bane's stormy eyes rolled. "Fine. I kind of deserved it. I did spray paint a statue of the mascot purple, but it was a blizzard and the warthog wouldn't cancel classes. Sorry— the dean's the warthog. The mascot is an elk. Anyway, I had friends without heat in their dorms who couldn't go home . . . Never mind. Text me when you're ready to go home. I need to spend some time in the office catching up."

I waved as he drove off and clicked open my emails on my phone, searching for the instructions of where I needed to go to finish my paperwork. Glancing through the sunlight dappling me and the sidewalk, I squinted, trying to make out the name on the nearest building.

"You look lost," a warm voice said.

I glanced up to meet the gaze of a light-skinned Black man. He looked about my age and wore an impassive expression, maroon pants, and a slim sport coat with rose-shaped buttons.

He held out a hand expectantly. "Maximilian Keep."

I snorted. "That's not a real name."

His perfect brows narrowed. "Like you have room to talk."

"You know my name?"

"You're Bane Leo's niece, Melbourne. Everyone is wondering about you," he said, his smile dangerous.

"I highly doubt that. It's just Mel, and there's not much to wonder about. How do you know about me?"

"I'm well connected," he said slyly. "I'm surprised you don't know. My name doesn't ring any bells?"

"Nope, sorry," I said, making to move past him. His legs

were significantly longer than mine, so he stepped before me again easily.

He sighed dramatically. "I'm Max *Keep*. As in Keep Corporation. Owned by my father, Travis Keep, who also happens to be the mayor of this fine city. And knows everything that arrives within or leaves its borders. Including you."

And according to the tabloids, the mayor reportedly hated Bane.

I cocked my head, surveying this boy up and down. Max Keep was gold all over. Hints of it gleamed throughout the artful, dark curls that arced away from his gilded brown forehead. There was even a touch of gold in his mahogany eyes. His smile was the kind that opened wallets, but softened on either side by boyish cheeks.

I squinted. "Fascinating. Do you know where the admin building is?"

Max's winning gaze blazed at me. "I have an errand there as well. I can escort you, if you like."

I shrugged, never one to turn down a stroll with a handsome man, and Max led the way out into the broad swathe of grass down the campus's middle.

"No doubt you're here because you're enrolling in Camden, right? Have you been regaled yet with our fine alma mater's storied tradition?" He started briskly down the sidewalk.

"I read what's on the website . . ." I started.

"Terrific. Then you know the main points. Now, *your* arrival is going to be what everyone's talking about all summer, so I'd be foolish not to learn the lowdown on Bane Leo's sudden and mysterious niece first. What's your deal?"

It was the most forward statement I'd heard in days. I shoved my hands in my pockets as we ambled. "I told you my deal. Are you enrolled in the summer program, then?"

"I'll be a sophomore in the fall and my current grades are not up to snuff for my father, so yes, I'll be joining you for this depressingly boring summer program," he said. "Regarding your story, you gave me a single, spartan sentence, with no enticing details. There has to be more. My approach must be refreshing. Isn't everyone else asking you what you think of Crown City and other superficial nonsense?"

His candidness *was* freeing, and I was getting tired of staying poised.

"That's fair," I said, "but what about you? You're the mayor's son. He's all over the news, which means you're probably all over the news, and you just alluded to a weird relationship with him, meaning you clearly want to be asked about it. What's *your* deal?"

Max stopped, pulling up short and facing me so I nearly ran into him. Our chests were barely an inch apart. His charming smile shifted slowly back to devious. I fought the urge to grin back.

"How about an even trade? You give an answer for every answer I provide."

"Deal. Why does your dad hate my uncle?"

Max blew out a breath and led the way into a tall building, labeled in stocky black letters as home to the communications program. "That's less interesting than you might think. I don't know the inciting incident of their rivalry, but basically, Bane stands for good and fun and chaos, and my dad stands for order and money and rules. But you Leos have money and sway in this town, so they, and by extension you, are a thorn in my dad's side. I don't know your uncle personally, but Bane seems immune to my dad's intimidation, and I think that drives him crazy. What do you think of your uncle so far?"

My chest felt like it was tilting at being grouped in with Bane as a Leo. I swallowed the sensation away.

It wasn't the angle I expected Max to take, simply wanting to know what I thought. Max was like a mischievous creature in a fantasy movie, poking to see what he could learn. I chewed on his question, considering my urge to be honest with him.

Max didn't press me for an answer as we walked past computer labs and classrooms. I watched the way he glinted as he moved. The fluorescent lights on his hair, his buttons, the watch, the sunglasses tucked into his collar. His expensive looking teeth. I trusted my instincts, and my impression of Max was that he didn't need anything from me, he just wanted to talk to someone else with an unusual life.

"Bane and I haven't had a lot of time together yet," I said finally. "I think we both have our guards up. He's like a tornado trapped in a human body . . ." My pause suggested the pros and cons of that. Max nodded. "But . . . it seems like he's doing this for me because he's kind. And if that's the root of him, everything else will work out." I phrased my question before Max could press me further. "What's your major?"

He led us across a glass bridge connecting to the next building.

"Business."

I could have guessed.

"And I minor in art," he added. The latter part, not so much.

"I'm going with economics," I said. "What's your dad like?"

He flapped a hand at a statue of a manatee resting contentedly in the middle of the lobby we traversed. "That statue is rumored to be lucky if you pet it during finals week. And it's still my turn. I didn't ask your major." He fixed me with his deep mahogany stare, leaning close as we walked, his voice low. "What activity thrills you the most?"

His proximity heated my skin. It'd been so long since I'd spent time in the company of a guy my age. "Honestly? Right now it's the idea of getting ahead on homework."

Max deflated. "You can't be serious."

"I want to do well."

He blinked, slowly. "Admirable, but boring. We're going to have to work on that."

I rolled my eyes. "I also watch a lot of movies . . . 'We?'"

"Two of the most talked about twenty-somethings in Crown City? I think we could be great friends."

I examined his face from the corner of my eye. "Maybe. It's my turn again. You and your dad don't get along?"

Max rubbed his chin while we walked through the gleaming hallways, considering my question. "My dad is a great leader. He believes the way he sees the world is the unequivocal right way. So, it's easy for me to step outside the bounds of behavior that he deems acceptable."

I ventured, "And being the mayor's son, you must have to be looking perfect at stately events pretty often."

Max grinned ruefully at my strategy; I didn't phrase it as a question. "Yes, I am paraded around all the time. You've heard that Crown is big on galas and fundraisers and all sorts of self-congratulatory festivals, right?"

"Kind of."

"Don't worry about being judgmental. Everyone who lives here knows it's true. If you stick around, you'll become one of us and sometimes susceptible to the draw. We *do* know how to party."

I bristled at the implication my stay might be cut short. Like Bane could decide to rescind his offer and not even host me through the entire summer. I shivered. He wouldn't. I'd find a way to stay before then.

Max cut through my musings with his next question.

"What are you most afraid of?"

I scanned the walls for any sign that we might be nearing our destination. "Not living up to Bane's expectations, I guess. Whatever they are. Or being a burden to him."

Max laughed. "I meant more like how I'm terrified of large birds, but those are both supremely valid answers."

A blush's burn crept across my cheeks. "Oh. In that case, dogs. I was attacked when I was little."

It was one of the few memories of my mom that was still vivid. I remembered walking with her when I was six, through a park in our neighborhood on a snowy day. I trundled along, barely mobile in a fluffy purple snowsuit while she looked chic and uncaring in an unbuttoned peacoat that swirled around her knees.

She laughed when I threw a snowball at her, the happy sound cut short by sudden, vicious barking. Her eyes widened at something behind me. She flung me atop a park bench and braced herself between me and the mammoth dog barreling our way. She threw her arms wide and tackled it to the ground, holding it down until its owner showed up.

I didn't scream or cry. I just stared in wonder at my mother, struck by how incredible she was. How quickly she calculated and protected me. I still had a slim scar on the back of one hand from where she had accidentally scratched me in her haste to move me to safety.

My eyes pricked. "Are we almost there?" I asked Max.

"Oh right, the admissions office. I took you on the scenic route."

I scowled. "What."

Max shrugged. "You were going to need to see campus anyway, and I'm the best tour guide Camden has." His perfectly pouty lips were almost enough to distract me from being pissed.

"I'll find it myself," I said, turning on my heel.

Max touched my arm gently, but it was his pretty eyes that pinned me. "I'm sorry. I'll take you there right now. Can you blame me for wanting to spend time in the presence of someone so beautiful?"

I kept my face flat and stared him up and down, aiming for unimpressed. "Is everyone in this town so disgustingly charming? I'm trying to figure out if you're the exception or the rule."

Max somehow widened his dangerous smile, and my stomach flipped in response. "Oh, I'm the exception. No one else is quite so insufferable. You shouldn't let me talk so much. Being in the presence of a good listener makes me rambly. Therapy says it's because of my parent's divorce." His hand still on my arm, he turned me gently and pointed toward a doorway down the hall. "That's where you need to go."

I fixed him with a stare, trying to look charming myself. "Thank you, Max."

"Any time, Mel." He made my name sound like music. "I have one last question."

I raised an eyebrow.

"What's your phone number?"

I fended off a blush with snark. "Do you practice disarming facial expressions in the mirror every morning?"

Max laughed brightly, only stopping when I held out my hand for his phone. As I typed, he checked his watch, a sprawling gold monstrosity. "I have to go, but I hope to see you around." He leaned in and kissed my cheek, and I was finally at a loss for words, staring at his immaculate attire over his fit body as he strode away.

I floated into the admissions office and had the dreamy look wiped off my face immediately by the counselor waiting for me.

I was so stressed as she looked over my information on her computer. She asked me a few questions that I stammered through while I fidgeted in my seat.

"Melbourne," she said finally. "You're a unique case. Between the late application, your lackluster high school transcript, and several years since you've been enrolled formally in any type of education . . . we'll admit you."

I released a long breath.

"On a probationary basis," she finished. My stomach

dropped. "At the end of your summer term, members of an academic review board will decide if you can formally enroll at Camden. Prove yourself over these next few weeks, and we'd be happy to have you back in the fall."

I nodded dumbly, trying to fix an impassive look on my face as I shook her hand and left. I'd have to fight even harder than I thought to stay in Crown City.

CHAPTER
SIX

I PACED BACK AND FORTH AT THE EDGE OF CAMPUS. AFTER several hours, my paperwork was done, my deposit submitted with the last of my savings account, and my classes registered. I got an actual, formal tour, though the guide wasn't nearly as fun as Max. I went through it all in a daze until I found myself on the sidewalk on the western edge of campus, chewing my lip. This was my one shot to stay in Crown City. When my stay at Bane's was up, I needed to be able to move to campus, to continue my education at Camden, and find the financial aid to make it possible. My head spun with panic.

A soothing warm breeze blew from across the street, tempting me to follow it. I definitely needed to clear my head before joining back up with Bane. I couldn't let him see me frazzled like this.

I walked out into the fading afternoon light, away from campus and into one of Crown's artsy neighborhoods. I surveyed brick buildings, murals by local artists on every spare side. The shops were all small and charming. There was a promising-looking coffee shop called Hardwired, quiet and content, closed for the night, but I made a mental note to visit later. I walked by a bakery, a metaphysical store, a community garden, a comic book shop lit up electric blue. The remaining daylight disappeared behind Crown's skyline, making me shiver as I stopped at a corner.

Craning my neck, I spotted a small park down the street, a few stylized lamps casting light over a reflecting pond. It would be a pleasant place to sit and think. Turning its direction, I cut across the front of a dingy gas station.

Briskly, I traversed the asphalt, jumping when the lights inside the small attached market went out. A young man backed out of the front door and I huffed to myself as he fumbled for a key, his other arm occupied by a stuffed paper grocery bag. The attendant was closing up to head home for the day.

I offered him a small smile as we crossed paths and he glanced up briefly from putting away his keys. I made it another few feet when I heard an intake of breath followed by a slam.

"Drop the phone," a harsh voice said.

I spun. A man pressed the gas station attendant against the side of a sedan, his bag of groceries in a split heap on the ground. A horrified expression on his face, the attendant did as he was told.

The phone shattered on the pavement.

I gasped.

The sound echoed around the deserted intersection as a lime rolled past my feet. The attacker's head turned my way.

"Keep on walking, kid," he commanded, a promise of violence twisting his face.

His threat pulled the air tight around us. My panic rendered his face murky. A real mugging wasn't exactly like it looked in movies.

Then I saw the gun he shoved against the attendant's chest. Instinctual fear tore up my spine, ratcheting up my heart rate. *RUN!* flashed in my mind, over and over in bubbled, neon comic-book font over the faces of the two men staring at me.

But there was another urge, a calmer rumbling beneath the first.

Help.

He punched the attendant in the stomach, doubling him over. "Wallet. Now. Then the cash register."

I stepped forward. The attacker turned his gun on me.

"I said *leave.*"

Both arguments died out in my head. My gaze focused on the single dark abyss down the middle of the gun's barrel, and I lost the ability to make a decision.

A black mass careened from the sky and hammered onto the car. The figure rolled down beside the two men, ripping them apart and sending the attacker flying across the pavement.

He skidded into a groaning heap, his gun forgotten on the pavement in the ruin of a dropped carton of eggs.

The figure straightened. Shock rocked through my body. I knew him.

I recognized him from blurry photos on the evening news and online articles and myth. It was the Shadow. His action figure hardly did him justice.

Up close, his helmet was tight and angular. Vicious. Large enough to protect his face and shield his identity. He was an imposing figure, covered entirely in matte gray, overlapping plates. One angular, palm-sized patch tinted faintly blue in the middle of his chest, shaped like a diamond with a chip missing at the top. He moved with unfailing purpose as he stalked toward the attacker.

Most frightening of all, he was entirely silent. His feet didn't even scrape on the pavement when he turned to assure his opponent was down for good.

The cowering attendant and I stood numb, gaping at the

Shadow. The attacker moaned from the ground, clutching his jaw. He rose unsteadily, facing the vigilante.

The attacker had several inches on the Shadow and threw a desperate, wild punch. The Shadow caught his fist easily, halting its momentum. He squeezed, and this prey seized up, pain tightening his features to one small, scrunched-up point in the middle of his face.

"You must be new here," the Shadow mused, his voice like steel gravel echoing out from his helmet. "I don't allow this sort of thing in my city."

The attacker's eyes grew wide. A snap sounded lightly, then another, and he began to howl and claw at his immovable, merciless captor.

The Shadow was breaking his fingers—mangling the hand he'd used to wield the gun only a moment before.

The Shadow released his prey, and the attacker collapsed.

I released my breath, exhilarated. My heart pounded wildly.

At the sounds, the Shadow looked my way and froze. An angular, postmodern gargoyle.

He gave a single, sharp dip of his helmet, his silhouette in perfect profile against the neon glow of a lottery sign.

"Don't catch my attention again," he told the attacker, resting his chin on his fist. The attacker cradled his busted hand, whimpering. Wisely, he fled.

Then the Shadow stepped back, fading into the darkness between buildings, and was gone.

The cool rush of wind left in his wake reminded me to breathe.

My chest heaved. I stared at the spot where he'd stood. The Shadow had stopped a crime. He had saved someone from a bad thing. No one could stop him. Trap him. Tell him what to do.

It was incredible.

"I'll call the police."

My head snapped around. The attendant poked his incredulous face outside the gas station, the lights back on. Interactions with the police would probably not work wonders for my argument to be admitted to Camden.

I nodded, and the minute he turned from me, I bolted up the street.

I scrambled for my phone, but before I could dial, it rang.

"Hello?" I tried to say brightly, my breath still uneven.

"Mel," Chezza said, chipper, "do you need a ride home from Camden? I'm in town on an errand. Bane says he'll be stuck at the office later than he expected."

"Yes, please." I hung up and sprinted back to campus. I made it back in good time, collapsing on a bench a moment before Chezza pulled around the corner.

"What errands were you running?" I asked as I climbed into the car, trying to be casual.

"Picking up dry cleaning," she answered, gesturing to a stack of black garment bags piled into the back seat. The top one had a glittering silver dragonfly embossed on it. "Most of our clothes are from one shop in town, Clare's. She provided all of what Bane picked out for you, too. If there's something you like especially, tell us, and we can get more like it. Bane insists."

Her statement halted my racing thoughts for just a moment. I assumed Chezza had picked out the stash of clothes that waited in my closet.

"He did a great job," I admitted, and rested my head against the window. Seemingly comfortable with the quiet, Chezza turned up the classical music she'd been playing. She wore pale blue scrubs.

"You work in the medical field?" I asked.

Chezza's gaze didn't dart from the road. "I work in a medical lab at the hospital. Vennie is content to stay in the house all day and consult for Bane and Leo Optics, but I like to explore. Analyzing pee and blood and stuff is a nice change." She winked at me, though her tone was oddly dismissive.

I stayed quiet the rest of the way home. Over dinner, Bane asked a hundred questions about my day at Camden while he pulled a tray of brownies out of the oven, dropping the hot pan unceremoniously to clatter against the stovetop as he tried to close the oven door with his foot.

Bane pulled out a black backpack, embroidered with Camden's elk and arrow crest. "I noticed your other one was ripped." Looking sheepish, he patted it.

His flurried appearance, thoughtful gift, and unabashed generosity rendered me speechless. I traced the gold embroidery on the otherwise simple backpack. The seams were thick and sturdy and it had plenty of pockets. Unadorned but highly useful. Exactly my style. "My hero," I murmured. "Thank you."

Bane waved off my compliment, his face sheepish. "Did you like campus?"

"Definitely. But since I applied so late, they want to treat my semester as probationary. I'll have a hearing in a few weeks."

"That sounds . . . structured," Bane muttered with a frown. "But I'm sure you'll knock it out of the park." He adjusted the cooling brownie tray with his oven mitt.

"Let me help with that," Chezza offered, her usual languid, unbothered self. Bane sat back across from me, his eyes on the grandfather clock in the corner, slightly unfocused. Vennie furiously poked at something on his phone.

Chezza dished out four double portions of brownies, heavenly steam wafting from them. As Bane poised his fork, I cleared my throat.

"Oh, I saw the Shadow today," I blurted.

I expected a dramatic response, but no one jolted or gasped. I felt redness creep onto my cheeks for the second time that day, which was two too many.

Bane tilted his head, his messy tufts of hair wilder than usual. "What happened?"

I stammered a bit. "Well, this guy attacked someone in a parking lot I was walking through. He pulled a gun on him, and the Shadow just . . . showed up and stopped him." I glanced down at my plate. "It was incredible."

Bane nodded slowly and considered me before diving into his dessert. "Well, you're an official Crownie now. Seeing the Shadow is basically initiation."

Vennie grunted. "Yeah, once you meet the mayor, you'll have met our two biggest celebrities." Bane rolled his eyes.

"I wouldn't be surprised if you see him again," Chezza said. "He's always around, helping. Did you put pecans in these?" she asked Bane.

He launched into an explanation on the delicacy involved with balancing nuts and caramel as he buried his own brownie in ice cream. He offered me some, but I shook my head and tried to pay attention, though I couldn't dispel the image of that dark helmet from my mind.

Exhausted on a variety of levels, I excused myself without finishing dessert.

"Hey," Bane called, following me into the foyer. "Why don't we have an adventure tomorrow?"

I tilted my head. "What did you have in mind?"

"Would you like to see how crazy Crown City can really get?"

I couldn't help it—I grinned in response.

CHAPTER
SEVEN

THE NEXT DAY DAWNED BRILLIANTLY BRIGHT. SUNLIGHT slanted through my windows to nuzzle me in bed. I rolled over at the sound of my phone buzzing.

My stomach clenched, suspecting another verbal assault from Sam, but it was a local number.

Morning, gorgeous. Nice meeting you yesterday. I hope to see you around Crown more. —Max

Interesting.

With a grin, I drew my covers tighter around me and thought about the shape of his lips when he laughed.

Eventually, I forced myself from bed only to frown at the contents of my closet, unsure of the appropriate level of festive for an infamous Crown City celebration.

I couldn't shake the spark of hopefulness that had responded to Bane's tone when he invited me.

"Don't get attached," I muttered, flicking hangers along furiously. "You still have plenty of time to screw this up. To give him a reason to hate you." My mind returned to the broken faucet, and I refused to let the questioning go further. *Later. I'll figure it out later.*

You bring destruction wherever you go.

That fast, Sam's voice was in my head and the memory of smoke flooded my nose, my mom's pleading voice fading with each command for me to run.

Shaking myself, I grumbled and focused on the task at hand.

I spotted the lone dress tucked at the end of the rack. I pulled down the fluttery thing, pale blue with short, wispy sleeves. I whisked it on and examined myself in the mirror, half hoping the gilt lion carved at the top of the frame would offer insight.

It was pretty and cinched gently at my waist, accentuating my wide hips. I tugged on leggings and boots and went to play with the makeup Chezza had left me.

Unable to resist the pull of the sun shining through my window, I found a hand mirror and leaned on the window seat while I wrestled with eyeliner. I nearly stabbed myself with a mascara wand when my eye twitched.

Unenthused at the idea of wandering the house alone, I waited until I heard the clanking of silverware echoing from the kitchen. Checking the mirror a final time, I was pleased to see pink had risen on my cheeks as I lazed in the sunshine. Bolstered, I headed downstairs.

Chezza and Vennie occupied either end of the kitchen. Chezza sat at the table ensconced in a robe, black and pink hair tangled into a high bun. With bags under his eyes, Vennie looked stoic as ever. His uneven gait brought him toward the table to set down a mountain of pancakes, a fuzzy slipper on his foot. He dished several onto Chezza's plate, and she nearly dropped her head off her fist into a pool of maple syrup. Jerking up, she caught sight of me.

"You look nice."

I braved a grin and joined them.

The morning paper lay picked apart in the middle of the table. One page was on top of the others. I craned to read the bold headline right as Vennie offered me a bowl of berries. It was a story about me and Max, an accusing headline sprawled over a blurry cell phone shot of us on campus.

I groaned, reading the salacious speculations. "Damn it. He's the one who started flirting with me."

Chezza winced. "We didn't know if it would be best to show you or scrap it."

Vennie flipped the article over. "It's none of the press's business. Or ours, frankly."

I shook my head. "I would have seen it eventually." Folding it into a tiny square, I stashed it under my plate.

So the press thought I was trying to wile my way into Max's pants. There were worse speculations. The warm feel of him leaning close flashed through my memory. I shook it off, reaching for the orange juice. "Late night?"

"Projects," Vennie said, eyes on his tablet.

Chezza nodded.

Of course. No details for the untrustworthy newbie. My sourness was eased a little when I took a bite of the pancakes and gasped. "Oh my lions."

Chezza grinned slyly.

Vennie's eyes crinkled at the corners, the only hint through his typical impassivity that he was pleased. "My secret is a squeeze of lime juice in the batter. The acidity—"

"Don't let him start on the science," Chezza groaned. "You'll be here for hours."

"Maybe Mel wants to know," Vennie objected. "She's smart. She could keep up."

My mouth was too full to share an opinion, thankfully.

"Of course she could keep up, but it's too early for a kitchen chemistry lecture. We don't even have mimosas," Chezza bit back at her brother.

Bane arrived in the frenzied way he always seemed to be

moving, saving me from having to pick a side. He shoved two pancakes in his mouth without a word, no plate, no toppings. His hair stuck straight up in the back.

"Morning," he mumbled, forcing a swallow. He wore a gray sweater with the wrinkled collar of a denim shirt poking up underneath, looking more put together than he usually did in the morning. "Ready to go, Mel?"

"The Summer's Start Soiree doesn't start for another two hours," Chezza said.

He grinned sheepishly. "Yes, but there'll be a lot of foot traffic. We'll park at Leo Optics and walk, so we should go like . . . now."

Chezza barked a laugh and dumped more sugar in her coffee. "That, Mel, is what we call a classic Bane-boozle."

Vennie agreed between bites. "Textbook. We're trying to break him of the habit with positive reinforcement, but since he's the one who bakes all the cookies in this house, it's hard to use them as bribes."

"I'm ready," I insisted. Bane shot me a grateful look for saving him from the roasting. I stood and brushed the crumbs from my dress. "I take it this is some sort of festival we're going to?"

Chezza nodded and pulled something from her robe's pocket and handed it to me across the table.

"Completes the look," she said wisely.

It was a simple gray scarf. Without another word, she drained her coffee, tossed three more pancakes on her plate, and buried her face in one of the local gossip papers.

I draped the scarf around my neck and made to follow Bane out the door.

"Hair," Vennie prompted.

Bane's hand flew to the back of his head, staring between us. "Is it bad?"

I said nothing as Vennie nodded gravely. "You look like an over-caffeinated cockatiel."

Bane swore and stopped by the front closet on our way through the foyer, yanking a Crown City FC cap over his hair.

The SUV was parked right outside the front door. I sank into the silky seat and breathed in the scent of new leather. The sun gleamed through the windshield, and as I situated the scarf, I realized it was the same heathered gray as Bane's sweater. Like we were a pair. An allied front. A family. My stomach twisted.

Bane grinned. "Nice. Is matching lame?" I shook my head, and he continued, "You look . . . especially confident today."

"Thanks," I said, smoothing the fabric. "I wouldn't have picked it for myself, but I like it."

Bane chewed his lip and kept his eyes forward. "I actually . . . picked that out. I thought it would complement your eyes. I thought you might like having options."

My throat squeezed so tight I couldn't fit a word of gratitude through it.

He cleared his throat again. "I went a little overboard, when I found out you'd accepted and were coming to live here. I actually . . ." He hesitated. "Bought this car?"

Gears ground in my head. I glanced back. Three rows of seats, lots of storage.

He bought a family car. One step removed from a minivan.

"I'm twenty-one years old," I said slowly, unable to suppress the hint of a laugh at the end. "I don't play sports. I don't even have enough friends to fill this yet."

"I know!" Bane shouted. "Chezza told me I was an idiot. I panicked. I wanted to have whatever you'd need . . . I thought it would be a good idea to have something safe for you to drive, too, since you said you don't have a license."

The thought of practicing my rusty skills on this expensive car turned my stomach. Would Bane still feel that way when I inevitably crashed it? What if he found out why my license had been suspended in the first place?

After a quiet moment, he spoke again. "I think it's clear that, despite my best efforts, I have no idea what I'm doing. All I know about teenagers comes from when I was one, and I was a nightmare. Chezza and Vennie keep me civil, but I've mostly been alone in that house for so long . . . My parental instincts." The word constricted around my chest. "Or guardian instincts, whatever. They're kicking in, slowly but surely."

He was worried about screwing up. "You've been wonderful," I argued. "I can see you're trying, and I'm grateful. You brought me here on such short notice, so I'm still trying to figure out where . . . *if* . . . I fit here in Crown City."

"I know, I know that. It's too fast for a drastic life change. But the minute I found out about you, I had to meet you. Then you hinted at how Sam was treating you." His hands tightened on the wheel and he looked over, seeing if he needed to apologize. He didn't. "I had to get you out right away. Even if you wanted nothing to do with me, I'd get you out of there. You deserve better. You deserve to make your choices for your own life. You deserve a *break*." He drew in a deep breath and adjusted his hat, going quiet like maybe he thought he'd said too much.

My insides still squirmed into knots. This break wouldn't do me much good if I couldn't find a way to stay.

The air in the car felt too heavy as we drove between buildings that grew taller and grander toward the city's center. Sun refracted off the windows, warring with sparse masses of dense clouds. Bane shifted. "Seriously, Mel, let me know if you need anything at all. You've hardly asked for anything since you got here."

It was too much. Too intense. Too close.

"For starters, the house could use a few more lions."

My tone sliced through our conversation's taut strings.

Bane laughed. A real, loud, startled-to-joy burst, his shoulders shaking, his head tilted back.

As he composed himself, Bane explained, "Your grandpa did all that. For a while I told myself it would be too much work to take them all down, but then I realized that as much as he frustrated me, I like those reminders. Sometimes it's like he's still here."

I thought of how I hauled my mom's battered old quilt to Crown City, even though it still smelled like smoke. How I couldn't bring myself to block Sam's number. "I feel selfish for how much I enjoy the batches of hours where I don't actively think about losing my mom," I admitted.

"Grief is exhausting. The constant pain," Bane said.

We sat in our shared loss as Bane drove downtown, among the bases of towering skyscrapers that I'd only seen hints of from Camden's campus.

Leo Optics was a towering group of silver cylinders like gallant, shining sentries. The familiar logo halfway up the tallest building's side watched us. Bane parked in the structure beneath it.

Bane led the way to a wide plaza in front of the central building. "All of Leo Optics's operations occur in the main tower, from product development to assembly," he explained. "That's partly why Mayor Keep and some other business leaders don't like us. We're not interested in making friends when we can do everything perfectly fine on our own. The outer towers house businesses whose missions align with ours, from startups to nonprofits to retail."

"That's a lot of variety," I observed, a question lingering in my tone.

"Rent is customized to what each business can reasonably afford," Bane explained. "For those that pay less, it's subsidized by the company. I want us to be surrounded by like-minded people."

"You instated that?"

Bane's mouth pressed into a tight line. "Some days I make it in on time and actually get some work done. Your grandpa built an incredible company, but he didn't often stop to think about people beyond himself. Our CEO is far too good to me, and she listens to my harebrained ideas and sometimes makes them happen. Lions know I couldn't figure it out on my own."

At the base of the main tower, a massive screen sat over the Leo Optics front entrance. It depicted a lion, of course, pacing lazily back and forth across a savannah. It blinked at the few passersby traversing the plaza at the early hour. As we walked closer, he looked up at us, his eyes fixating on our approach. A gentle curve in the screen and some clever proportion work on the part of the artist made it look like the lion was lounging in a luxurious exhibit and could pounce on us at any moment.

"This is Goldy. One of the first marketing efforts I helped launch," Bane said, a hint of pride in his voice, "His programming is top notch, but my favorite component is the philanthropic initiative. If you scan that code by the doors and donate to the Leo Family Foundation, you can have an approved message put up and Goldy will paw at it, or do a variety of behaviors, depending on the size of the gift. The money is distributed to causes around the city. Conservation, food pantries, scholarships, things like that."

"That's incredible." I stared up at Goldy, who after a deep stretch plopped onto his haunches and shook out his mane.

Bane smiled. "I want to show you something else."

We circled around one of the smaller towers. Bane tugged my elbow and turned me toward a shop front, opening the door before I could read the sign over it.

I hit a near palpable wall of scent, heavy with warm sugar and cream and dark, rich chocolate.

It was a bakery, quaint and clean and bright.

"Pick anything you like," Bane said. His eyes lit as he

stepped up to a long display case, the staff greeting him with familiar smiles.

I could definitely get used to Bane's fondness for sweets.

Ten minutes, two massive cookies, and an espresso shot each later, we were jogging down the sidewalk.

I gasped around a crumbly bite and thought back to our conversation in the kitchen at the Leo house. "We're late, aren't we?"

Bane grinned back at me, his collar sticking up beneath his sweater. "Late is kind of my thing! People expect it by now. If I was on time, it would really throw them off. And *that* would be rude."

Shaking my head, I followed his frenzy through the city streets, the smatterings of people growing thicker. We skidded around a corner and I froze. A blockade was set before us, keeping milling passersby back from the platoon of gargantuan parade floats, lined up patiently like bright soldiers for five blocks in either direction.

I swallowed my last bite of cookie. "It's a parade?"

Bane gave a bashful shrug, panting lightly from our jog and looking invigorated. "Did I not say that, explicitly?"

"No . . ." I trailed off, noticing there were far more event staff than crowds. This was the loading area. "Oh, we're *in* the parade."

"Ah . . . Yep."

A classic Bane-boozle, indeed.

He ducked under the blockade and I followed, nearly nailing my head as I stared up into the stern face of a thirty-foot-tall lion made entirely of yellow and orange flowers interspersed with huge triangular screens. Cohesively, they made a brilliant mosaic of organic matter and glittering technology. The screens depicted undulating ribbons of gold light, making it look like the lion's fur flowed in the light breeze. The Leo Optics logo spun and flashed along its massive flank. Its emerald eyes glared straight ahead, wreathed in a mane of countless red roses.

"The hell kind of town is this?" I breathed.

"You said you wanted more lions?" Bane offered weakly. "Embrace the odd, Mel. It only gets stranger the longer you live here." He clapped me on the back and walked to greet a person marching toward us wearing a crisp suit, hot pink lipstick, and a severe expression.

"The line starts moving in *three minutes*," they hissed.

"And we're here with three minutes to spare, Logan," Bane said with a lopsided, placating grin.

Logan rolled their eyes. "It's *so* good to see you, too, boss. I hardly recognized you, you've been in the office so little lately."

Bane shifted his weight and held an arm out my way. "Mel, this is my *assistant*—"

Logan pointed their laser stare toward me, stroking their goatee. "Ah, yes. The niece. Lovely to meet you."

Before I could respond, Logan herded us toward the float and urged us on board. We circled to the front, standing between two massive orange carnation paws, where a railing circled as a safety precaution. "Smile, *like you mean it*," Logan said, shooting Bane a pointed look. "Please try to keep from looking like you'd rather be anywhere else."

"I *have* done this before." Bane looked down at me. "For once I wouldn't rather be somewhere else."

Logan faux gagged. "How endearing. Keep that up. The media will be paying even closer attention than normal." They eyed me. "They'll jump at any chance to critique you both."

My thoughts flitted to the morning's article speculating about Max and me.

Bane rolled his eyes, his knee bobbing. "And as usual, they can go to hell."

Logan glared evenly. "But unlike usual, your actions now affect their perception of *her*."

"I'm right here," I said.

Logan continued. "Given all our talks a few weeks ago, I assume making her life any more difficult is still *not* your goal?"

Bane scowled and leaned against the railing, resting his chin on a fist to pout. "Of course not."

"Great. So we're in agreement. Turn on the charm, Bane. If it helps, imagine how happy you'll make me on the indulgent vacation I'll take when you give me another raise." And with that, they turned sharply on their heel and stalked off, muttering, "Thirty years old and still as petulant as a teenager."

Bane turned my way. "Logan doesn't give me enough credit. I play nice for the press at least half the time . . . Reporters blow it out of proportion when I don't smile." He gave me a sarcastic version of his lopsided smile, his eyes squinted nearly closed.

"That's horrifying. Please stop," I said lightly, wringing my hands around the railing. ". . . Though I have been wondering if you brought me here as a publicity stunt."

Concern contorted Bane's face. "Oh, Mel, no. Though I feel like an idiot for not warning you about them. I've grown up with the media basically up my ass. I'm used to it, but I didn't think about how they'd want to know about you. This is why I hire people like Logan. They're harsh, but they think about what I don't. The company and my life probably wouldn't run without them . . . You'll get the hang of ignoring the cameras in no time. This'll be fun."

He sounded like he was convincing himself as well as me as a marching band blared to life somewhere ahead of us.

The float lurched into motion and Bane steadied me. "Seriously," he said, leaning close conspiratorially. "Don't be nervous. Everyone's excited you're here."

I raised an eyebrow. Bane remedied his statement. "Well, *I'm* excited you're here. There's never been much of a likable Leo in Crown City before. They'll be grateful for the change. Maybe you'll make me more palatable." I observed him with my usual flat face. "They'll at least appreciate that you're always on time."

We trundled forward, following the path of a local bank's giant astronaut balloon and a two-story tall rubber duck representing Jolley Good vegan cleaning supplies. Buildings climbed all around us, their windows bright like mirrors in the sun. I craned my neck to try and take it all in.

I mulled his words, frowning. "Are you actually excited I'm here? You don't even know me yet."

Bane gaped. "Of course I am. I—You're—" He floundered. "You're my family. That means I like you. That makes you enough. Have I not made that clear?"

I chewed my lip, considering saying I didn't know him that well, either.

"You fit," he said finally. "And that's got nothing to do with me."

I cut a glare his way. "What?"

"Earlier. You said you're trying to figure out where you fit. It's with us. The minute I found out you existed . . . I danced around the room like an idiot. I shouted for an alarmingly long time. You make me *so* happy. Just seeing you every day . . . You've met us. We're an odd bunch, and you fit."

I offered a smile and squinted as the float in front of us turned. The weather was as glorious as the sun outside my window had projected. Bright enough to cause the watering in my eyes, I told myself. Hints of true summer were arriving on the breeze, as if the parade really was going to shepherd in the season.

"Do you believe me?" Bane asked breathlessly.

"Yes." My response was hoarse. I cleared my throat. "This festival celebrates the summer? We haven't had a solid string of warm days yet."

Bane respected the shift in topic. "Crownies will take any excuse to celebrate. Like if we party hard enough, the sun will decide to come out early and stick around," He looked skyward. "We might be in luck, if those clouds stay back. Some years, it rains. One time it snowed."

I shuddered, silently cursing the Midwest's capricious moods.

Our float turned onto a wider avenue that commenced the formal parade route, and cheers rose in a thundering wave. Flocks of people lined both sides of the street in vibrant colors busted out for the Summer's Start Soiree, brightened by the sun streaming perfectly between the rows of buildings.

"Time to be charming," Bane muttered sourly. He fixed his own smile and lifted an arm in a jaunty wave. The first row of onlookers tore their eyes from the Jolley Good duck to stare in awe at our lion. Its hide flashed bright and mesmerizing, a grand roar echoing from hidden speakers.

After the initial wonderment, their gazes roamed downward to admire Bane, and then settled on me, full of questions. I waved and tried not to look awkward.

My cheeks quickly ached from the smiling and the chill breezes whipping down the wind tunnel created between the buildings. I flinched every time someone pointed a finger my way.

Bane steadied me, touching my shoulder lightly. "Focus on the kids," he said. "It helps."

He was right. When I made eye contact with them, it was easy to mirror their smiles of delight. Letting my eyes scan quickly over every other face as I looked from child to child helped.

Every few minutes, the procession would halt as a float or group of performers stopped in front of City Hall to be formally announced. My anxiety grew as we approached. It was where the bulk of the reporters and cameras huddled. Lights and cameras were strewn across rigging and a wide, temporary stage crawled with people. The congregation moved again, and we inched closer to the designated spot. I tried to look confident. One reporter saw me and a flash of recognition jolted across his face. He mouthed my name. Then all at once, a group of them pushed into the street and began shouting at me.

"Melbourne, what do you think of Crown City?"

"Tell us about your relationship with Max Keep!"

"What does your dad think of all this?"

I gasped. "How do they know about him?"

I shrunk back, and Bane shifted to shield me, glaring at the press. "I don't know. Time to be selfish," he muttered. He pulled out his phone. "Take a photo with me?"

"Sure."

He glanced into the screen while reporters squawked, adding his name to the mix. "Lighting's all wrong," he muttered, and slung an arm around my shoulders, gently pulling me back between the lion's paws, beneath the shadow of its mane. Security officers finally got control of the small media stampede and urged them back behind a barricade. "Much better," Bane mused. He lifted his phone high between us. "Say 'lions'!"

I allowed a small smile of relief and Bane snapped a photo.

The reporters properly herded, and we moved forward again, inching into the designated spot over a purple and gold city emblem pressed into the pavement. Cameras flashed in earnest and I let my eyes roam the crowd of reporters and officials, looking for something to find solace in.

A pristine smile flashed brighter than the cameras, and I locked eyes with Max. He stood on the stage, just off center. He grinned at me wickedly as I blinked in surprise. Max flicked his hand, gesturing down to his sharp gray suit, the fibers subtly metallic in the sun. He inclined his head and winked. I raised an eyebrow and tried to look unimpressed.

The woman standing next to him looked my way. She was tall like Max, though her brown skin was several shades darker. She held up a massive faux check—written out to a Crown City charity—to cover her mouth as she spoke to Max. From the tilt of his head, it looked like she was asking him a question.

The announcer bellowed. "Next we have Leo Optics! Innovators of the world's most advanced screens. Leo Optics: See more, clearly."

Max's composure faltered for a moment as someone strode up to him. His mother's face soured and she stepped away to speak with a group of volunteers.

Even if he hadn't been standing right next to Max, I would have recognized his father. Mayor Keep was the same height as Max but with wider shoulders, and his skin was white to Max's light brown. He had hair like steel, and it was styled as meticulously as Max's. Heavy lines dragged at the corners of his mouth and eyes.

He stared right at me, his lips a thin line, his thick brows low and disapproving. Clearly his distaste for Bane extended to me. He certainly read the morning papers.

My spine iced. Mayor Keep was on the board at Camden, the one that would decide whether or not I'd be fully admitted.

Bane followed my glare and hugged my shoulders. "Don't let that old blowhard get to you. He doesn't like anyone." With that, he winked and directed finger guns right at the mayor, whose frown deepened before he turned away. "Good riddance, you over-veneered nightmare," Bane said through a grin.

"Why is Max's mom here?" I asked.

"You know Max Keep?" he asked.

I shrugged. "He goes to Camden." I would *not* be having that conversation with him.

"Right, um, she runs a nonprofit and plays nice with the

mayor for photo ops and things. It helps assure they get funding."

We lurched forward and stopped abruptly. Bane and I craned to see the disruption. The duck float ahead of us stalled, a giant faux bubble caught under its wheel, rendering it immobile. The reporters prepared to swarm again, taking advantage of the lull. A storm of camera flashes blinded us.

Bane sighed. "Sweet fucking lions, you've got to be kidding me."

One of the reporters took a tentative step toward us, gesturing for her camera operator to follow.

Bane scowled, staring daggers. "How would you like a better view?" he asked me.

He nodded toward the top of the lion. Thin strips of metal climbed up its side in a neat, subtle row, leading up behind its neck. Rungs, like a ladder.

"I can *ride* it?"

Bane's eyes twinkled. "And get some space from the press. We Leos do love a spectacle."

Without a moment's hesitation, I placed my hand on the first rung. It was lovely and warm from the sun. I began to climb.

Bane remained by my side, one arm hovering protectively behind me. "Be sure to buckle in at the top."

Pulling myself up was easier than I expected. I hauled up the rungs. In a flash I was at the top, beside a wide seat molded just behind the lion's mane of flowers.

I glanced around, hoping the sounds and faces of the crowd would be quieter higher up, but they echoed louder, magnified somehow. I hoisted myself into the seat, having to pull myself the last few inches to accommodate my short legs. I kicked my feet and managed to haul one leg over. I sat up and smiled, a little out of breath and extremely pleased that I'd opted to wear leggings under the dress. From my perch, I could see Crown City's splendor for blocks, shining in the sun.

I squinted and twisted, searching for the safety belt Bane mentioned.

A blast of wind buffeted me, built up from rolling down the parade route. Gritting my teeth, I gripped the iron bar that served as a handle on the seat's front, hating the air's frigid traces along my bare arms. Looking up, I saw it heralded a batch of grumpy clouds.

Dismayed, I watched them inch over the sun, blotting its rays, plunging the street into shadow. The wind picked up, tearing the scarf from my neck.

I shivered as the heat leeched from my body. The crowd grew disgruntled. People frowned and tugged sweatshirts from backpacks, blankets from strollers.

They all looked put out, except for Bane. He grinned up at me like a lunatic.

The wind rushed again, shoving against me like a bully.

Then I felt woozy.

The familiar fainting feeling swept up my torso. With a scowl, I groped behind the seat. Where was the damn safety belt? My left hand was wrapped tightly around the iron handle, my knuckles tinged blue. I felt frozen, like I couldn't move. As my vision swam, I stared down at Bane in panic.

"Mel?" he shouted, worry drawing his eyebrows close together.

And strangely, something like recognition.

A particularly icy blast slammed into me. Black tinged the edge of my vision. I heard screeching metal and the first note in a chorus of gasps as I blacked out and slumped sideways off the float.

CHAPTER
EIGHT

My eyes snapped open to a hulking shadow ringed in sunlight. It moved closer and Bane's face became clear. He hovered over me, laser focused.

"How many times?" he demanded.

"What?" I fought to sit up, my well-trained fainting recovery process nearly automatic. The sun glared down on us, the clouds having fled while I'd been unconscious. I was lying on the float alongside one of the lion's massive, flowered paws.

Bane's grip was gentle as he moved us both so we were shielded from the crowd's view, his hands like ice. He swore and whipped off his hat, settling it on my head.

"How many times have you fainted like this? Is this the first time?" He spoke fast and low, his eyes steely.

I looked around him, trying to make sense of what happened. Two security officers tried to approach us from the back of the float. The street teemed with people, but the cheers had morphed to shouts of alarm. Officials tried to hold back the crowd. Someone yelled for a doctor.

"She's fine," Bane snapped. "Give us some space!"

The guards paused at his tone, looking at him like he was a wild animal.

He shoved his face in my line of sight again, interrupting my attempts to act normal or survey the situation, positioning himself so he was all I could see. He helped me sit upright against the lion, the scent of flowers flooding me.

"Mel, focus! How often? When did it start? How long do they last?"

I froze, meeting his stare. "This happens sometimes."

But somehow he already knew that.

"It started last year," I continued. "It's happened six or seven times."

His eyes left mine as he looked around. Logan's spiky head bobbed through the crowd. "No paramedics. *No* media!" Bane shouted to them.

Logan nodded tersely and turned to call to the crowd. "She's just dehydrated. Everyone relax. Please stay back and prioritize safety."

The Bane I'd come to know was chaos, but the man before me was all cool control. As if, upon seeing me fall, something had clicked into place.

"I'm not hurt," I said slowly. I didn't feel any pain except a receding pounding in my head.

"How's your headache?"

"I didn't say I had one. How do you know that?" I demanded.

"Because it's what happens when I faint," Bane said matter-of-factly, then continued with intensity, "Mel, I caught you when you fell." I stared at his eyes that matched mine. "Things are about to get super weird. Like, infinitely wild. I need you to trust me. I haven't earned it, but I'm asking you to anyway. Can you do as I say? Until I get us out of here. Then I'll explain. I promise."

I opened my mouth to ask a question, but he cut me off.

"Please." It was the look on his face that stopped me.

Fear. It was shielded behind determination for self-preservation at all costs. It was a face I made often.

I snapped my mouth shut and nodded. Bane glanced around, then grabbed the collar of his sweater. In one quick motion, he tore it down the middle. He shrugged it off and handed it over. "Put this on," he said tersely, straightening the shirt he wore underneath.

I obeyed silently, sliding my arms into the makeshift cardigan.

He held his hands tentatively toward mine. "I need you to give me that."

I followed the movement with my eyes, to my hands clenched tightly in my lap. They were wrapped around the iron rung I had used to cling to the float, the edges torn and mangled. I opened my hands to reveal ten perfect imprints of my fingers pressed into the metal, complete with fingerprints.

Bane gently tugged it from my grip and didn't look the least bit concerned as he tied the solid metal bar into a knot, then crumpled it in his fist as easily as if it were a napkin and tucked it in his pocket. "I have something I need to tell you."

🔥🔥🔥

LOGAN IMPRESSIVELY WITHHELD THE CRUSHING WAVE OF MEDIA with their voice alone, subtly pointing out a break in the crowd. Bane helped me from the float, and I leaned into him as we escaped. Once clear of the crowds, he picked up the pace, both our short legs straining. With an unfamiliar iron focus, Bane kept his eyes straight ahead, urging me on. We dashed across streets closed off for carnival rides and snack stands that would be swarmed after the parade. Bane kept one arm protectively around my shoulders, though not quite touching me.

He pulled me into an alley between major streets. Rear entrances to a handful of dive bars lined either side. Whiffs of food waste and fry oil floated around us, rendering me both hungry and nauseated.

Bane spun on me, his face wild. "Are you okay?"

"Unclear," I muttered.

I focused on where my feet met the ground, trying to make sense of what had happened. The woozy fainting feeling was slipping away, leaving the dregs of a headache.

I brushed my fingers along my forehead, marveling at the lack of pain. "I think I'm okay."

"Are you going to pass out again? Are you cold?" Bane's stare was intent on my face.

"It doesn't feel like it . . . You told them I was fine already."

"I lied. I don't care about them. I care about you. Are you okay?" he asked again.

I spoke slowly, as his eyes had gone huge. "Beyond wildly confused and fairly certain those cookies were laced with hallucinogens, I'm all right."

"The sun. The *sun!*" Bane said, whirling to pace along the alley. "I'm such an idiot. Of course we're the same . . . only *opposites*. Like me and—So your mom . . . Holy shit. The press is going to have a field day with that fall . . ."

I opened my mouth to ask a question when his phone rang. He looked concerned for a moment, then answered.

"It's already on the news, isn't it?"

A pause. Then Vennie's voice confirmed Bane's fear across the line. I heard him as clearly as if the phone were pressed to my ear instead, and a second voice I recognized as Chezza's.

"Is Mel hurt?"

"She's fine, I think." Bane glanced back at me, and I offered a noncommittal shrug. "No evident injuries. Because she *is* like me. Well, more like my dad."

That startled me. He only ever referred to Sydney by his name or as "your grandpa."

Chezza spoke again. "Well, fuck."

"We're idiots," Vennie added.

Bane nodded enthusiastically, as if they could see. "She runs *warm*. That's why we haven't seen her show signs. Not in the house, the way we keep it."

"The way *you* keep it," Chezza corrected. "I wouldn't mind turning the heat on every once in a while."

My phone buzzed adamantly from my dress pocket, making me jump. Max's name lit up the screen. I jabbed the ignore button, and the glass shattered beneath my finger, its interior giving out a startled electric shriek. I stared in horror.

"Uncle Bane?" I asked. His face snapped toward mine, yanked out of his flurried focus.

I held my palms out toward him, still red from their tight grip on the float's rungs, my phone a fractured wreck in my left hand.

Bane floundered. "You were due for an upgrade, right?"

"Please tell me what the hell is going on."

He hung up his phone and pulled me into a hug. "Of course. It's scary the first time. I completely forgot."

I was afraid to squeeze my arms around him in return. "The first time *what*," I demanded, abruptly very done with his inability to stay on topic.

"The first time you realize you have superhuman strength," he said simply, his head settled on top of mine. My face contorted as he pulled back and glanced around the alley, reading the doors. Before I could ask for clarification, he ushered me through one marked Jardello's.

We stepped into a restaurant's darkened annex. With the dinner rush a few hours off, there was no one around except a server folding napkins at the host's stand. She eyed Bane. "I like your other outfit better," she remarked.

Bane walked toward a booth, all charming smiles. "Is Don here? Would he mind if we sit for a minute?"

"I'll tell him," she said, and disappeared through a set of

double doors to what must have been the kitchen, given the sprawling gleam of stainless steel.

I sat across from Bane and started talking before he could continue with his trademark half-thoughts. "Uncle Bane," I said again, "how did you know about my fainting, and what does that have to do with the fact that I somehow wrecked your parade float? Did you say *superhuman strength?*"

Finally, Bane looked a shade worried. "Mel, you and I are—"

The kitchen doors busted open and a man with a lot of hair and even more belly sauntered over with a gloriously full basket of breadsticks.

"Bane-o!" he boomed. "It's nice to see you during daylight. About time, but I'm sorry to say we don't have any sauce ready. It's too early."

"That's fine, we just need to avoid the photographers for a little while," Bane explained.

"Ah, the press. They're almost as scary as what usually chases you through these streets." Don turned his friendly face on me. "Finally, a new recruit? I've always said you're a fool to act alone."

Bane covered his face with his hands, and his voice came out muffled. "She was grandfathered in, so to speak."

Don sauntered away, and rather than sort through their cryptic exchange, I double-fisted breadsticks. Mercifully, they stayed intact in my grip. Bane set the warped knot of metal on the table between us. My instincts itched to touch it, but I crammed another breadstick in my mouth then sat on my hands.

He held my gaze. "That float was made brand new by Leo Optics this year. State of the art, with the finest materials."

He waited.

"And I . . ." I began, having trouble admitting what I'd witnessed, what I'd felt and done, because it was impossible. I released a breath and pointed at the metal scrap. "I ripped that . . . with my hands."

"Yes," Bane said, and stared at me for a while, seeming to decide where to start with whatever wild explanation he could offer. He tried a few times, glancing away, then rubbed his hands together. He fidgeted worse than my mom had when she gave me the sex talk. Finally, Bane spoke, folding his napkin neatly into smaller and smaller squares as he did. His eyes never left mine.

"A long time ago, Sydney Leo underwent a gene altering procedure that gave him superhuman strength, among other enhanced abilities. He didn't realize that those attributes would pass down through our bloodline. I have them. I wasn't sure if you had them, until today."

I stared. The word *superhuman* was strictly reserved for comic books and movies . . . based on comic books.

"We're superhuman?" I said slowly.

"You don't sound upset."

"There are worse family secrets."

Bane eyed me, then grinned. He leaned forward excitedly. "Well, superhuman is a broad term. More accurately, we're Extrahuman."

I grabbed another breadstick. "Extrahuman."

Bane continued, "Your grandpa coined the term. Because we're humans, with a little extra." He lilted the phrase like an ironic slogan.

"But you weren't sure I was," I repeated.

Bane spoke around a bite. "Since I have powers, there was a decent chance your mom did, too, but we know so little about Adelaide. With no evidence that she had them, we couldn't guess if they would pass down again to a grandchild. Plus, your signs are showing earlier than mine did."

"Signs?"

"When was the first time you passed out like that?"

I fidgeted. ". . . After my mom's funeral. Not even a year ago."

I avoided thinking about that day as best I could. How I'd run for the church's doors, burst out, and collapsed in the snow. Sam's disgusted face as I came to. Thatcher watching over me in a side room while the service finished.

Bane frowned. "And how long until the next time?"

"A little over a month. They're getting more frequent."

He nodded as if that's what he expected. "Mine started in my mid-twenties. I didn't think much of it. I contributed it to my lifestyle. I was a nomad, at the time. Living all over, learning as much as I could, but not paying too much thoughtful attention to what I consumed. How much I slept."

According to whatever sci-fi movie Bane lived in, my fainting spells were *normal*. He'd had them too! Hope spiraled out of control in my chest, with no way for me to reign it in. "I'm super strong?"

Bane gestured to the crushed hunk of metal. "Clearly."

My memories unspooled backward, trying to make sense of my sickness. "But not all the time."

"You feel sick pretty often, right? And you can't find an explanation why?"

"Who told you that?"

"No one. When you fainted off the top of the float, I recognized it. The same thing used to happen to me all the time until I figured it out."

"Grandpa didn't tell you about this?"

Bane shook his head. "Not before he died. I suspect he didn't think the powers could be passed down. He was older than me when he underwent his experiment. The abilities must emerge earlier in each generation. I didn't think I'd have to explain this to you for a few years."

"This is why I feel sick? Why I pass out all the time?" My heart surged at the idea of finally having an explanation for my frailty.

Bane nodded. "What does it feel like? Lethargy . . . A sour stomach?"

I wrung my hands. "Yes, exactly . . . I thought something was wrong with me."

Bane shook his head. "There's nothing wrong with you, just your surroundings. Our enhanced abilities are revealed in proper environmental conditions. In our case, temperature. I'm only strong when I'm cold. You are the opposite. Like Sydney, you're strong when you are surrounded by heat."

"What."

"Think about it. You climbed that float no problem today, because the sun was out and you're wearing layers. Climbing built heat, too. But when the clouds and the wind cut through, you lost it."

I stared off, working through the implications. I finally had an answer about my frailty. An outlandish, impossible answer.

Bane sprang up. "Wild, right? Here, it's better to show you."

I trailed him to the kitchen, trying to process the revelations as he spoke over his shoulder. "It seems that when the abilities are passed down through each generation, the impact of temperature extremes switch."

He stopped at a tall freezer. The hostess eyed him warily. "I'll pay for anything I ruin, Judy," he said, flashing another smile. She rolled her eyes and left.

"We had a bad date once. Entirely my fault," Bane explained as he opened the freezer's door and thrust his hand in among the pints of gelato and cuts of meat. I stepped back from the waft of chilly air.

"See?" he said. "It's instinctual."

Bane withdrew his hand and grabbed a fork off the counter. He pinched it delicately between his index finger and thumb, and like it was made of pudding, they met in the middle and the fork clattered to the counter in pieces.

"Your turn," he said quietly, tilting his head toward a pot of boiling water on the stove.

"People are going to eat out of that," I chided, and looked for something that wouldn't be wasteful. A full pot of decaf steamed in the coffee machine.

Lifting the pot and feeling incredibly foolish, the thought came to me that this might be the moment I learned all the rumors circulating about Brisbane Leo were true, and that he was insane. Sucking in a breath, I poured a thin stream of scalding coffee over my palm, dripping a small puddle onto the floor.

Despite the foreboding steam, it felt pleasantly warm on my skin.

Bane set a knife in the middle of my palm. Without thinking, I shut my eyes at the same time I closed my fist around the handle and squeezed.

A second passed, and I heard the dull clang of the blade hitting the floor.

Slowly, I looked down to see the mangled handle in my palm. Bane looked triumphant, and I went into a sort of disbelieving shock.

The colors before me bled together, and a hollow rushing filled my ears.

Bane touched my elbow. "I think it's time we head back to the car. Better to freak out at home."

I nodded numbly and let him tow me through the back door. Don called us a cheerful farewell and said to come back soon.

The pavement sent reverberations up my legs and brought me back to the present as we tore through the streets.

Extrahuman. The word ricocheted around my head, moving too fast for me to grab onto and examine. I kept my eyes focused on Bane's back and tailed him, fiddling with the edges of the sweater he'd wrecked to keep me warm. He kept glancing back at me.

The fifth time he did, he nearly plowed into the corner of a florist's shop by taking a turn too soon. Not great, considering I wasn't sure the difference between up and down, because I'd learned that what I thought was an undiagnosed, debilitating mystery illness was actually undiagnosed, sometimes-debilitating mystery . . . powers.

"I'm fine," I told him unconvincingly. "No matter how weird this is, my new bed is too comfy for me to bolt on you now."

That startled a laugh from him, and he kept his eyes on the sidewalk. He led us down another long, shaded alley, and I could see the Leo Optics sign glaring at us at the far end as we neared the underground parking structure.

"Hey," I started, tugging Bane's sweater tighter around me.

Bane turned back abruptly, and I saw it then, killing the question in my throat. He'd dropped some of his carefulness since I'd fallen off the parade float. Since my arrival in Crown City, I'd thought he had walls up because I was new, an outsider, a family member he didn't know he could trust. For the past twenty minutes, I'd thought it was because he had been hiding his powers.

But that was only a shade of the full spectrum of the secret, and I saw it then, with the sun completely hidden behind the buildings. The way he filled that dark space, his stature fearless, looking double his size and so sure of his surroundings and himself. His legs shifted and weight recentered at my call, in case I was alerting him to trouble. I saw it the second his head swiveled sharply to me, the same way a helmet had just yesterday. I halted suddenly and shouted, arms flung out, acting more related to him than ever.

"This is why everyone thinks you're a lunatic!" I shouted.

"Not *everyone* thinks I'm a lunatic. Just the vast majority of people."

Missed meetings. A schedule that never added up. Sudden

disappearances. Private doctors. No close friends. No long-term relationships. No one on the property, ever.

"Lions," I breathed. "You're the Shadow."

That uneven smile crept over his face.

"A superhero," I ventured.

A single sharp dip of his chin.

The dread that constantly occupied my stomach shifted then, draining away to make room for a sensation I wasn't super familiar with—brilliant, epic potential. Bane waited.

"I get to be a superhero, too?"

His eyes like mine flared, like my response was all he ever dared to hope for.

"If you want to be."

"I do. Right now," I said, shooting a smile back at him.

"Okay then."

CHAPTER
NINE

THE CAR RIDE BACK WAS SILENT. BANE TURNED UP THE HEAT on my side of the car and let me process. As we circled the big marble lion out front of the Leo house, I chose the first of a thousand questions I had for my uncle.

"Chezza and Vennie know about you . . ." It was still hard to say out loud. "They must help, then?"

Bane nodded enthusiastically. "I couldn't be successful without them. With her experience in a medical lab, Chezza is our first aid resource, as well as a brilliant problem solver. She generates the ideas for a lot of our equipment, and Vennie helps refine the designs and make the tech actually happen. He's also a prolific hacker."

"Chezza's the idea person. Vennie then makes her concepts a reality."

"Exactly."

"Who else knows?" I asked as we climbed out of the car and headed through the front door.

Bane scratched his head. "A few others—Don graciously operates his restaurant as a safe house when I need it. There's a woman who helps us with hard-to-procure supplies. My doctor knows for the rare extreme medical emergency. I suspect Logan has a hunch."

I stared at my hands. "If I stay warm, I shouldn't faint anymore?" Hope flared in my chest. It was still so hard to believe.

Bane nodded, a grimness taking over his excited demeanor for a moment as we went inside. "While heat makes you stronger, cold makes you weaker. I'm the opposite. I haven't been in high heat for more than ten minutes in . . . years, probably."

"How is that possible?" I asked. He always wore sweaters, and while it was still chilly in Crown City, I'd read its Midwest summers became impressively hot.

"Thanks to the genius of my few friends," Bane explained as he tugged his shirt's collar sideways, revealing the rounded corner of a slim, nearly translucent patch. A thin strip of wires leading away from it disappeared beneath the rest of his shirt.

"Am I supposed to know what that means?"

"It's called a Tempatch. Chezza and Vennie developed it. I'm wearing seven right now. They pull heat away from my skin and keep me cool all day. You see how intense these social functions can get quickly," he said, his humor unfailing even as he tried to explain that we were basically mutants.

I followed him through the kitchen and into the back hallway that connected to the garage. On our left, carpeted stairs led upward to Chezza's rooms. Bane turned to the other end of the short hallway, where a neat, patterned rug lay in front of a portrait of, of course, a lion.

This one depicted a lioness, finally. She perched on a wide, sun-drenched rock, scanning the horizon.

Bane gripped the right-hand side of the thick frame, wrapping his fingers around it. A moment passed, then something whirred softly, and green light flashed behind the frame, scanning his fingerprints.

The light turned white, and Bane pulled. The entire painting swung open like a door, revealing a staircase that matched Chezza's, except this one led down.

Bane pulled the painting aside, standing back to point an open hand down the dark stairwell. Bright light leaked up from the distant bottom, and familiar, mischievous voices floated up to us.

"After you," he said.

Bane stayed close as I descended. It was a long stairwell, but it didn't warrant the light-headed feeling that consumed me as I carefully stepped further into the gaping cavern beneath the Leo house.

Nearly as long as the house itself, the room's uneven walls were gouged directly from the bedrock, melded at sporadic intervals with sprawling metal sheets. Slim pillars dotted the space, disappearing into the ceiling to support the house above. The area was littered with random commodities: thick padded mats, a patched blue sofa, a freestanding exam table, and medical equipment that looked directly transplanted from a premier hospital. An intimidating metal door was tucked into a back corner, and closest to me was a row of metal shelving divided into tall cubbies, a wide bench before it. Hung neatly in the first was the Shadow's suit, the pointed blue emblem gleaming innocuously.

Bane rested a hand on a shelf next to the Shadow's helmet —*his* helmet—and ruffled his hair.

I spun slowly. The Leo family crest was carved into the wall next to the stairs, accented with gold. It was as tall as me, and better than any iteration elsewhere in the house. This one has been graffitied. The lion's mane was painted vibrant colors; mostly pink, some fluorescent yellow, a single strand of black. A bandage was scribbled across its forehead, and a small hoop through its left ear. Its eyelids were tinted with green glitter and flared lashes. The typical regal banner waved beneath it, but the word *Glory* had been crossed out with a violent red *X*, and in the hectic handwriting that had changed my life, Bane had remedied it to read *For Good*.

Bane eased up beside me, his hands deep in his pockets. "I had an intense punk phase."

"*Had*," Chezza's snort rang.

Across the room, she leaned against a table, grinning knowingly. Vennie perched on a stool, angled away from a massive curve of glass that dominated the middle of the room. "Welcome to the family, for real this time." He gestured to a full spread of takeout before them. "We figured you'd be hungry."

Bane dove for the food while I explored. Photos and articles were taped all over the cubbies. The blurry image of the Shadow leaping between rooftops from the day I arrived was taped on top. Next to it, someone had displayed my old senior school photo from Upstate High. I conceded a small smile and surveyed the other articles. Some were yellow and brittle, the print indistinct.

"Shadow sightings have been reported for over forty years . . ." I said, confused.

"And I don't look a day over twenty-nine?" Bane asked.

I ignored him, trying to make sense of all he'd told me. He was sprinkling in bits and pieces, trying not to overwhelm me with the ramifications my grandpa's choices had wrought on our family.

My grandpa. His experiments were the reason we had powers.

"Grandpa was the Shadow, too," I realized. "He was the Shadow *first*."

Bane nodded, a satisfied set to his mouth.

"Here," Vennie called, pointing to the expanse of curved glass. He sat at a sleek workstation before it, another sheet of glass beneath his hands. I walked to the curve and saw that it was of course a giant screen. It was massive, nearly transparent, and unlike anything else I'd seen from Leo Optics. Vennie pulled up a legible scan of the faded article. It reported a bizarre, masked figure had assaulted a crew of thieves in the middle of an art theft.

I tilted my head. "Was Grandpa trying to become a superhero?"

Bane shook his head. "He was trying to explore the limits of the human body. He wanted to be stronger. Live longer. He worked with a research partner named Eleanor Kavoh, who was a brilliant geneticist. Your grandpa didn't keep great records, or he destroyed them. From what we do know, we think that at the beginning, he didn't think the experiments worked. He split from Dr. Kavoh soon after their experiments. But a few years later, Sydney started fighting crime. We think it was self-serving, mostly. That he was testing his limits rather than trying to help people. Those first thieves were stealing from *his* collection at the museum."

Chezza frowned. "Those guys were working with a drug cartel. It was probably better that they didn't have the money they'd get from selling the paintings."

"Yeah, fine," Bane conceded. "So Sydney occasionally busted crimes on and off for years. I didn't discover this place until after he died." He trailed off, lost in thought.

I stepped closer to the giant curved screen, lifting a hand to touch it. Vennie made a noise in his throat but was quickly muffled when Chezza kicked him. Vennie coughed and remedied what he'd been about to say. "That's the Luminous Ultra Mainframe Arc. The LUMA. It's an advanced computer and screen hybrid. My favorite pet project . . . You can touch it."

I tapped the LUMA. A search bar appeared. I wrote directly on the glass with my finger.

SHADOW VIGILANTE CROWN CITY

Dozens of headlines appeared. They populated above my head, then scrolled quickly downward in neat rows, filling the entire screen. I tapped a handful of the most recent, popping them open and dragging them to different parts of the glass, spreading them as far as I could reach. The headlines spanned scores of thwarted crimes. Muggings, drug deals, theft, homicide. Most were coupled with photos of a tidied crime scene. Only a few included grainy photos of a figure in black.

Through the glass, Bane's hair was wild above stormy eyes. He had his chin propped on a fist, gauging my reaction. Only his subtly shifting weight betrayed his nerves.

"You saved all these people," I said. The words *you saved me* stuck in my throat as I remembered the Shadow ripping an assailant away from me. "You must save a lot of people."

"I try to," he said, his face unreadable.

Chezza nudged me. "Don't let it go to his head." She held up a flat gray node the size of an ice cube. "May I?"

I nodded, and she tugged aside Bane's ruined sweater to press it against the inside of my bicep, where it stuck on its own.

She looked at the curved screen expectantly, and after a moment, a series of readings populated across it. My vitals.

"This is like . . . your Shadow Cave?" I ventured.

"We call it the Den," Chezza said, reading my data intently.

"This family and the strong branding," I mused, then turned my gaze on Bane. "You're a vigilante," I confirmed.

Vennie winced, "Don't say the *v*-word. He doesn't like it."

Bane rolled his eyes. "When I discovered my powers, and what your grandpa had been doing, which was just busting crimes when he was bored, I decided to take it further. It gives me a purpose."

I knew how singular focus kept grief at bay. How devastating loss made you desperate for an anchor when yours was suddenly gone.

Bane loosed a long breath. "How are you holding up with all this?"

I looked down at myself. Wide hips, short legs, same as always. But a deeper potential underneath, apparently. I breathed in deep through my nose. My thoughts felt watery and hard to grasp, as if there weren't any more room in my head for revelations.

"I'm okay," I decided.

"We should start her on five Tempatches." Chezza peeled the node off my arm.

Vennie rubbed his chin absently and picked up a soldering tool and a network of patches like Bane wore.

"If my temperature affects my strength . . . Sometimes I've been warm and not broken things, and sometimes I've been cold and not fainted."

"Well, if you're like me . . ." Bane started.

Shadow's suit was visible over his shoulder. I wanted to be like him more than ever.

"When my abilities started," Bane said, "they weren't consistent. I would feel sick sporadically, sometimes worse than others, and I'd randomly break things by accident."

"Like my favorite Gamebox controller. I custom built that thing," Vennie said, not looking up.

Bane continued, "We found this place soon after I discovered my powers. We deciphered a little about my powers from the clues we found down here. I found ways to be cold consistently, and my body's reaction evened out until I could control my strength."

Chezza sighed longingly. "Ah, those days before Tempatches, when you were scantily clad most of the time." She sauntered up to Bane and rapped his sternum with her knuckles. "Come on, hero. Show her the layout."

Turning slightly pink, Bane unbuttoned his shirt.

An impressive network of patches and flat wires sprawled across his skin. Chezza whistled appreciatively at the lines of his abs, and I crinkled my nose. She tapped a finger on a patch over his chest. "The Tempatches are one of our best inventions. We think Sydney just wore layers all the time, and his suit was insulated to retain heat, since he ran warm like you. But we can't send Bane around naked and covered in ice packs all day. These keep him cool, so he's not passing out, or conversely breaking things."

I reddened, thinking of my mangled faucet.

"You'll grow used to your own strength, and moderating it," Bane said.

Vennie came over with a small stack of wireless patches. "These should work for now. I modified Bane's to reflect heat onto the skin instead of dispersing it away. I'll get started on your own set. In the meantime, these will help you be more comfortable on a day-to-day basis. Do you mind?" He motioned toward me, and I conceded, rolling up my sleeves.

He peeled backing away from a patch, then smoothed it along my arm. It was the size of my palm and slim, bending easily with my skin. He placed another at the base of my neck, then prompted me to take off my boots and shift my leggings so he could place two against my shins while I stuck one on my other arm.

"Let's see how you like these. They're short term and function completely on their own. A full set is wired like Bane's can run indefinitely and be controlled with an app I developed," Vennie said, rubbing absently at the spot where his leg met his prosthesis.

"Speaking of, can you order Mel a new phone? Hers was one of the day's casualties," Bane said as he pulled his shirt back on.

Vennie nodded. "These are good if you're in a rush, or if you're wearing clothes that won't conceal the wires, or only need the temperature for a few hours. How do you feel?"

Warmth radiated from the patches. I arched my head back at the sensation flowing from the one on my neck. I flexed my arms experimentally, not sure what I expected to happen. I still shook from nerves and the thrum of blood through my arms as the pads leaked warmth into my skin. My heartbeat thundered in my ears.

They were all staring at me.

"So good," I said finally.

"I'd like to see what you're capable of," Bane said. "From what we can glean from your grandpa's notes, my capabilities extend a little further than his. We've been wondering if the powers' capacity increases with each generation."

"You think I could be even stronger than you?" I asked. From the reports, the Shadow could lift a truck.

Bane grinned. "I know you are, but I want to know how much."

"Um. What should I do?" My first thought was to karate chop the table, but that seemed cliche on top of being rude.

Bane's eyes darted around the room. Vennie gestured to a dilapidated toaster on the table, perhaps thinking if I smashed it, he wouldn't have to admit that he couldn't figure out how to make it work.

Bane tentatively placed his hands on my shoulders and turned me toward one of the exposed brick walls, where the concrete featured a small depression at my eye level. A burst of thin cracks echoed out from its center.

"We think this happened the first time your grandpa tested his powers. This used to be his weight room."

"How did you discover your powers?"

Bane smiled. "I accidentally ripped a sapling in half coming off the ice-skating pond at the back of the property. Vennie was the only witness."

"I nearly shit myself," Vennie said.

"Since you and your grandpa share powers, this seems fitting," Bane said.

I broke his gaze and faced the wall. Settling into what I envisioned as a fighter's stance, I hesitated, then withdrew my arm and drove it blindly forward.

The impact hurt, but not as much as I expected, especially with the dramatic boom and shower of dust.

Where my fist had made contact, the face of two bricks had dented and begun to fleck away. I struck again, aiming slightly to the left. More of the mortar surrounding my target brick came loose.

Addictive heat built as I moved. A warm, powerful sensation bloomed across my skin and sank into my muscles.

Using both hands, I scraped around the brick's edge. The mortar gave way beneath my fingers, crumbling to dust. There was little resistance as I got purchase and pulled. I forced the brick from its snug home, and it groaned. My eyes widened as the wall stopped resisting me and yielded. A brick that had supported the Leo house for a century rested in my palms. My breath caught as I clenched my fists, silently determined that the concrete wouldn't impede their closing.

The brick dissolved to dust between my fingers.

I broke into a disbelieving smile, and Bane mirrored it.

"Want to do another one?"

"Woah, that wall is load-bearing," Vennie said around a mouthful of noodles. "She thrives in the heat. Damn, Bane, imagine what an asset Mel would have been at the Sayto Sciences fire."

I spun. "So you—the Shadow—*were* there."

Bane rubbed his neck. "We investigated it. The circumstances were definitely suspicious. We couldn't figure much out though. Fire is hard for me to be around."

"I could go with you next time," I offered, a fiery feeling welling in my chest, "while you're the Shadow."

"I planned on going out tonight, actually . . ." Bane stared blankly, then his face lit. "Yes, of course, absolutely! We can make that work, right?"

Vennie shrugged. Chezza nodded.

"One of Sydney's suits would probably fit."

"Give me a couple hours. It'll be rudimentary, but functional."

Chezza continued to run tests on my strength in between us all scarfing the mini Italian buffet they'd ordered. After much tinkering on Vennie's part, Chezza looped an arm through mine and led me to the cubbies where Vennie worked. Next to Bane's cubby was another, and my grandpa's suit hung inside it.

A rush of nerves bubbled through me, raising goose-bumps. I was going out with the Shadow. To help.

Chezza lifted out the stiff, dark bodysuit, deep wrinkles carved stubbornly where it had hung for so long. She held it up, nodding absently, then pushed it into my hands.

I stared dumbly. "I just put it on?"

She nodded and turned her back. Bane and Vennie surveyed my readings on the curve, pointedly not looking my way.

I pulled off my dress and stepped into the suit, hauling up the material. It had a heft that suggested it was heavy, but I didn't struggle to pull it on with the Tempatches radiating heat into my skin. It was wildly too long, bunching at my ankles and wrists. Sydney had been taller than Bane and I both. I shimmied in as best as I could manage with the unwieldy built-in gloves. It was snug in the hips, and a little loose in the chest. Steeling my nerve and hugging the chest part around my torso, I cleared my throat.

Chezza and Vennie leapt on me as Bane visited his own cubby. Chezza used a pat of dark, moldable strips as impromptu seaming to adjust the fit. She overlapped the edges where the upper part of the suit was too big while Vennie took a pocket knife to the ankles and wrists.

"You don't have to do that," I insisted.

Bane shrugged. I couldn't see his face as he pulled on his own suit, a jacket and pants instead of my singular jumpsuit. "We have plenty of his old ones. This is temporary."

Both suits were gunmetal gray and scraped in places, the finish on Bane's more muted. The suit I wore was plain except for the seams, while Bane's was uneven plates of material overlapping in a chaotic non-pattern, like large, bulletproof scales. My gaze roamed to the emblem gleaming in the middle of Bane's chest. It wasn't clear in any of the media's Shadow photos. Up close, it was a slim diamond shape, dyed a deep, faint blue. Two sharp points jutted off the top, arching toward each other.

I looked down at the emblem that now sat across my own chest, slightly off center with how Chezza made the suit fit. The crimson paint was faded, but the shape was similar, though curved. Like a sharp water droplet.

Bane followed my stare. "Your grandpa designed his emblem like a flame. I made mine the frozen version."

I touched the symbol on my chest reverently and finally met Bane's eyes. There was warmth in his gaze, like the first day I'd shown up. He looked proud.

He snapped out of his daze and started pacing, his helmet under his arm. "Okay, okay, okay." The suit turned him into something dark and imposing, a brute force that juxtaposed his sweet face. "We'll go somewhere low-key. Just have you run around a bit. Get a feel for things."

"What about Oakton?" Vennie suggested.

"No skyscrapers," Chezza added.

"No skyscrapers," Bane agreed. He pulled his helmet on, touching a switch on the bottom so that the visor withdrew.

"Oh," he said with a pause, "I don't think we have a spare helmet. I busted the last one."

"Landed right on his head," Chezza mused. "I might have an idea."

Chezza stepped around me, scanning up and down. After a moment, she shrugged off her chic vegan moto jacket and held out a hand to her brother. He plopped a pocket knife into her palm, and she began to saw off the hood. Once it was removed, she came around behind me and attached it around my shoulders with the fabric strips. "I prefer to look edgy anyway," she said before I could protest.

"What is that stuff?" I asked instead.

"Superseam. One of my brilliant inventions." Her palm pressed around my neck, adhering the hood to my suit. "It's a fully waterproof adhesive and makes a nearly impenetrable seal." She finished and reached over my shoulders to tug up the hood.

"But what about shielding your face?" Chezza mused to herself, then tore a short piece of Superseam and laid it on the counter. She carved with the knife, rounding the edges and cutting two small holes. She peeled it from the surface and handed it to me, a makeshift mask.

"I promise I can remove it when you get back."

Along the widest wall of the Den, where the practice mats sprawled, a stretch of wall was made entirely of mirrors. I had a rough idea of my bearings; this wall aligned with the front of the house. I carefully smoothed the mask to my face.

The figure that stared back at me was . . . interesting. I stepped closer to the mirror, away from the lights over the workstation, into the shadows.

With the hood shading my face, and the mask obscuring my features further, I looked pensive, moody. If you didn't focus on the raw edges or ill-fitting areas, I looked intimidating, except for my socks.

Bane came up with the boots I'd worn all day. "These will work for now," he said, and I was thrilled by the idea of whatever would come at the implied *later*. Sitting on a slab of rock that jutted out from the wall, I laced up the boots, being careful not to pull too hard and snap the laces as heat built in my suit.

When I straightened again, Bane had a funny look on his face.

"What?" I asked, slightly self-conscious.

"I'm really happy." A smile dominated his face.

I grinned back.

"Are you ready?" he asked, the reckless glint burning in his eyes.

"Ready for what, exactly?"

Bane flung his arms wide. "To save Crown City, of course!"

Vennie rubbed a hand over his face. Chezza made a sound like a morose tuba.

"Fine, fine. It's rarely as grandiose as that. We'll try to stop a few crimes that will make a big difference for some of our citizens."

"Perhaps Mel doesn't want to be tossed in the deep end?" Chezza offered.

"I can just observe you to start," I offered.

"Absolutely," Bane said. "Great point."

"Press your emblem," Vennie instructed me. I did, and a tightening happened in the suit, and the material gently hugged my limbs. I nearly hummed with joy at the snug comfort. "Heat won't escape now. With Bane, I can adjust his temps to fit any situation, but I don't have that ability with you in this version. So the heat building from your patches will be retained and reflected in the suit. That means you're super strong and super fast, plus some other stuff, starting now. It'll get more intense as you start moving. If you need it, the button on your wrist will release a one-time blast of super high heat, if things get dicey."

Bane laughed. "With me around? Never."

I eyed the triangular button just above my right wrist.

"Why not be at extreme temperatures all the time?"

"We tried that for a while," Vennie said. "We threw Bane in a suit that kept him constantly freezing. But you gotta remember how that affects every move you make. What if you needed to put someone in a headlock to incapacitate them, but strangled them instead?" I shuddered, but Vennie maintained his serious eye contact. "Even at a moderate heat, you need to be careful. Save the maximum heat button for when you need it. You don't want to go for a high five and fracture someone's wrist on accident."

Bane rolled his eyes. "I've apologized for that a hundred times already."

As the heat built around me further, I buzzed with an unfamiliar energy. What was I capable of in my makeshift supersuit? Could I lift a boulder? Smash it to pieces? Both?

Chezza handed me a small nugget of black plastic and tapped her ear. I stuffed it into mine as she stuck a tiny microphone to the inside of my hood.

"Check, check," Bane said, and I heard him in the room and also in my ear.

"Um, I can hear you," I confirmed.

"There's a camera lens above your emblem. We'll be able to see what you do." Vennie explained.

Bane tilted his head a particular way, and his visor snapped closed over his wild eyes. His voice echoed out, slightly warped and metallic, raising goosebumps across my shoulders.

"This will be fun."

CHAPTER
TEN

BANE WALKED TO THE MIRRORS AND PRESSED A PALM TO THE glass. A section of the wall split to allow us into a plain, meticulously clean elevator without buttons. The back wall looked to be made from the same rough stone that surrounded much of the Den, but it shifted downward as the elevator ascended. I reached out and felt smooth glass beneath my glove.

"Another screen," Bane explained. "We're viewing it from behind, like a two-way mirror."

The rock fell away, and it took a moment to make sense of what opened before us. We were in the garage. The SUV was always waiting at the house's front door, so I'd never been inside it. Dim headlights stretched in a neat row. There was a practical sedan, an elegant black coupe, and a cobalt sports car, faintly glittering with white racing stripes down the middle.

On a lofted second level, a muted gray behemoth shaped like an arrowhead leered.

"Is that a *plane*?"

"Technically it's an aircraft," Vennie corrected in my ear.

"For emergencies," Bane said.

We stepped from the elevator and the doors closed silently behind us, taking on the exact appearance of the plaster walls.

"Wow," I murmured.

Bane shrugged. "Best screens in the world."

He headed toward a back door that opened into the yard on the side of the house and checked something on the forearm of his suit. "This might make you question if you even need a driver's license," he said, a grin in his voice. With that, he dashed into the darkened yard.

Frantic, I burst into motion and followed. Familiar dread swelled in my chest at the prospect of physical activity. I had been so weak for so long. I couldn't remember the last time I had willingly done any sort of exercise, always too worried I'd faint, draw attention, and become further entrenched in Sam's vortex of control.

But *now*.

My body reacted the instant I willed it. The suit's warmth buoyed me, keeping me upright and tall. The flex and pull of my muscles was deeply satisfying. I *wanted* to exert. In a second, I closed the thirty yards between the house and the trees, nearly smacking my head on a low-hanging branch. I regained my composure and dashed after Bane. He sprinted ahead, weaving among the trunks and laughing like a lunatic.

I pumped my arms, enjoying the rush of air in my lungs. My entire body burned in the best way. I tried to lengthen my minimal stride and my limbs happily complied, putting on a burst of speed so I could catch up with Bane. His voice buzzed in my ear.

"Feeling good?"

"Never better!"

"Good!" he said, chipper. "Now's the fun part. Get ready to jump."

"What?" That syllable came out winded.

"Yeah. Over the wall?" Bane's voice faltered a bit like my own.

"There's no tunnel or gate or anything?"

"Not on this side of the property. Jump!"

The wall appeared between the trees, imposing as ever. I panicked and leapt a beat after Bane. He soared, touching a foot lightly along the top to maintain momentum over the other side.

I left the ground and promptly panicked as the forest floor dropped away. A bizarre sound of distress escaped me as I shot over the wall, arms windmilling. The ground raced up, somehow faster than it had fallen away. My feet made contact and I barely kept them moving as I shot forward. I careened toward a massive oak's trunk and managed to put my arms up in time to avoid breaking my face all over it. The impact sent a flurry of bark off the tree in a small explosion.

"Ouch," Vennie crackled over our line.

Bane was at my side in an instant. "Are you okay?"

I pushed away from the trunk, bones reverberating. "This is *amazing.*"

The stinging in my arms faded as Bane let out a relieved breath. "That was my fault. I got excited. We'll go slower from here." He tugged my elbow and started into the Shadow's idea of an easy jog. I kept up easily, one hand holding up my hood as we flew across the landscape. The last hints of daylight disappeared and thrust us from twilight into darkness.

Bane explained as we ran.

"Our enhanced strength affects our bodies in a lot of ways. Durability, endurance, speed. We can see perfectly fine at night, and further away than the average human. All our senses are enhanced. Am I forgetting anything?"

"Faster reflexes," Vennie added.

"Pain tolerance," Chezza reminded them.

"Which component of your powers makes you stealthy and able to move through the shadows so quietly?" I asked.

"Oh, that? The powers don't help much with that." Bane grinned wickedly. "That's just practice."

He must have run to the city a thousand times. He hardly looked away from me as we talked and ran. Roads became wider and more frequent, and the darkness grew less dense as we neared downtown.

We reached the barrier along a major highway. The trees halted on our side while cement took over on the other. Crown's skyline soared above, vastly different at night. Its quirky angles turned foreboding without the sun against them.

"How do you decide where to . . . patrol?" I asked.

Bane veered left, following the highway. "Vennie is inside almost all surveillance tech in Crown City. He keeps an eye on what's going on. Manufacturing districts like where we're headed are common hot spots for crime since everything is closed at night. Sours tend to target areas like that."

"Sours?"

"Bad guys."

We remained quiet as we darted through an empty intersection and dove down a wide, dark avenue, commercial buildings on either side. "Technically this is illegal . . ." I ventured.

Bane sighed. "Yes, that's the difficult part."

Chezza snorted in our ears. "The only one?"

"You know what I mean," Bane countered. "It's complicated, and an issue I have to reassess constantly. But with these abilities, I can help in ways no one else can. There are rumors about other people with abilities—not exactly like ours, but special in their own way, and dangerous—in Crown City."

"Others? Other Extrahumans?"

"Your grandpa's old lab partner, Dr. Kavoh—there are still some zealots around here who believed in the work she was doing enhancing human abilities. They try to replicate her work. As far as we know, there haven't been any experiments as successful as us, but some of the sours we've encountered show signs of Extrahuman abilities. They're no match for me." Bane's helmet twitched to the side. I think he winked at me, failing to remember I couldn't see it.

Chezza groaned.

We zigzagged northwest through the quiet streets. The air was musky and dense, and I heard the soft rush of the river, though with my enhanced hearing, I wasn't sure how close we were. Bane slowed and swerved between two buildings and I followed, panting as we stopped.

"How are you feeling?" Bane asked, only a little breathless as he withdrew his visor.

Though I was hunched over, I couldn't help but grin wildly. "So good."

He lounged against the alley's wall, the picture of assured badassery while I curled in on myself like a shrimp, stitches creeping up both my sides.

"I forgot how hard the adjustment is, in the beginning," he admitted. "Suddenly you have all these abilities. You *can* complete amazing feats, but you have to learn *how*."

"Ah, yes," Chezza drawled in our ears, "take it from the Shadow, the prince of finesse."

"Isn't it past your bedtime?" Bane shot back.

"I don't have to work tomorrow, and I want to see how she does."

"Ask him how many times he's nearly concussed himself," Vennie added.

Bane ignored them. I straightened gently. Under the light layer of fatigue, I felt terrific.

"We have a bit of a . . . haphazard . . . approach to heroism," Bane said. "We have excellent resources. Chezza and Vennie are invaluable, with their skills in technology and medicine."

"And we try to *never* say any of the team's real names over the comms channel," Chezza drawled. "In case of a security breach."

"Not on my watch," Vennie said with a snort.

Bane gave a lame laugh. "Yeah, uh, that's a perfect example of when to not do what I do. Where was I? Right. The team. We have a discreet source for procurement and production. My salary funds everything. With your grandpa gone and most of his records missing, we can't unravel the extent of our powers—maybe he didn't even understand them fully—but we do our best. We try to do what's right, and be safe while doing it. I'm not the best at planning."

I cocked my head, trying to raise an eyebrow, but they were sluggish under the Superseam mask.

"It's a bit of a shitshow sometimes, I guess is what I'm saying."

I shook my head vehemently. "A shitshow that accomplishes a lot of good, it sounds like."

"I like to think so . . . That being said, I don't have a superhero lesson plan. It's a lot of weird internet searches and mixed martial arts video tutorials. But here's a good lesson to start: alleys are your best friend. Learn to love them."

He brandished his arms, presenting the grandeur of overflowing trash cans and a pile of busted pallets.

"Groundbreaking," Chezza deadpanned. "If you're done with your lesson, teach, and you have both caught your breath, it looks like there's a break-in a few blocks over. An alarm pinged on an auto parts shop, then shut off. Could've been a glitch, but it's worth checking."

Nerves flooded my gut. Bane caught the twist of my mouth.

"Don't worry," he said. "You just watch."

Bane raised his left forearm. Of course, a hand-sized rectangle on the suit, that a minute prior had looked like the rest of the suit's material, was actually a screen. Vennie pushed an overhead map of the neighborhood to it, and a small gold skull marked our destination.

"How do you like that interface?" Vennie asked. "Sexy as hell, right?"

I couldn't tell what most of the data around the border meant, and the skull seemed a smidge sensational, but I was saved from answering by Bane, who dropped his arm and stepped into the street.

"We can stop crimes because we're super-strong, right? But we operate by a set of rules to mitigate damage. Protecting innos is the top priority. Innos are bystanders or victims of the crime. Next is immobilizing the sours. If we're not careful, we could kill someone. There are plenty of ways to incapacitate with minimal harm."

Chezza coughed.

"Fine. If they're preying on innocent people, I usually break bones in the hopes that they think twice before doing it again. But you've got to consider the situation. We run facial IDs on the sours before engaging. What if they're desperate? What if they're stealing something to support their family, and I break their arm and they don't have health insurance? We take the time to assess and go from there."

I considered. "You want to take down the people who prey on others."

A dip of the helmet. "Exactly."

My chest swelled as I tailed Bane down the street, keeping tucked close to the walls. We crept from the shadow of one building to the next, following the sides of manufacturing buildings that faced the river, inching toward the gold skull on Bane's map.

He slowed as we approached a corner separating us from the auto parts shop. Our suits were near-silent. Stray pebbles didn't crunch beneath our boots; the material absorbed and dispersed sound.

A metal shriek echoed from the street beyond us, and I jumped. Bane steadied me with a hand on my arm and peeked around the corner.

"Four sours. They forced up the garage door of the shop front. Did the facial scans register?"

"All of them," Vennie said. "Each with violent crime records, bailed out by Sprinkles."

"Local crime boss, and yes, that's his real name," Chezza added for my benefit.

"They're all holding crowbars, it looks like. They may not have guns," Vennie said.

Bane turned to me. "When I engage, slide around this corner. There's a small alley on this side of the street. Hunker down inside it and watch. Jump in if you feel like."

"Jump in?" I mouthed, but he had turned away from me. "That sounds like a terrible idea," I muttered.

Chezza coughed in a way that sounded suspiciously like it shielded a laugh.

Bane was eerily still, all kindness masked by his merciless visor. He assessed for nearly a minute. Gruff, muffled voices sounded, and extreme silence followed every sound, the tells of a group trying to go unnoticed.

Then he moved.

Bane's suit must have been cranked down to freezing with how fast he bolted into the street. His disappearance was immediately followed by a grunt and several yells of alarm.

I poked my head around the corner.

The men were grouped around a shiny passenger van with its rear doors splayed open. The steel, roll-up security door in front of the shop was raised and mangled along the bottom, its lock dangling in a contorted mess.

One sour was already curled on the ground, and Bane was a blurred bullet that wrought havoc among the rest. He spun and leapt from one sour to the next, smashing his palm into one's chest and grabbing the man's arm as he fell backward, swinging him forward to career into one of his cohorts. He spun and *kicked a guy in the head*. He touched each sour only a few times, and they sprawled on the street and stayed down. One tried to pull a gun, but Bane kicked it from his grip before he could aim.

"You wanna get moving?" Vennie prompted. With a jolt, I realized his question was directed at me.

Steeling my resolve, I sidled along the building. Bane ducked as one of the final sours swung bolt cutters at his head.

Darting my eyes away from the action, the alley Bane mentioned opened on my left. I dared a few hopped steps and sunk into the deep shadows with a sigh of relief. I ran my fingertips along the edge of my mask as Bane felled another sour.

I whispered into the darkness, "Why steal auto parts?"

"They can sell them for a lot of cash," Vennie said.

"Or they could be building something," Chezza added.

Bane was a blur of limbs that warped from one sour to the next, one direction to the opposite, one fighting style to the next. The Shadow's battle rhythm was a sporadic cyclone, breathtaking and extremely effective. The sours rarely landed a blow, and when they did, Bane moved through it like he hadn't felt a thing, though I heard his grunts over our comms channel. If any of the other sours had a gun, Bane moved too fast and the sours were too close together to risk taking a shot before he had them unconscious.

I was entranced, so much so that I didn't register the crunch of boot soles on concrete until it was right behind me. An arm snaked across my chest and pulled me tight against a large body. Its owner jabbed me in the side, huffing the breath from my lungs.

"Hey there," a gruff voice said in my ear, accompanied by the icy whisper of a blade against my throat.

CHAPTER
ELEVEN

I GRAPPLED FOR PURCHASE ON THE ARM ACROSS MY THROAT, realizing Vennie or Chezza couldn't see my assailant since my camera faced forward.

"Are you trying to die, small fry?" the man growled. "I have a knife. That means I'm in charge."

Bane dispatched the last sour with a punch to the gut as my captor's voice registered through my mic.

"What is that?" Vennie demanded.

Bane spun our way and froze while Chezza swore.

The sour pressed, and pain was a single freezing needle-point at my throat amidst the panic roaring through me. I couldn't think, instinct overriding so that all I could do was desperately retract my head in vain. In two seconds of not paying attention to my surroundings, my life was forfeit.

Extrahuman strength flooded my body, but there wasn't a scrap of thought in my head. Bane's silence didn't give me confidence that I was knife-proof. I was stronger than this creep, but I had no idea if I was faster than the pressure he needed to slice my throat open.

My sense of helplessness triggered a memory of my

mother sprawled on the floor, her face obscured by smoke as I ran away.

Bane's voice cut through the terror-filled haze of my memory, projecting, warped but casual, through his mask. "I'm sure we can settle on a trade." His helmet turned slightly toward the half-loaded van.

My captor's snort ruffled my hood. "You better hope we can. I'm leaving here safe and rich tonight. I didn't know you had a pal. Didn't anyone tell you it's no good to have friends in this line of work?" He jostled me, and Bane started. "Hold it right there. This is exactly why."

I realized Vennie was murmuring in my ear. "Keep him talking. The second he moves that knife away from her, you could make it. You'd have to cross about double the distance you could in the amount of time—"

"What is it you want?" Bane asked while Vennie continued.

"Is there anything on the ground near you? Something you could chuck at him?"

As Vennie continued to list options, I realized he wasn't talking to me. They were plans for Bane to rescue me, and none of them sound promising.

Bane took a step forward.

"Don't move!" my captor shouted as he pressed on the knife. I gasped at the sharp pain and sudden wet warmth streaking down my throat. Rage flared in every inch of my body at being *handled*.

The sour continued, "I'm gonna walk this one over to the vehicle with me. You can have her when I'm out of here. I'll be on my way, and you two can continue to disappoint the city, or whatever you were up to."

His grip across my waist slipped lower, grazing my hip. I swallowed a howl of frustration.

Vennie recited numerous stats and odds while Bane turned slowly to check the van's interior. I gritted my teeth and ignored them, glancing down. My hands were side by side on the sour's arm, the ridges of my gloves just visible along the bottom of my line of sight. I shifted my left hand, turning my index finger toward my opposite wrist.

I slid my finger slowly over the triangular button that rested there, and pressed.

Heat more intense than I'd ever felt engulfed me. Fire ripped along my limbs and nestled my spine. Power roiled through my body, slamming through my extremities.

I latched onto the sour's arm and pulled, focusing solely on keeping the knife's point away from my throat. With a roar, I hauled him around my shoulder to smash against the wall. His momentum was so intense I lost my grip. He rebounded with a snarl, shoving away from the wall to swing wildly at me. I dodged back, barely staying an inch from the blade with each violent pass.

He swung again, and I ducked. Throwing my arms over my head and closing my eyes, I charged into his torso, pushing with all my might.

He flew against the brick wall, breath huffing out of him to match the cement that shook from the bricks. He collapsed to the ground, and I stepped forward, gasping, to rip the knife from his hand. His eyes stared up at me, incredulous, then rolled back in his head. He slumped over.

Adrenaline buzzed through me, crackling along the edges of my nerves. The sour's knife was mangled in my grip. With a shudder, I chucked it away, accidentally sending it flying into the front window of the store behind me, which promptly shattered, triggering an alarm.

"Oops."

Bane was still in the middle of the street. He withdrew his mask away from his gaping mouth.

"Or, that," Chezza said smugly.

I managed a shaky grin.

Air vacated my lungs a second time when Bane barreled into me, crushing me in an embrace.

I hugged him back, careful not to squeeze too hard. "I'm alright, I'm okay," I insisted. "I handled it."

"Clearly!" Bane shouted, throwing his hands toward the sky. "I certainly couldn't." He grabbed his helmet like he needed to rub his forehead.

Lights began flashing from the store's interior in tandem with the alarm.

"That's our cue to scram," Bane said. He closed his mask, jumped through the broken display, and retrieved the knife. "We'll ditch this at home. Is there blood on the pavement?"

I scanned the ground alongside him, the pebbles in the concrete crystal clear in the dark with my heat-enhanced vision.

"We're clear," Bane said grimly. "Let's go." We took off as the whine of police sirens joined the shop's alarm. We'd be gone before they could show up to find the small sea of unconscious sours.

I wanted to see more of a typical night for Shadow, but Bane was clearly distressed, pushing us faster and faster. I kept up easily with the heat circulating in my suit. I touched my neck, feeling my blood, though it blended nearly seamlessly against my dark glove.

When we exited the elevator into the Den, Bane finally combusted.

"I am such an idiot!"

Chezza swept toward us, taking my arm. "Yes, but why are you shouting?"

Bane dropped his voice but not his desperation as he followed us. He whipped off his helmet and searched my face with wild eyes.

"I almost got you killed."

Chezza scoffed and shooed him away, cutting off my protests. "Drama queen. Go take a time-out."

She led me to the exam table and patted it. I hopped up and pulled down my hood while she dug in drawers underneath. "How are *you*? That improvisation was pretty awesome."

I grinned, my gaze following Bane as he stomped toward Vennie and the LUMA.

"I'm great."

Chezza nodded. "Because you are a lady, and therefore extremely tough. Give Bane a minute. He's still a new papa bird, and you scared him."

She lifted my chin and dabbed at my throat, the towel coming away red.

"How did you become team doctor?" I asked.

Chezza flipped her pink and black tresses with her free hand. "I have many talents. While I am not legally licensed to practice medicine, I'm an enthusiast of the space, and also the best you've got."

"I trust you," I murmured as she swabbed ointment over my cut.

"It's just a scratch. You could say you got it when you fell off the parade float." She handed me a bottle of sharp-smelling liquid. "Use this to peel your mask off."

As I peeled away my mask, Bane returned, seemingly cooled off.

"It's not entirely fun," he said, resting his hands on his hips.

I yanked a bit of Superseam from where it clung to my cheek, wincing. "What?"

"The superhero thing. It's fun, but that's not the point. It's very, very dangerous. I've almost died . . . a lot."

Chezza's mouth was a thin line as she pressed a bandage to my neck.

"Well yeah," I said, staring at them dumbly. "But that's what helping people is, right? Especially like this. It was still amazing."

Bane's frown deepened. "You liked it?"

I hopped down, crossing my arms. "Yes! No wonder you can't focus on anything else!"

Doubt shattered my excitement like lightning. What if I neglected school the way Bane did his work? Camden would never fully admit me.

Bane sighed. "You see the problem."

"But isn't it worth it?"

"Not if I lose you. Tonight wasn't one of the ones where we save lives. What if you'd lost yours?"

My rage had barely receded, but it bubbled to the surface at the doubt on Bane's face. "So you're not going to let me be a superhero?"

"I won't not *let* you do anything!" he stammered, cringing at his convoluted thought. "I invited you here so I could help! Not to make your life worse. Not to put you in danger. If you want to do this with me . . . I'll give you everything I have. I'll give you everything I have anyway. I just don't want you to get hurt."

"I'm prepared to get hurt. I want to do this more than I fear that. I want to help people!"

Bane didn't say anything.

"*That's* when you look the most alike," Chezza cut in. "That mulish, fuck-all face you both have."

Vennie came over, a tangle of plastic wires and straps in his arms. "Yeah, plus you're nearly identical on the inside. Mel's gonna be a hero like you, Bane. And she's going to keep going back out, in spite of everything, like you do. So rather than wasting time arguing about it, why don't you get started on a training plan so we can prepare her the best we're able?"

Bane frowned at all of us, his stormy eyes doubtful.

I took a shaky breath, my hair falling across my face. Tangled bits from under my hood stuck to Superseam residue I missed on my forehead. "Lately I've constantly felt like there's so little I can control for myself. This—" I flexed my palms, collecting my thoughts. "This means I can help people who feel the same way. I can stop those who insist on being the controllers.

"I want to do this," I insisted again, glaring, my resolve diluted by the wisps of my hair sliding across my face.

Bane stared at me for a long moment. Finally, he reached into a slim pocket at his hip and held something out to me.

A tiny, clear elastic.

Bane pulled one of the tendrils away from my face. "Can I help?"

I nodded, and he gently gathered the strands of my misbehaving hair, taming them neatly and gathering them together with a small section above my forehead. He smoothed them and fixed the elastic around the bunch, pulling just a little so it sprouted out of the top.

"You saw what it's like out there," he said. "It's dangerous. Sometimes it's scary. On the worst days, it's heartbreaking. If you want to help, I won't stop you. But we start training right away so you're better prepared."

What would happen at the end of summer if I didn't find a way to stay?

I ignored the thought. "Why do you have hair ties in your suit?"

"He had an epic bun last summer," Vennie said, tapping my suit's emblem. "I'd like to run some tests if you're feeling up to it."

Thinking of the hour, exhaustion washed away the remnants of my receding adrenaline. But I didn't want to sleep, so I shed my grandpa's suit. Chezza offered a zippered sweater jacket to go with my leggings. "Hope you don't mind I raided your closet," she said.

"As long as you left me more cute stuff," I countered.

Bane had disappeared up the stairs into the house. He trounced back down, a cupcake in his hand, the pink frosting nearly indiscernible under a thick layer of sprinkles.

"I keep a stash of plain ones in the freezer and decorate them when I'm feeling stressed." He held it out to me. "I've already had three. Listen, Mel, I've felt so alone for so long, and here you are, a miracle. Someone who is my family, and who shares my secret. Who is *just* like me." His smile was sad. "Except you have better judgement than I do. I'm sorry I put you in harm's way."

I took it from him with a smile. "We'll be more careful next time. Tonight was one of the best nights of my entire life, Uncle Bane."

His crooked smile started to show. "You've never called me that before today."

I took a bite of cupcake and considered as I chewed. Finally, I spoke. "I didn't know you very well before today."

Bane grinned fully. "I'm really glad you're here."

He looped an arm around my shoulders and guided me toward Vennie and his tests.

CHAPTER
TWELVE

MAX PLOPPED DOWN ACROSS WHAT HAD BECOME MY USUAL table in Camden's student union over the first week of the summer program.

"The Carbati brothers are throwing a party tonight. You should come. Loads of Camden students will be there. It's a great way to meet people."

He was sparklingly flawless, as usual. His jeans fit impeccably, and his black and white sneakers posed a cocky contrast to his blazer.

"Hi," I said.

The start of my college career had been intense but otherwise uneventful. Bane drove me to and from campus, only sometimes late, and often encouraged me to drive the SUV. Most afternoons, I'd settle in the union or at the local coffeeshop, Hardwired, to study. In spite of keeping to myself, the press still released a few nasty pieces suggesting I was latching on to Bane's money. I tried to avoid the papers, but Sam texted me the headlines. His most recent included a message: They're onto you. Won't be long before he realizes why you're really there and puts you out on the street.

Max surveyed me across his foamy triple espresso, brown eyes expectant.

"I'll think about it," I conceded finally. I was desperately in need of some fun that didn't revolve around running through Crown's streets at night.

Max gave me a close-lipped, wickedly dimpled grin, leaning in conspiratorially toward me, his beautiful face stealing my focus from my textbook. That smile sealed the deal, and he knew it. "I'd be happy to introduce you to more of our esteemed classmates."

"Free of charge?" I snorted. "How charitable."

Max smoothed his immaculate lilac shirt over his chest. "Well, I do require an exorbitant fee in compliments."

Shaking my head, I focused again on homework, acutely aware of his presence. His scent wafted over me—beaches and boutique shopping and meticulously folded pocket squares. Promises to escort you down grand staircases and across sweeping lawns.

His soft laugh centered me back in my seat. Max came around the table and leaned over my shoulder. "And don't you dare use homework as an excuse to bail. You have all weekend to work on that. Please?"

The last word was nearly a purr. It sent goosebumps up my arms beneath my long sleeves.

"Fine, I'll come," I conceded, tipping my cup high to finish my coffee. "Where is it?"

"They live down the street from me." He began walking away backwards, smoothing his lapels without looking away from me. "I'll text you the address. See you later."

🔥🔥🔥

"STREET" WAS TOO PLAIN A TERM TO DESCRIBE THE glamorous boulevard Bane drove down later that night. Gargantuan homes lined either side, with rolling, groomed lawns spread wide between them. An immaculate plain dotted with sculpted pillars and archways and grand windows. Not a single one looked properly lived in.

"I don't plan on being out late," I said, nerves at being around so many people already making me want to demand that Bane turn the car around and take me home.

Bane spared me a thoughtful look before answering. "What if that's when the party starts getting good? This is all a part of the college experience. Text me when you're ready. I'll be up." He dropped me at the curb a house away, though I didn't care if anyone saw me leave his car. His eyes twinkled mischievously at me through the window. "Cause some trouble, Mel."

I laughed internally at the idea of the Shadow stopping mid-crime busting to come pick me up. "I'll do my best."

Light leaked out of every window in the Carbati mansion, and a bassline pulsed all the way out to the street.

I schooled a pleasant, indifferent look onto my face and followed a group of Camden students through the front door, relieved that I was dressed similarly to them. After scouring my new wardrobe, I'd settled on a cropped black sweatshirt with leather accents at the shoulders. I liked the way it looked with my jeans and sneakers. I resisted the urge to wrap my arms around my three bared inches of midriff. I wore a few Tempatches, keeping off the chill, though their heat wasn't as strong or steady after a full day. I'd forgotten to swap them out for ones with charged batteries.

I craned my head to stare around the sprawling foyer, complete with abstract art and a blown-glass chandelier. Gleeful shouts and slurred responses echoed from every corridor leading away. I set my shoulders and went in search of a drink.

🔥🔥🔥

"WHERE THE *HELL* IS THE KITCHEN?" I MURMURED TO MYSELF ten minutes later, hopelessly lost somewhere between a screening room and two different mini home gyms.

"In need of my brilliant tour guide abilities yet again?" a satiny voice asked behind me.

I spun, scowling at Max, who leaned against the wall at the end of the hall, tracing his fingers idly over a painting featuring slapdash lines and squares that probably cost more than our combined tuition.

Max smiled at my scowl. "Hello, granite face," he said, somehow making it sound like a compliment, like I was a prolific statue, a work of art. Heat twisted in my exposed stomach. He'd ditched his blazer from earlier, and I didn't know anyone could make a simple striped T-shirt look so . . . hot. I watched him out of the corner of my eye, appreciating his incredible posture. I had a sudden urge to pull him into a closet to make out for a while, then steal his confidence to use as my own.

His face was a little flushed from his walk over. I wondered which gargantuan palace along the street was his.

"This house is ridiculous. How many closets could one family need?"

"Depends on the skeletons they're hiding," he said, stepping toward me. "Care to join me to frolic with our peers and rejoice in our youth?"

I raised an eyebrow. "I need a drink, especially if you're going to keep talking like that."

Max's laugh was like champagne. "Fair enough, let's go."

Max swirled me in front of dozens of faces across three more massive rooms full of low, chic couches and abstract vases in the corners. Most smiled politely at me and asked Max about a recent skiing trip, but a few stared a little longer after Max introduced me, clearly knowing who I was related to.

At one break in a hallway between rooms, I sagged against

the wall, huffing a sigh of relief. Nothing awkward had happened. I was even at risk of enjoying myself.

Pausing with me, Max asked. "I expected you to be a little nervous . . . New town, new school and all that, but were you really that worried?"

Of course Max never worried whether or not people would like him. Charm oozed from his nearly invisible pores.

I mulled over his question. "I haven't been in a good position to make friends before. My life has been too weird to explain." He looked at me thoughtfully and I groaned. "I'm making myself sound like a complete charity case."

Max barked a loud laugh and set a warm hand on my shoulder. "But you're my charity case, and even though I don't want to share you . . ." Heat flared in my chest, both indignant and ignited by his tone. "I have great news for you. This is Crown City. No one is particularly concerned with any concept of 'normal.' The Carbati brothers' parents don't even live here. They stop by for a weekend every few months because they feel the boys can handle themselves. They work on a farm in Utah developing rare varieties of potatoes."

I forced myself to not rub the spot when his hand disappeared and he whisked us into a game room packed with people and pool tables set up for beer pong.

"Max Keep! You got next?" a tall boy called from the edge of the table nearest us. He and his partner were close to fully annihilating their competition.

Max turned to me. In the crowded room, he was much closer than the span of the table at Hardwired that usually divided us. "Want to be my partner?"

"Absolutely," I said without hesitation. I'd been to plenty of parties in Upstate City before Mom died and I'd stopped going. I'd never realized until now how much I missed casual conversations about movie releases and gossip, and the light buzz of a crappy contraband cocktail.

"We need drinks," Max hollered to his friend, who I

recognized from one of my classes as a boy named LeRoy. "Then we'll take you on."

Max tugged me through a doorway, my arm burning at his touch.

"Are you even old enough to drink?" I teased.

"Of course," Max scoffed. "I'm older than the others in my class. I did a gap year in Italy."

"Of course you did," I muttered.

The kitchen had a wide, silky marble countertop haphazardly covered in bottles. Max handed me a cup, then someone called to him from the other side of the room.

He turned to greet them. I didn't want to pry, and seized the moment with myself. I breathed deep through my nose and surveyed the minefield. A gallon of orange juice stood at my elbow, looking safer than the two liters of cola that stood partway empty in sticky pools of their own remnants. I frowned at the bottles, all full of clear liquor. I preferred whiskey—it was like a heated blanket in a cup. Sighing ruefully, I dumped a measure of vodka into my cup and splashed juice on top.

Max's conversation continued behind me. I didn't want to cling. I could make friends on my own. Max didn't need a shadow and I didn't need a babysitter.

I squared my shoulders and walked into the next room, which expelled flashing lights and thrumming beats and hysterical laughter. It was a good move because the room was full of my friendly looking peers. It was a bad move because they were all *dancing*. Mostly in pairs. Some of them on the floor. I was ready to smile and introduce myself . . . but not to someone entwined with someone else.

Leaning against the wall, I sipped my drink that tasted like a cleaning product, trying to look like I belonged.

I jumped when an arm wrapped through mine.

"Can you *believe* that exam in Advanced Soap Carving Principles?"

I looked up into huge hazel eyes like crystal balls. Their owner's voice was casual but her hand clenched tightly around my forearm. Her brown hair waved past her shoulders and a fleet of freckles splattered across her white skin.

I recognized the kindred flash in her eyes, the one of someone watching out for themselves. She needed my help.

"And it won't even be graded on a curve? Ridiculous," I said carefully.

"Mhmm," she mused, taking a long drink. "Go with this for, like, thirty more seconds." Her request echoed from the inside of her cup. She shimmied her eyebrows impressively.

I nodded toward the dance floor. "What are the odds I could convince them all to join me for the macarena?"

She spat a laugh into her cup and glanced around. "Great, he's gone. This kid can't take the hint that I'm not interested." Her eyes strayed from mine to follow the swaying hips of a girl who walked past us. "Like, as a pansexual queen, I'm interested in a lot of folx, but I can't get behind any she, he, or they that cares *so* much about golf, you know?"

I groaned. "Was it regular golf or disc golf?"

She groaned too. "Does it *matter*? Both are a nightmare."

"True," I said. "I'm Mel. I'm in the summer program at Camden."

"Neat! Gem Jellis, sophomore class president. I'll see you in the fall." She squeezed the arm looped through mine in lieu of a handshake.

"Gem . . . Like a diamond?" I clarified over the electric beat.

"Exactly," she said with an expression that looked like it certainly could cut glass.

I immediately wanted her to be my friend. "God, these parties can be sensory overload, but alas, I don't like spending my server paycheck on booze when one of these kids' parents will do it." Her eyes somehow got wider as she stared past me. "Max Keep is coming this way. Do you need me to scare him off?" To illustrate, she narrowed her eyes to vengeful slits.

I snorted. "He's alright. Thank you for the offer though."

"Ahh." She nodded knowingly. "The untouchable Max Keep sheds friends like a snake does its skin, but I've never been able to tell if it's because the people who try to be his friends are just in it for his money, or because he's a bit of a jackass."

I mused as he came over. "It's at least seventy percent the second factor, but he has his moments . . ."

"And he's a handsome jackass, nonetheless." Gem shifted her hair and winked at me. "If you've caught his eye, you should go for it. I certainly would! Thanks again for saving me. I'll leave you to this handsome enigma—I'm going to see who's drunk enough to loan me their timeshare in Malibu for spring break. Want to swap numbers? You seem normal."

I nearly choked on my drink, thinking of how I spent my nights lately, but I swapped phones with her to type in our numbers. As we traded back, Gem gave a lingering look over my shoulder, surely at Max. "Text me later—I want to hear *all* about Max Keep." With a flick of fingernails painted like galaxies, she disappeared into the crowd.

Max took her place against the wall, brows knitted together. "Who was that?" he asked.

"That's Gem. A new friend to share me with," I told him with a pointed look.

He winced and tapped his cup against mine. "I'm happy for you. Did you come in here because you want to dance?"

I grimaced. "Absolutely not."

Disappointment flashed across Max's features. He quickly recovered his charm. "How about that game of beer pong, then?"

Despite my encyclopedic knowledge of teen party movies, I was hopeless at beer pong. Max was decent, and more importantly, a graceful loser. He laughed with me as my shots careened off cups' edges. LeRoy and his partner were also a few drinks deep, so Max carried us for a respectable amount of time before they delivered the death blow.

As our final cup was cleared away and I chugged the remainder of my drink, Max unceremoniously tossed his ping pong ball at LeRoy's head and stuck his tongue out at him, his perfect-boy facade slipping to something lovely and disheveled.

"Ah, well." He ran a hand over his curls. He frowned into his empty cup. "Refill?"

I nodded. We surveyed the pathetic state of the pilfered drink station and I frowned into my cup.

"Not seeing anything you like?" Max asked.

I scrunched my nose. "I prefer whiskey, but I think the last of that is in some guys' belly button in one of the sunrooms."

Max looked thoughtful, then grabbed a fresh cup and backed out of the kitchen, motioning for me to follow.

He ducked into a darkened room off the foyer, and I followed, bumping against him as he fumbled for something. His phone's flashlight flared, revealing that we stood close. I stepped back involuntarily, and Max busied himself with a lamp on the desk. Warm light flooded the stately office.

"In a house like this, there's always a pretentious, rarely used office." Max scanned the room, then reached for the cabinets over the back of the desk. He pried one open and shoved aside a stack of documents.

I waited skeptically.

"And," he said, shooting his wicked grin over his shoulder, "there's always a stash." He withdrew a bulbous bottle with a black label.

"Oh, you beautiful genius," I murmured, eyeing the caramel liquid inside.

Max's smile flared. We were both quiet as he tipped a measure into the cup.

He stepped close and offered it without a word. I had to

tilt my head back to meet his dark eyes. I felt warm even though I hadn't taken a sip.

"Bro, how many scallops do you think I can fit IN MY MOUTH?"

The shout echoed around the hall, moving closer as footsteps stampeded by. Max closed his eyes and breathed out long and slow through his nose.

"Don't want to miss that spectacle," I said hoarsely, mentally running through all the reasons it would be smart to not kiss the one friend I had.

Gem is now your friend, probably, I thought.

Max reached behind me and tugged the door gently open, our chests barely brushing together.

A couple careened down the hall toward us, tangling their limbs and mouths and noticing us at the last second.

"By all means," Max said, stepping aside so they could slink into the office.

I finally took a sip, savoring the smokiness. "Air?" I asked.

"Air would be good," he said, his voice dry, something extra in his fading smile as he fiddled with his watch.

We headed back to the kitchen, the doors off it flung wide to reveal an elaborate stone porch. Emerging into the backyard, we traversed the crowd to where someone had erected a massive bonfire in the middle of a too-small decorative pit.

Max lifted a hand in greeting to those milling around, but I froze, reminded of the fire back in Upstate City. How in my memory it now seemed so much smaller, and so distant in my past.

I stopped behind Max, his form blurred dark as the flames danced behind him.

I took another drink, basking in the warmth both inside and out. I offered the cup to Max, holding my free hand out to the flames.

He shook his head. "I can admit I'm partially to blame here," he began.

"You're going to have to be more specific. For making me drink shitty vodka, waiting to help me find the good whiskey, for the unfortunate chill in the air, the state of the world in general?"

He cut his head to the side, shooting me with that smile again, seemingly not offended. "I should have mentored you on the strategy behind throwing a ping pong ball."

I elbowed him, accidentally sending him stumbling to the side. "Oh, that loss was entirely your fault. I made one cup, right?"

He steadied himself with a hand on my arm. "I hate to correct you, but it's my duty as your beacon of leadership in this transitory time. I don't think you made even one." He rubbed a hand over his eyes. "Don't worry. I'll buy the Carbatis a case of beer to make up for it. I should go tell them."

"What do you mean?" I asked, following him back toward the house, the fire's comforting warmth receding, highlighting the bare wisps of heat coming off my Tempatches. I shivered.

"Well, the standard party rule," Max said, making air quotations and rolling his eyes, "is that if you make no cups in beer pong, you owe the host a case of beer . . ." He helped me up the patio steps.

"*Or,* you have to do a naked lap around the house!" LeRoy trumpeted, shoving between us.

I brought Max to a reeling halt with the touch of my hand on his bare arm. "You can't be serious."

"I am, but it's barbaric and awful, so we're not upholding that rule tonight." Max shot LeRoy a look, but he was too distracted chugging from one of the bottles he held in either hand. "Seriously, ignore him. It's a stupid, made-up thing. Dying slowly with the patriarchy."

"Not quick enough," I muttered, watching two classmates wrestle in the grass, both of them shirtless and covered in Jell-O shots.

The words "naked lap" stuck in my head like a burr. Max gently touched my elbow.

"I'm sorry. I shouldn't have mentioned it. You must think we're such assholes. The Carbatis throw the good parties so we have to deal with their bullshit. Plenty of kids lose on purpose for the attention. I'll buy the case. You won't hear anything more about it."

"Wait—" I put my hand on his arm to still him, trying to make sense of what he was saying, but my head swam a little from the whiskey. "Of course I'm not going to run around this house naked. That's insane. It's harassment *at least*." Max had the audacity to look relieved. "But you're actually going to buy them a case of beer?"

"Yes?" Max said with a slow blink. Though the end of the word lilted up, like it was a question he definitely did not know the answer to.

I stared unflinchingly into his eyes, the same color as all the fancy wood furnishings inside the Carbati mansion, his hair tinted the same shade as my whiskey in the fire's distant glow.

"That's impressively stupid. You can't buy them beer. It's reinforcing their idiotic rule. It's hardly better than if I actually did the naked lap. I only run around naked when *I* feel like it, sir, whether I've won a game or not." The last part was definitely the alcohol.

I rooted myself on the patio, bodies whipping around us. I was right, and Max's hesitation made it clear he knew it, too. But he wanted to buy that beer to not make waves with our peers. Who stood up for a matter of principle at a house party?

I did.

A breeze whipped around us, rustling the manicured bushes and drawing unpleasant goosebumps along my skin wherever it was exposed.

"Guys, guys," LeRoy slurred, "it's a paaarty! Don't fight."

He slung an arm around each of our shoulders and spilled half an icy wine cooler down my back.

I gasped, and Max's brow furrowed. He finally opened his mouth, but I didn't hear what he said because at that moment the world tilted. I tried to grab Max by his overpriced sleeve but missed before I fainted.

CHAPTER
THIRTEEN

I JOLTED AWAKE IN UNFAMILIAR SURROUNDINGS.

"Mel?"

Max perched on the corner of a bed I didn't recognize, bedside lamps casting shadows along the high walls. I was curled on a plush leather sofa in the middle of a cavernous room. The French doors across from me had the blinds up, looking out into the pitch-black evening.

Max's statuesque face was pinched in the middle with concern. A pounding started in my head, followed quickly by a thick stomach stew of dread.

"What time is it?" I croaked.

Max frowned, coming over to sit on the glossy black coffee table, sweeping aside music magazines with satiny covers. "You fainted—"

"I know what happened," I muttered, groping at my pockets under the blanket Max had tossed over me. Groggy and grumpy at having let my guard down, I found my phone and lit up the screen. It wasn't long after midnight.

"I'm confused," Max said carefully, his perfect face even more charming in the throes of weakness. "Did someone put something in your drink? We need to find out who—"

"I faint all the time," I said, shaking my head vehemently. "I have a . . . weak constitution." I swallowed back a maniacal giggle at how my understanding of the issue had changed so much in recent days. "Is this your house?"

Max nodded, and I cut him off before he could speak again. "Can I use your bathroom?"

His forehead scrunched. Max pointed to a door across the sprawling room.

He caught my elbow as I stood, but besides the headache, the swoony feeling didn't linger. My Tempatches were totally dead, but Max's room was deliciously warm, just like his hand. "I'm fine," I told him, though I leaned into his touch as I made my way to the door.

Max trailed me. "When you collapsed, I didn't know what to do, but you talk about not wanting to draw attention, so I carried you here."

I mustered a weak smile. "Too bad I was unconscious for that part."

Max's face broke into a pleased smile as I shut the door. He continued while I leaned on the sink, splashing my face with warm water and studying where he immaculately groomed himself each day. His bathroom was all tiny dark tiles and shiny surfaces and a collection of product bottles that would make even Chezza jealous.

"You only had two drinks, I thought. Are you *sure* . . ." Max's worried voice echoed through the door.

"This happens all the time," I reiterated, patting the back of my sweatshirt, which had mercifully dried. I opened the door. He leaned against the frame, his amazing face closer than I was used to. It took me a moment to remember my priorities. "Did anyone see my little spectacle?"

Max's smile failed a fraction. "No one sober enough to remember," he said. Then, after a moment, he asked carefully, "Mel?"

"Yeah?" I'd been a little dazed just staring at him.

Max kept his mahogany eyes, stained darker in the dim light, trained on the floor. "When we got here and I laid you on the couch, you were coming in and out. You managed to insist you were fine, and then you passed out again. That was twenty minutes ago. I nearly dialed the hospital half a dozen times. And all I could think about was how badly you wouldn't want me to call someone." He lifted his eyes to mine. "Why?"

I sighed and headed back to the couch, motioning for Max to follow. He sat close, one leg curled up so he could face me. He laid an arm along the sofa's back, its heat radiating against my shoulders. Max's attention sent a thrill through my bones, but I couldn't have him paying too close attention. How could I have let myself get so close to that fire? What if I'd revealed my Extrahuman strength? I'd put Bane and his entire Shadow mission at risk.

Gingerly, I laid my head against the warm brown skin of Max's arm, and lied.

"Everything about my stay here is temporary, right?" Before Max could protest, I continued, "Bane invited me for the summer. My stint at Camden is probationary. But I can't go back to where I came from. This is my one chance. I can't risk having to leave Crown City, And I already made a fool of myself at the parade . . . Look, after my mom died, things were awful. I didn't act my best, and with my shitty attitude and circumstances, people weren't inclined to think well of me. So, I don't want to draw any attention. Especially from anyone at Camden. I need to keep a low profile. I don't want them to have any reason to dig into my past."

There. My statements were truthful. The parts of the truth I could trust Max with, I hoped.

"What would they find?" he asked, his hand curling to stroke my hair.

I pressed my face between my hands, focusing on the feeling of sinking my socks into his plush carpet. Max had removed my shoes while I was passed out.

". . . There could be an instance of assault," I moaned.

To his credit, Max looked surprised, though he kept his voice light.

"I take it someone deserved it?"

"This guy laid hands on a girl at school and no one was doing anything to stop it. I punched him."

"Well that's justifiable—"

I lowered my head between my knees and muttered, the words coming out muffled, "They also might discover that I've been under investigation for arson."

". . . Oh." No charming comment for that admission.

I swallowed, swearing I could taste ash.

"You know a little about my dad. He's only around to torture me because my mom died last year . . . It was a house fire. I made it out. She didn't. The police wouldn't have looked my way if it weren't for my record . . ." Max waited patiently as I tried to find the words so hard to utter. "A few years before that, when I was in high school, something similar happened. I was partnered with the school bully in chemistry class. Our lab station caught fire—she'd mixed some chemicals wrong. She got badly burned, and I was totally fine."

I kept my hands over my face, hiding the incredulous O my mouth had dropped into as I realized the truth of these past traumas and how I'd escaped unscathed.

"I got lucky, I guess," I continued with a hollow laugh. "I've never faced charges, but this stuff is all still on public record. Plus, I failed that year of school, and had to repeat it. That's why it took me a while to come around to the idea of college, and my mom died not long after I started looking into it . . . After that the fainting started . . . Anyone can decide I'm too much trouble to keep around."

Max shifted his hand to my back. "That does make sense. Though I think Bane would be first to sympathize with a troubled past . . . Do you read the papers? He has a troubled *present.*"

I remained sullen. Max brushed a strand of hair from my face. "I'm so sorry about your mom. Thank you for telling me."

I sighed. "On the bright side, I'm realizing it's not so bad to talk about her. I think about her all the time, but sharing her with other people feels good. I didn't think it would."

"What was she like?"

I smiled idly, seeing her impish face. "Perpetually unbothered. I hardly ever saw her worked up. She was distant, sometimes, and mysterious. She was an accountant, managed books for all these companies, sometimes working sixty hours a week, but never skipping our evening movie dates. I think she'd work in the middle of the night so she could spend more time with me." My voice lilted a little, and I stopped. I didn't often let myself think of her so freely, and the yawning pit of pain in my chest filled with my roiling grief and threatened to spill over. I swallowed.

Max took the hint and changed the subject. "I get it, you're anxious about Camden, especially with the summer program being a trial, but still, thinking that Bane—someone who has faced his fair share of judgement—would desert you because of your past is . . . what did you call me earlier? Impressively stupid."

I slumped deeper into the couch, and Max's arm tightened, pulling me into a comforting embrace. But I felt the heat beneath it, the sudden pounding in both our chests. I turned my face up to his, and he tilted his face just an inch closer to mine, a gentler smile playing around his lips than the troublesome one he usually flashed around freely.

Max mulled over my words. His perfect facade had smudged even more. I'd smelled whiskey on his shirt—I must've spilled on him. And the perfect lines of his clothes were wrinkled from carrying me. His shoes were kicked off in a corner, and his hair was a mess. I liked him better this way, a little wild.

There was hardly any distance between us, and I wanted Max to close it.

Instead, he spoke. "We can't all be perfect all the time, even though I make it look possible. If you believe it, I have a tendency to smoke massive amounts of pot when I'm stressed. Drives the mayor wild." He stared out into the night, his jaw grinding back and forth. "Do you want me to take you home? We can act like you had a standard night of college debauchery. Nothing abnormal about that. I bet you that no less than three people at that party are vomiting into rare and expensive potted plants at this exact moment."

"You've been drinking," I accused.

Max shook his head. "I decided not to, tonight, actually. I was drinking water." His cheeks tinted faintly as he picked at the knees of his jeans. "While I like to blow off steam as much as the next Camden student, I didn't want to do anything embarrassing . . . in front of you."

Ah. So there would be no kissing tonight, with the imbalance of my fading tipsiness between us.

I pulled away and considered him. Max the sparkling enigma. "Well, that's sweet of you. Thanks for taking care of me."

Max stood, offering a hand. His fingers were pleasantly warm around mine. "Oh, I'm glad to take care of you anytime." His trouble smile was back, and it set off a fireworks show throughout my entire body.

He kept my hand and led me across the room. I spotted a smattering of purple spots along his forearm and cringed as I remembered grabbing him to stop my fall. He checked his appearance in a massive mirror on the way, frowning and wrestling his clothes back into place with his free hand.

Max dropped my hand to disappear into a second room I

assumed was an office, but must have been a closet, because he returned with a piece of clothing.

"Did we wake anyone up?" I asked, chilled at the thought of running into the mayor.

"My dad isn't here. He's probably still at the office," he called. "I'm surprised he doesn't sleep there. My sister would normally be up playing video games still, but she's at our mom's this weekend. But who cares what they or anyone else thinks?" He said, "Here's a few things to know about Crown City. Most anyone who'd think negatively of you is awful already. And, this might be one city where you actually could blend in. You think fainting is an oddity? We have vigilantes and mutants."

He passed me what he'd been rooting around for in his closet. The fancy kind of coat male models wore while walking the streets of London. I couldn't pronounce the name scribbled across the label.

"You can borrow that, and I won't even charge you for dry cleaning," he told me with a wink, holding his door open. He led me through the house, and I remained silent, not wanting to risk Max returning to his last comment. Thankfully, he stayed quiet as we made our way through the corridors to what seemed to be Max's own personal garage.

Max, of course, drove a sleek black convertible coupe.

"Subtle," I said drily. "You really are a man of the people."

Max laughed as he got my door, then slid into the driver's seat. He glanced over at me, his grip easy on the wheel. "Prior to the whole fainting part, did you have fun?"

I assured him I did, filling the rest of our drive with chatter about various classmates, while Max patiently reminded me of peoples' names.

Max grew serious as he checked the intersection at a four-way stop.

"I'm glad you came to Crown City, Mel."

"Oh?"

"Dysfunction doesn't make you squirm. Some of our classmates who would listen to me whine would also likely tell the press. I don't think you'd do that."

Max turned and the familiar foreboding security wall appeared through the trees.

"Definitely not," I said, glaring through the windshield. I was fully sick of the press myself.

Max inched up to the looming gate, cranking his window open to prompt the speaker box. It buzzed to life before I could punch in the code Bane had shared with me on the phone app to open the gate.

"Mel?" Vennie's voice burst through the speaker, sounding surprised. The Shadow was still out on the prowl, then.

"Um, yeah," I called over Max's shoulder. "Max brought me home."

Nothing from the speaker for a long moment. Vennie was likely paying much closer attention to whatever the Shadow was doing.

"Uh, Vennie?"

"Yeah?"

"Can you open the gate?"

"Oh. Right! Sure thing." The speaker cut out, and the gate opened.

Max glanced over with a raised eyebrow. "Maybe I'm wrong, and you really are the strangest family in the entire city."

"Everyone in Crown is weird," I said, parroting him.

Max seemed pleased. As we traversed the drive, I slipped off his coat and folded it over the console. It left a trace of his cologne along my neck.

As we pulled around the lion statue and I undid my seatbelt, a certain intensity gleamed in Max's eyes through the car's silky dark interior, making it feel half the size.

"Thank you," I said finally, "for everything."

I stepped from the coupe before it could shrink any further.

"Good night!" Max called through the open window.

I waved, allowing myself to savor a last glimpse of him before his tail lights painted the front door a brighter red.

Since Bane was out, I sent him a quick text letting him know I'd made it home safely and traipsed to my room, thoughts bubbling with sensations of Max near me. All the bubbles popped as I spied the stack of textbooks on my desk, waiting expectantly. With a sigh and a glance at the clock, I sat at my desk and got to work. Between romance and being a superhero, homework had to fit in somewhere or I wouldn't be in Crown long enough to see either endeavor through.

CHAPTER
FOURTEEN

"Remind me again what the mayor called me . . ." Bane asked as he dispatched a sour with a quick jab between their shoulders. "A garage sale vigilante?"

I nudged my own prone sour with my boot, assuring I had effectively rendered them unconscious. "Bargain bin vigilante," I corrected, quoting Mayor Keep's most recent statement to the *Crown City Chronicle*.

The moonlight played across his helmet's angles when Bane sighed. "Can't charm them all."

The mayor was heated over a shipment of drugs Bane had stopped from being delivered earlier that week. I'd watched quietly from the top of a stack of shipping containers, prepared to tackle anyone who tried to run. No one got the chance. It was awesome.

Still, Mayor Keep insisted it was a job for the police, and didn't appreciate the added flourish of half the sours being kicked into the lake.

I frowned as Bane scanned the rest of the street for threats. The muggers' victims had sprinted the instant we appeared. In the days following the party, I'd eventually told Bane about my fainting in front of Max, and he'd shrugged it off with the same nonchalance.

I followed him silently up the narrow iron stairwell along the building's rear. Bane stepped onto the railing at the top of the staircase. He grabbed the roof's edge and heaved himself up.

If Mayor Keep hated Bane, did he hate me, too? How much could Mayor Keep sway the rest of Camden College's board regarding my admittance? My stomach clenched.

I placed a foot on the railing and boosted myself up. Bane grabbed my hands to help cover the few inches between my fingertips and the roof. I huffed a thank you and stood beside him. From our spot in Midtown, Crown's skyline was close and enormous, glinting ominously, like it had a secret it dared us to ask about while we caught our breath. The air was crisp with the city's signature scent of evergreen and metal.

"Despite what most action movies suggest, I say you should always be cautious of rooftops," Bane said, adopting his vigilante teacher voice.

"Why's that?"

He explained as we walked, jumping from the roof of a pizza restaurant to a record store to a watch repair shop. "Higher ground is usually an advantage, but it's got to be worth it. You need to be sure you can make it back down safely. Always spare a second to think of an escape route. It's not like we can fly."

". . . Can any of the other Extrahumans fly?"

Bane shook his head. "Of the few we've had to handle, they've mostly had enhanced strength, though nowhere near ours, and unfortunate physical deformities that seem to be side effects."

He noticed the question in the tilt of my head. "When we can pull it off, we try to subdue them subtly, outside of media attention. Give them the option to leave Crown and live their lives quietly, relocated and away from people that would try to harness their abilities for nefarious purposes. Most let us help them move somewhere sunny. For the more contrarian Extras . . . we have connections with an organization that can detain them."

I chewed on that, my mind veering to other questions. "How come Kavoh never figured out Grandpa was the Shadow?" Bane twitched minutely whenever I called him that, but it was growing less pronounced.

Bane took a running leap to the next rooftop, explaining as I followed. "Kavoh left Crown City before Sydney began his escapades as the Shadow, and for once in his life managed some subtlety. Plus, we've planted the idea that the strength comes from the suit itself in the online Shadow conspiracy forums, so lots of folks think I don't actually have powers, just an outfit with impressive capabilities. In a techy town like this, it's not hard to believe. No doubt if Kavoh had known her experiments with Sydney were such a success, she would have come back for her prized test subject."

I shivered. "Was she the closest thing we had to a supervillain?"

"Besides Mayor Keep, whose only power is a super-sized stick up his ass," Bane said, adjusting the fit of his boot. "I'm relieved she died before I had to deal with her."

Vennie made a noise of protest over our earpieces. "Her company only released a statement *saying* she died. Then nearly all the information on the internet about her disappeared."

Bane sighed, as if this conversation had been hashed out before. "Exactly."

"No, *exactly*," Vennie countered. "Real death isn't that tidy. Records and miscellaneous listings stay up online, bills and insensitive mail get sent for months, traumatizing family members left behind. She 'died' the perfect death of someone who wanted to disappear."

"Fair point, but let's say you're right," Bane argued. "By

now she's at least eighty, so whatever she wanted from disappearing, she must have accomplished, right? She's well into retirement, if she's even alive. Is there evidence that she's connected to the other Extrahuman activity we've seen?"

"No, but it doesn't add up, and that bothers me. Every equation adds up somewhere."

Sensing Bane's building frustration, I cut in. "Doesn't this city have enough conspiracy theories?"

"You two *are* conspiracy theories!" Vennie stammered.

Shaking his head, Bane tugged my arm and pointed across the street, where a couple followed a young woman down the sidewalk, staying out of the pools of light cast by streetlights. "Maybe Kavoh simply wanted to be left alone?"

Vennie gave up. "You always get me there. I would understand that. Being left alone sounds delightful," he grumbled.

Bane rested his foot on the building's edge. "So no, no supervillains. Just regular villains, and they keep us busy enough."

On cue, a shout echoed from the dark avenue.

"You'll develop an instinct for when bad stuff's about to go down," Bane explained. We scrambled down the building's front, using its sign's massive letters like a ladder.

As we crept across the street, voices echoed through the chill night air.

"Aw come on, you should know better than to walk alone at night," a woman crooned at their captive, while her partner held the inno against a closed shop front, a switchblade pointed at her chest.

In between whimpers, the inno managed to speak. "I could walk alone fine if it weren't for people like you."

The sour woman backhanded her. "Stop *talking*. Where's your wallet? Phone too."

The man jostled her again and she squeaked, reaching for her pocket as we approached.

Bane jerked his head toward the man. "I'll handle the

knife," he said quietly, his voice more in my ear. I nodded assent, my hood billowing. Chezza's Superseam still held my makeshift suit together, though it was beginning to chafe. My grandpa did not have my awesome thighs.

Bane stepped up behind the man, silent. I mirrored his movement.

He tapped the man's shoulder.

The sour spun with a yelp, and Bane clocked him in the face. I ripped the woman away from the inno, twisting her arm like I had learned from one of the LookToob videos Bane had shown me. She yelped and squirmed out of my grasp, turning to face me with a vicious snarl.

Bane tackled his bear of a sour while I dodged punches. He wrapped his arms around the man, struggling with him as the inno remained petrified and frozen against the wall.

I kicked my sour in the ribs, sending her flying into a lamp post. She crumpled to the ground.

"When this happens," Bane explained, quiet enough that I heard him in my ear but not through his helmet. He had his arms crossed over the sour's chest. "You can utilize your suit's built-in electronic immobilization device. Middle button along your left wrist. Like so."

Electricity buzzed. The man jolted, eyes rolling back. He dropped his knife and followed its trajectory to the ground.

"Woah," I stared.

"Since you're wearing one of the old Shadow suits, you don't have one," Vennie piped in to explain. "But your new one will. Only two jolts before it needs to be recharged. It sucks a lot of life from your suit's brick." Bane turned away and gestured to the thick gray block between his shoulder blades that served as a computer and power source.

Spindly arms wrapped around me. The female sour had regained her footing. She scratched at my face, her nails finding purchase along my cheek, under the edge of my mask. I spun, splaying my arms to dislodge her hold. Grabbing her shoulders, I flicked my thumb up to one of the pressure points along her neck. We struggled and she flailed, landing awkward punches as I strained to position my hands right to render her unconscious. I checked her with my hip, and finally her snarl of indignation died as I pressed the right spot and she pooled to the ground.

The inno ran off, shouting "Thanks!" over her shoulder.

Bane crouched before the sours, peering at them, his form seeming to inflate with intensity. He hissed at them, "Stop preying on Crown citizens if you want to keep full use of your limbs."

We dragged them behind a dumpster to regain consciousness unbothered, before sprinting away, back into the shadows. I gasped, regaining my breath from the sour's punches, and shuddered at the feel of her nails against my cheek. Luckily, she hadn't drawn blood.

"Sorry about that," Bane murmured, dropping the Shadow's intensity. "I should have been watching your back . . . Sometimes I am so bad at paying attention."

"Understatement of the century," Chezza chimed in.

"Go back to *bed*," Vennie whined.

"I *was* going to offer you some of this ice cream, but now I've changed my mind."

Their argument devolved into muted tones as Vennie lowered the volume on their microphones.

"I mean, I'm alive," I offered lamely.

"There is that," Bane said, though he was pensive the rest of the way home.

🔥🔥🔥

WE'D DEVELOPED SOMEWHAT OF A TRAINING PLAN FOR ME that we fit in most evenings after I'd finished my classes and homework. When we'd "go out" to patrol in Crown, I'd hover and watch unless it was one or two sours we'd be fighting.

When we weren't dealing with sours, Bane would lead me on running tours of the city, provide tips for scaling walls, and point out the locations of our handful of safe houses. In between, we'd spend our evenings working on a variety of exercises. Shadow's training regimen involved a weird amalgam of fighting styles. Bane was proficient in tae kwon do, and Vennie shared his old private security training with us. Most everything else we learned from LookToob.

We practiced boxing, yoga, pilates. We ran and lifted weights. We climbed the cliff that served as the southernmost wall of the Leo property. We did sit ups until I thought I would puke.

I learned how to fall, how to balance, how to punch, repeating each motion over and over until I got it perfect, and that perfection became habit.

Before long, my resting stance changed so that my feet were always spread just so, my balance centered, the balls of my feet solid on the ground, even in the shower, where I threw punches at imaginary opponents beneath the hot spray.

Chezza revived a digital sticker chart she'd designed to keep Bane focused during his early days as the Shadow. It glowed on the LUMA when we got back to the Den. I frowned at my row that had been added beneath Bane's. I had green stars, indicating entry-level knowledge, in only half of the training categories. Bane showed gold stars in nearly every discipline, though in the "strategy" column, his star remained resolutely red, signifying "needs improvement."

After our outing, I strolled to my cubby, unfastening my suit and tugging the elastic that kept the front of my hair out of my face. Bane's suggestion had become my preferred way to wear my hair while vigilante-ing, and he procured a jumbo pack of elastics for me.

I shed my suit, savoring the excess heat before hauling it onto a steel hanger and pulling on a sweatshirt and leggings over the sports bra and bike shorts I'd taken to wearing as a base layer. The more of my bare skin that was exposed to the suit's warming lining, the better. Bane had changed into a T-shirt and gym shorts by the time I joined him back at the LUMA. Chezza handed me a cup of salabat, ginger tea flavored with brown sugar and honey. She sipped her own, eyes skeptical on the LUMA beneath her messy bun, pink and black strands slipping out. Vennie tapped his prosthetic against his desk, a light dinging that signified he was immersed in thought. Meanwhile, Bane was elbow deep in a bag of licorice.

Chezza frowned at the LUMA. "That was tidier than some of your recent rescues," she muttered. "But you need to start thinking of the two of you as one unit."

Vennie nodded in agreement.

Bane sighed. "You're right. It might be time to retire my old mantra of 'Guess, assess, and hope for the best.'"

"Yeah, how's that been treating you?" a deep voice asked from behind us.

I whirled, nearly dropping my mug.

A hulking, olive-skinned man in a leather jacket with waves of thick black hair and a chin like a semi's fender grinned smugly at us from the base of the stairs. A bulging duffel bag rested at his feet.

His teeth flashed blinding white as he crossed his arms, shoulders swelling beneath leather. "When the hell were you gonna tell me you became a daddy?" he demanded.

Bane whooped and launched himself at the stranger.

The man held Bane at arm's length while they laughed. Chezza smiled on, shaking her head. Vennie dutifully ignored the spectacle and punched buttons on his keyboard.

The man's dark eyes found me. "This her?"

Before Bane could do more than nod, he sauntered my way and held out a massive hand. I took it tentatively. He squeezed, a wisp of a challenge in the gesture. Still warm from the suit and my layers, I squeezed back, hard.

His eyes widened. "That's what I'm talkin' about." He pulled me in for an embrace that lifted me off my feet and cracked my entire spine pleasantly. He set me down as Bane hovered in our vicinity, looking sheepish. "Nice to meet you, kid. I'm your Uncle Roger."

I raised an eyebrow at Bane.

Bane affectionately rubbed the newcomer's shoulder.

"Mel, this meathead is my old friend, Roger. We used to work private security during my gap year . . ."

Roger's laugh boomed. "Turned into a gap couple of years, didn't it? Worked together, played together. How have you not regaled her with the legends yet?"

Bane rolled his eyes. "Because I knew you'd tell her the minute you got here. When I actually got around to inviting you. Which I haven't done yet."

Roger grinned and shed his jacket, tossing it on the couch. "You know I keep tabs on the news around here, so I heard about her arrival and thought I'd give you guys some time. But then I got to thinking, what are the odds she's a freak like you? I got impatient and decided to swing by." He shook out his hand. "Looks like I was right. Per usual."

Chezza swept in and gave him a kiss on the cheek. "Good to see you, Rog. I'm going to bed. Your usual guest room is probably a little dusty, but the linens are all clean."

Roger returned the smooch. "Thanks, sweetness. Good to see you too, Vennie. The security system is looking great. Should keep anyone out, except me of course."

Vennie just grunted.

Roger turned back to us. "I have excellent timing." He eyed the star chart. "Looks like you definitely need my help."

Bane slung an arm around my shoulders. "We've been doing alright, thanks." He explained, "Roger works for a private security firm based out of California. They take care of some of the Extrahumans we neutralize, actually. He's got an expansive set of skills."

"That I do," Roger said, nodding solemnly. "Now, show me what you've been working on."

Bane looked unsure. I shrugged.

Roger rubbed his massive hands together. "Aw come on, you two, I made sure not come on a school night."

Vennie sighed and pulled up our favorite pizza joints' website on the LUMA and ordered our usual.

🔥🔥🔥

ROGER STAYED WITH US TWO NIGHTS AND MADE THEM count. He ran me through a variety of combat and calisthenic drills, breaking down each movement to the minutiae and having me repeat until I could perform them flawlessly from memory or with a glance at the notes he scribbled on the LUMA. The latter made a vein pop out on Vennie's forehead until he grumbled and retired to bed.

Roger pitted me against Bane. We'd sparred before, but with pads and much trepidation on both our parts, which Roger found impractical.

"I always tell you, Bane. Your priorities are in the wrong order. You gotta bleed a little to learn. C'mon, Toasty," he told me, and had me launch a kick that caught Bane in the chest. My uncle rubbed his sternum, impressed.

"Excellent," Roger said.

Still regaining his breath, Bane grunted in agreement.

Roger rubbed his chin. "You guys cover weapons yet?"

"We don't use weapons," I started. "They're—"

"Dangerous and too easy for the cops to use as a way to frame you as threats, I know, I know," Roger interrupted. "Defend and incapacitate, I've heard the spiel a hundred times. Bane, where are the guns?"

Bane frowned, his mouth tight.

Roger didn't back down. "Seriously? You haven't done this

with her yet? Just cuz you're not using them on others doesn't mean they won't pull them on her."

Bane's gaze tipped to the floor.

"Oh my God, she's already been held up? Fuck's sake, Bane. You two aren't *that* bulletproof. Where'd you put the locker?"

"But it was *before* we knew about her powers—Never mind. They're in the safe room, with the Cube," Bane admitted, not looking at me.

Roger sauntered to the giant metal door, and Bane begrudgingly pulled up a keypad on the LUMA and typed a complex chain of symbols. The door swung open after a series of resounding thuds. I peered around Roger's massive frame to the Cube mainframe, where it sat on a refrigerated pedestal. Vennie had affectionately mentioned it before: a giant hard drive that stored all their Shadow data. The Cube was a foot square and held every piece of information pertaining to Shadow. It lived behind the imposing security door in the Den's corner. In a minute, Roger emerged, hauling out a large, military-grade storage bin. Bane gave in and helped him carry it alongside our ring of practice mats, then placed his palm on a screen set into its lid.

The lid slid back to reveal a small armory. Rows and rows of guns and grenades and other dark devices I couldn't identify. Sweat pricked along my forehead just looking at them, thinking about that first sour that had turned a gun on me, the night I met the Shadow.

Roger pulled out safety glasses and tossed them to us, put on his own, and pulled out a wicked looking pistol. He also tossed us earplugs. "For those bat ears of yours." He walked me through safety precautions, then how to use, fire, and dismantle each type of gun in the case. Bane begrudgingly refreshed his skills, too.

Keeping the safety on and the barrel pointed toward the far end of the Den, Roger lifted the gun and wrapped my fingers around the handle. I tried not to grimace and adopted the stance he'd shown me.

"Excellent, Toasty. You've got it. You should eventually head to a range and actually fire them, so you know you can aim if you ever need to." He turned to Bane, "Now that you've got a partner in crime-fighting, are you gonna reconsider my advice about adding a ranged weapon to your utility belt? She could be a sniper, non-lethal bullets or something."

Bane shook his head as vehemently as I did.

"Fine, fine," Roger took the gun from my hand. "You're going to be glad I taught you all this," he told me out of the corner of his mouth.

I forced my trepidation down, shifting my perspective to focus on learning another useful skill to help keep Crown citizens safe. I was glad to have my grip free of the repulsive metal, but the faster I could render a firearm useless, the more effective I could be.

As it neared two in the morning and we covered the mechanisms of the final weapon, Bane and I sagged in relief.

"How about some shots? The alcohol kind?" Roger suggested, cracking his neck with a series of loud pops.

"Yes, *please*," Bane said.

I politely declined and headed to my room to do reading for my classes, which I was barely keeping up with, but I fell asleep with my head between the pages.

CHAPTER
FIFTEEN

THE NIGHT AFTER ROGER LEFT, BANE SLEPT OFF THE CHAOS, his snores echoing out into the foyer. I couldn't sleep, so I padded to the Den where one person would almost always be up.

I cleared my throat at the base of the stairs, and Vennie turned his head from his tablet, but his eyes darted back every other second. "Hey, Mel."

"Can I see all you have on the Shadow's history?"

Vennie brightened. He helped me drag the battered blue sofa over so he could situate me in front of the LUMA.

Its massive display demanded my entire attention. Videos flashed across its curved surface in an endless stream. News segments, blurry night vision footage from Bane's helmet camera, and amateur documentary clips made by members of the Shadows' fan club speculating on his origins and identity.

Vennie queued up every piece of information he had on the Shadow. His legacy. Our history. My potential. As the night wore on, a pile of cupcake wrappers littered my lap, growing as I devoured the Shadow's lore. Vennie took the time to run more tests on my powers. He was convinced my strength was evening out the more time I spent with

Tempatches on, so my risk of fainting shrunk each day. He wrapped a thick band around my arm, with looping wires connecting it to a spring-loaded device in my hand.

Vennie worked quietly on his own project, occasionally pausing to polish off the last of the chicken adobo he and Chezza had made for dinner and ask me questions about how I felt as he set my Tempatches to different heat levels. The device measured my grip strength at increasing temperatures and sent the information to the Cube. My drooping eyes flicked to it every few minutes as the clocks ticked toward morning.

🔥🔥🔥

MAX SNAPPED HIS FINGERS IN FRONT OF MY FACE.

I started and almost fell backward out of my chair.

"Late night?" he asked, smirking. The gentle clamor of ceramic cups and an ancient radiator that defined Hardwired Cafe registered and centered me back in the present. It was the afternoon and I'd finished with my courses for the day.

Gem sat next to me, capturing the muted brilliance of the coffee shop with watercolor markers in a massive sketchbook while I struggled through calculus equations. We'd met up for coffee, and she'd agreed to help check my work.

Max had texted a few times, wanting to hang out.

"*Invite him!*" Gem had insisted, curious to study the elusive golden child of Crown City.

I couldn't blame her. He was stunning even in his subdued outfit of an olive polo shirt and khakis.

"Couldn't sleep," I muttered, running my fingers through my hair, trying to will some volume into it. "So much studying to do."

The barista called Max's name, and he sauntered to the bar for his drink.

"He is *so* into you," Gem hissed, capturing the walls of the cafe in a perfect rusty orange, even as she turned her eyes on me.

I didn't have time to reply as Max pulled out the chair across from mine and took a sip from his drink, while sliding over a steaming to-go cup. The delicate scent of cinnamon seeping through the lid, a respite from the empty coffee mug at my elbow. I perked up. "If that's a dirty chai, I promise not to call you a terrible name for at least the next fifteen minutes."

"It is indeed." Max grinned and leaned close as I popped the lid off and took a long drink. He slid an iced matcha to Gem as well, and she batted her long lashes at him. "I'm worried you're going to burn yourself out." The warmth in his tone roused a squeeze in my chest.

My body ached all over from training and I needed a nap. No wonder Bane missed so many commitments. Still, he had been up early to wish me a good day before heading to work.

I met Max's warm stare, nearly forgetting how to speak. "I can handle it," I insisted.

"Even the great Melbourne has her limits . . ." Gem suggested, perfectly shading the chrome components of the hissing espresso machine in her drawing.

I groaned. My heavy workload was a nightmare when all I could think about were my new powers and my time with Bane. Even the pleasant hum of heat from a handful of Tempatches beneath my clothes was no match for sleep deprivation. Camden's summer program was halfway over, and I hadn't missed an assignment, but my grades were only passable.

Max nudged my side and I tried not to wince. He hit the same spot as a sour had a few nights prior, though Max's touch was infinitely preferable.

Max dipped his perfect face conspiratorially, taking up my entire field of vision. "Why don't you skip studying today?"

My mouth twisted in two different directions.

Gem snapped her sketchbook closed. "That's a great idea! You've gotten the last four equations right without my help." She checked the time on her phone. "I have a manicure appointment. I'll see you two around."

I smiled at her gratefully, though I was fairly certain her appointment wasn't for another hour. She winked at me as she floated out the door.

Gently, Max closed my textbook, brushing my hand out of the way with the back of his. I scowled at him. "I need full admission to Camden at the end of the program. You know that."

Max flashed his smile. "Don't flunk calculus and don't rob a bank. You'll be fine."

"Spoken like someone whose parents donated enough money to the place to have their name on a building," I muttered, though I set my pen down.

Max sighed, and continued to read my mind. "You haven't missed a single class or assignment." He examined his latte for a moment, then said, "You know college isn't your only option, right?"

I narrowed my eyes. Many conversations with my old Upstate High counselor of the week started this way. "How do you mean?"

He leaned back. "Like, what's the fixation? I mean, I get it. I'm doing college, too. It's preferable to any other route. But say you didn't make it in—" I scowled and he put his hands up. "I'm sure you will. You're brilliant. But say you didn't. Your life wouldn't be over. You know that, right?"

I made my granite face. Max blabbed while I tried to unravel his point.

"It wouldn't mean you're not smart, or successful. You'd be great at so many things. Trade school, just entering the workforce. They're all good and valid options. This college thing seems so . . . life and death with you."

I swallowed a manic laugh as the half-healed cuts under my sweater twinged.

I unstuck my face and glanced up brightly. It was sweet, Max trying to understand me. "Thank you for saying that, but this is all I want. I was told I couldn't do it, when I know I can. It's important to me that I prove it." And permanently stay away from Sam, I added silently.

Max looked prepared to argue, then sighed. "I understand that I don't understand, and I'll help however I can."

I nodded and turned my eyes back to my paper, but all my motivation had left. "Fine," I sighed. "I'll be done with school work for the day."

Max stared at me for a moment, considering. I raised my eyebrows as I tipped my cup high.

"Why don't we catch a movie?"

He knew my kryptonite. "Do you have one in mind?"

He shot me his sneaky grin. "Have you seen *Woman on Neptune*?"

"Obviously not. It's not out yet."

The corner of his mouth crept higher, his eyes the same color as his latte. He took a leisurely sip. "Ah, finally, I can show you the perks of my . . . resources."

I squinted skeptically.

He rolled his eyes. "I have a screener copy."

I sat straight up. "Really?! You're the best."

As I chucked my papers into my bag, he touched my side again, more gently. I hesitated.

Max stared into his cup. "No, that would be you," he coughed and clarified. "You're actually the best. That's what I think."

The compliment paralyzed me. Blood rushed to my face, broadcasting my intense feelings about his statement before I could sort out what they were.

He slowly lifted his eyes to mine, and I rolled back through our friendship in my mind, comparing how he'd looked at me on the first day we'd met to now. The affection there that made appearances more and more frequently. When he'd glance over at me as we walked across campus, trading snarky comments. Every time I revealed a messed-up tidbit from my past and he'd concede one of his own. It's how he'd looked at me for the entirety of our time at the Carbati's party.

I liked Max, and very much had not considered what it meant if he shared the sentiment. I was busy with my long-lost uncle and prolific fainting spells and the discovery that superpowers were real and that I also happened to have them.

And calculus.

I remembered my unfinished mouthful of chai and unceremoniously swallowed it with an audible gulp.

Disappointment flashed across Max's face. He drew his bag over his shoulder, pushing in his seat without meeting my eyes. "Or I can drop you back at home, if you like. If you need to catch up on sleep," he said hurriedly.

Was that a trace of a *blush* on the untouchable Max Keep's cheeks? I set a hand on his arm before I could make the situation any more awkward and simply told the truth.

"I want to watch a movie with you."

Max's blinding smile reappeared. "We have to get it from my dad. Forgive me if I made myself sound important—he's the one with a Hollywood contact. He doesn't watch them, he just likes having access. *I'm* the cultured one." He finished with a mocking half-bow.

"And how lucky I am to have some of that esteemed culture rub off on me, you ass." I rolled my eyes and shoved him toward the exit, my palms lingering on the smooth muscle beneath his shirt a little longer than necessary.

🔥🔥🔥

MAX DROVE TO THE NORTHERN EDGE OF DOWNTOWN IN silence, parking in the same neighborhood as Leo Optics. As we traversed the sidewalk, Max kept his hands shoved in his pockets.

I slipped into that calculating mental space where I was so comfortable. What did I know? Max liked me, and I liked him. I felt good around him and wanted more.

Would it detract from schoolwork? What about superheroing? Well, he'd never know, so it didn't matter. Shadow shenanigans had nothing to do with Max.

But did I remember how to have a more-than-friend? Back in Upstate City, I'd had my fair share of hookups but few deeply romantic interactions.

You also used to not have a family, and you seem to be figuring that out fine, a quiet voice mentioned in the back of my head.

The solid comfort of resolve clicked in, and the ensuing possibilities had me feeling warm, but an entirely different sensation than the one from the Tempatches.

My thoughts were interrupted with a slight tug on the elbow of my jacket, pulling me to a stop. Max dropped his hand, and I looked up. We were dwarfed beneath a broad, beige building twenty stories high, the words KEEP CORP emblazoned across the top in sharp red letters.

"Ah," I said lamely.

Max snorted and opened one of the glass doors for me. "My dad spends more time here than at City Hall," he explained as we stepped into a wide, marble-tiled lobby, complete with obscene gold elevators, two fancy restaurants, and an expansive security desk.

"What does Keep Corp *do*?" I asked as I gaped at the distant ceiling. Sharp, abstract shards of black glass dripped water onto each other and then into a wide gold basin in the middle of the space, surrounded by a small forest of miniature, precisely trimmed shrubs.

"Real estate management, mostly," Max said as we walked. "But this is an umbrella for a bunch of other companies. E-commerce, consulting, all sorts of things."

"How does your dad run an entire city and a giant company?"

Max ran a hand over his hair, frowning at the water feature. "He makes sure to do a good enough job as mayor. He takes action to appease enough of his constituents. It's genius, really."

I mused as Max waved at the security guard on duty, and they waved us past. We stepped into one of the elevators, and my moment of awe was broken as the doors slid closed. Max pressed a button for the highest floor and put his hands right back in his pockets. He stared at the ceiling, away from me.

I wrenched up my bravery, preferring to face three sours in an alley than figure out how to flirt with Max on purpose.

"So . . ." I began brilliantly. He glanced my way, holding my gaze for the first time since we left campus. I faced him as the elevator rose. "Back at Hardwired . . . Was that a need-lessly snooty way of confessing that you have a crush on me?" Mercifully, the words stayed steady and turned to a smile on my lips.

One broke out on his face, too, and he faced me. The bouncing light within the elevator illuminated gold in his eyes as we passed the glass shards and the water that splashed off them. "That's exactly what it was. I didn't expect you'd have a complaint." He took a step, bringing his body an inch from mine. "Would you prefer something more direct?" he asked quietly.

"Yes," I said.

He leaned down, and I shifted up on my toes to close the distance.

Like the rest of him, Max's lips were pure gold.

I wrapped my arms around his neck as his circled my waist. Max's kiss bubbled through me like champagne, warming me from top to toes. His mouth moved in such a purposeful way that made me light-headed as the elevator continued up.

The elevator halted with a light *ding*, and I slowly pulled back, dropping my arms. Max smiled at me gloriously. The doors opened and I fought to make myself breathe normally.

"Ready to meet the mayor?" Max asked, taking my hand.

The mayor. Fuck.

What did I know about the mayor?

His son was a stellar kisser. Not helpful.

He'd stared daggers at me in the parade, and I tried not to shudder at the memory.

He famously hated my uncle, and Bane didn't seem to think much of him either. Not great to think about after kissing Max.

Kissing Max.

My heart thrummed, heat bolting up my cheekbones. I didn't notice much of the lobby we stepped into. Instead, I felt the ghost of Max's hands on my waist and tried not to reverently trace where his lips had met mine.

Max flashed one more smile over his shoulder, then dropped my hand as we crossed the room. Stiffness crept into his posture. The light on his face subdued. I wiped the idiotic grin off my own as we approached a marble counter manned by a small fleet of assistants, tailored jackets and tiny black headsets on all of them. Most were locked in intense phone conversations while simultaneously stuffing a mountain of envelopes.

"Is my father available?" Max asked the least occupied staffer, who tugged on her blonde braid as she read a document. She glanced up from her binder, pursing her lips.

"He's on a call," she said dismissively, "but you can wait." She brought us tiny bottles of sparkling water, which Max ignored while I fidgeted. Finally, we were given the go-ahead to walk down a wood paneled hallway behind the reception area.

The Honorable Travis Keep's office was all closed blinds, reddish wood, and sports memorabilia in thick glossy frames.

His eyes flicked to us from a muted, non–Leo Optics TV in the corner as we entered. He lounged in a massive leather chair, tossing a golf ball from hand to hand.

"Maximillian," he said by way of greeting.

"Dad." Max inclined his head and held an arm toward me stiffly. "This is Melbourne Alloway."

I extended my hand over the desk. Mayor Keep leaned just an inch forward and pressed one massive palm to mine. He squeezed and held my grip, studying my face without conceding a millimeter of movement on his own.

"Nice to make your acquaintance, Melbourne. How are you liking my Crown City?"

I dislodged my grip from his, twisting my hands behind my back. "What I've seen is wonderful," I said stiffly.

Max was uncharacteristically silent somewhere behind me.

The lines around the mayor's mouth tightened infinitesimally. "I'm sure. Don't let Max be a bad influence. Your time with us is so uncertain and he takes you to a trashy party with those Carbati troublemakers. How is your free spirit of an uncle handling the adjustment of being a sudden caretaker?"

The mayor's clipped savagery sliced at the tendons in my knees, turning my lower half to water.

"We're both thrilled," I offered blandly, trying not to shake.

He nodded and glanced out the window. "I sincerely hoped that the tendency for spectacle wouldn't prove to be genetic. Your fall at the Summer's Start Soiree was unfortunate. All those cameras, all that distress on a nice day designated for celebrating."

"Luckily, I recovered," I said.

Mayor Keep said nothing.

Max cleared his throat. I looked away, needing a moment to blink and breathe before my composure dissolved. My eyes roved to the muted TV in the corner. It was tuned to a program I knew well, the familiar face squeezing the last of my breath from my lungs.

My dad grinned cheerily out at us, holding a rattlesnake and likely lecturing on the importance of giving reptiles a wide berth.

Mayor Keep was watching Chanimal. The message was clear. He knew all about me. He ran this town, and he didn't want me in it.

My stomach turned sour, but I had escaped my own father. I could handle Max's as well.

"Thank you, I'll see you at home," Max was saying as he fetched a stiff, square envelope from a pile of mail on a table in the corner.

Mayor Keep called to us as we left.

"I hope you enjoy your visit, Melbourne."

Like he was certain I wouldn't be staying long in Crown City at all.

CHAPTER
SIXTEEN

FOR THE BRIEF MOMENTS I PAID ATTENTION, *THE WOMAN ON Jupiter* was fantastic. It was easy to be a generous critic of an afternoon spent sprawled across a cushy recliner alongside Max. It was made even better by the endless supply of popcorn from the machine in the corner of his personal screening room.

But my fizzing excitement was overcast by my encounter with the mayor. It plagued me even after I suggested to Bane that we take the night off from any Extrahuman business so I could catch up on sleep and schoolwork. Bane agreed and even decided to work late with Logan to learn the happenings at Leo Optics he'd been neglecting for who knew how long, and to help with preparations for the upcoming Tech Expo.

I couldn't focus at my desk, every few minutes longingly staring at my bed, where I could sink into sleep and reminisce on the feeling of Max's lip between my teeth.

With a scowl I gathered my books and stomped to the end of the hallway and up the stairs, emerging into the mysterious office with its unending fire in the hearth. Between the dust and Bane's avoidance, I was positive it was my grandpa's personal study. Since no one else went near it, I'd commandeered it as my own.

Settling into the armchair, I stared into the fire and massaged a knot developing in the muscle between my shoulders.

I grinned, hearing one of Bane's standard laments about Sydney in my mind. "Pompous ass, never one to skip on a tribute to his own genius." He had added with a grumble, "Never wanting to be forgotten. *Always* needing attention."

I saw Bane's point, but I appreciated the flames in a way I imagined my grandpa did. The fire's design was brilliant. It burned for years without causing an issue, likely electrical or solar powered.

He'd probably be pleased someone minded the fire.

I halted. Maybe Sydney *wanted* someone to notice it.

Slipping from the chair, I crouched before the fireplace, eyeing the gently dancing flames as they whistled and huffed. If I squinted, I could make out the electric components beneath the faux logs.

I shoved up my sleeve and reached in. The flames licked lovingly along my arm, letting me know I could crush the metal pieces if I wanted. I traced my fingers along the logs until I felt what I suspected. A switch.

When I pressed it, the fire didn't go out. Nothing happened. I sat back on my heels with a frown.

"Hello, Melbourne."

"Agh!" I toppled onto my ass.

My grandfather stood in the corner of the room.

I scrambled behind the armchair. Superpowers were one thing, but my psyche could not readily handle the existence of a ghost.

"Please don't be alarmed. This program is designed to be nearly indiscernible from reality." Sydney chuckled. "Judging by your reaction, it's highly effective."

I stared, and my grandpa kept talking.

"I can't say I'm not pleased at your alarm. I was unable to test this system while I was alive. Leo screens are the best in the world, aren't they?"

Heart pounding, I crept forward. Sydney's apparition wore a suit with a dated cut and a bright red pocket square tucked against his chest. As I passed the window, the sunset's flare did strange things to his figure. He looked transparent for a moment, the light leaking through his pale hair.

"Please don't get too close," he said. "The glass is ultra thin. You will likely break it. I didn't prepare replacement sheets. I don't know if anyone at Leo Optics would be able to recreate them."

My grandfather's proportions didn't stay quite right depending on the angle I viewed him from. He stood in one corner of the small room, his lower legs and feet indiscernible behind a faux plant in a broad pot.

"You're an image on a screen."

"Very good," he said pleasantly. "I'd expect nothing less from one of my own. But I am more than that. I'm a trained and educated response and advisory system." His bright eyes roved the space. There had to be a hidden camera mounted in the room that enabled his interface to "look" around. His face was impassive for a moment before he spoke again. "You were able to activate me, but the everlasting fire hasn't been extinguished. I could not be more pleased that you inherited my exact abilities. What a fun twist of genetic fate."

Goosebumps tore up my arms. "How do you know that?"

The image blinked blandly. "The Cube hard drive you use was my invention. I planted this program within it a long time ago. I've seen the media coverage of your arrival, as well as the tests Venancio ran this weekend on your strength. This is more than I ever hoped for. My abilities survived genetically, coupled with such an excellent name Adelaide chose for you. I am happy to be of service. Since I'm sure my son won't deign to speak to me, you have a monopoly on my expertise and advice." His gaze flicked to the ornamental carvings behind the desk.

"Oh my lions," I said, imagining Sydney as a ghostly program, floating around in the Cube with all of our Shadow data, a digital stowaway. "Your records aren't missing. You hid them."

Sydney smiled broadly as a soft click echoed through the room. The wood slowly lowered on silent hinges, revealing a dense row of notebooks. "Now they're yours. I scanned most of them to my digital memory and am happy to pull any information you require quickly."

Sydney kept up his proud smile as I scanned the shelves, pulling out a notebook. I opened it reverently. Sydney's handwriting was smaller and neater than Bane's. "I am a wealth of knowledge and experience, though my corporeal encounters are a bit outdated," he said. "I am the first and foremost expert on the Shadow. I made the persona, though I must admit Brisbane has improved on the venture. He was always so thoughtful of others, even when it did him a disservice."

I collapsed back into the armchair, the words in the notebook blurring as my head spun. "These are the complete account of how you became Extrahuman?"

Sydney smiled. "A brilliant first question. Surely you know some of our family's history—how I came to Crown and built Leo Optics."

"Uncle Bane told me."

Sydney chuckled, "'Uncle Bane,' how delightful. I hope he's a good influence." He waved his hand and the bulky computer on the desk hummed to life. A photo appeared on the screen as Sydney spoke. In black and white, it depicted a much younger Sydney, all charming smiles, standing next to a stony-faced woman with glinting eyes and dark hair.

"After several years of Leo Optics continually dominating domestic markets, I grew bored. I dabbled in a variety of sciences. My interest in genetics drew me to a brilliant scientist, Dr. Eleanor Kavoh. We had similar aspirations in exploring the limits of the human body. She was convinced she could expand them. Of course these explorations would have been frowned upon by governing boards of all kinds, so we conducted them in secret." He scoffed. "The small-minded . . . Always inhibiting the growth of humanity. We created a cover story that we were researching gene therapy treatments to prevent certain types of cancer."

"That's fucked up," I blurted.

Sydney shrugged. "Our shared genius and drive led to a highly productive partnership. Kavoh developed a gene therapy and determined I was a strong candidate for a successful procedure. I needed little convincing. Our abilities were born. Though Kavoh was not pleased with our results. She wanted to push our experiments further."

I studied the pixelated flat line of Kavoh's mouth. "She wasn't satisfied with your super strength?"

Sydney sighed heavily, "No, she was after something else. Something grander." He let the silence stretch.

"The flair for the dramatic in this family," I muttered under my breath. "What was she after, then?"

"Immortality."

My eyebrows drew together.

"Is it such a farfetched idea?" he asked. "You can reach through fire and come away unharmed."

I absently ran my fingertips over Sydney's notebook in my lap. "Did she figure it out?"

Sydney adjusted his pocket square. "Thankfully, no. Her manic devotion to her goal made me uneasy. Much like when your and Bane's powers developed, my abilities were inconsistent. They came and went seemingly without cause, leaving me faint and weak at random. Realizing Kavoh's goal, I convinced her my strength was temporary, that my abilities faded." He pulled up a different image on the computer screen, a scan of a medical file on Sydney, a dark stamp reading "FAILED" stained the front. "She was immensely frustrated. We parted ways soon after that. Eventually I discovered that temperature affected my strength, that, like you, I was strong when warm and weak when cold. I conducted some other experiments on my own and birthed the Shadow persona, but eventually I turned my focus to being a better husband and father, but not soon enough."

The AI's face went eerily blank after the allusion to his own death. And my grandma's. I changed the subject.

"What happened to Kavoh?"

Sydney's eyes narrowed. "She fled the country, and took her experiments to more remote locales. I don't think she had other scientific triumphs. Though, as you've seen through some of the mutants within Crown, some zealots are trying to continue her work, with varied success."

My head spun and my eyes burned with exhaustion. "Will you be here forever now? I have more questions, but I need to focus on my homework."

Sydney brightened. "Appropriate respect for academics. I'm so proud. Indeed, I am at your disposal. I'll go into rest mode when we're not speaking. I could even complete your assignments for you, if you like, in record time. You do have other priorities, it would seem. The mutant infestation in Crown City is troubling. We should be the only ones."

Tempting, but I shook my head.

The projection sighed. "You're more like Brisbane, aren't you? That's probably for the best, though don't forget that we wouldn't have these powers were it not for me."

"Thanks, I think."

Sydney inclined his head as I gathered my things. "And Melbourne, please don't tell Brisbane about me. Unless something drastic has changed since our last meeting in life, I don't think he could refrain from smashing my mechanism immediately, and my development was quite expensive. Again, I did not prepare a replacement."

"I won't tell him." I stared awkwardly, wondering if it would be rude to try and shut my grandpa off.

"I must say, I'm so glad you made your way to Crown City, Melbourne. I've enjoyed following your escapades. You've certainly had an exciting stay so far."

Apparently the public fainting was going to haunt me forever. I snorted. "The *excitement* just won't stop." I thought of my day alone. "Do you know why Mayor Keep and Uncle Bane hate each other?"

Sydney's face went blank again as he processed. "I never formally met the current mayor. I vaguely remember the name Travis Keep . . . I think he and your uncle were friends during Brisbane's depressingly short time at Camden College."

My head throbbed. "It's fine. I'll ask him about it eventually. Can you shut off until the next time I need you?"

"Of course. I will transmit full accessibility credentials to you. You will need a pass code."

"Er, like what? Does it need a number and a special symbol?"

I swear the image looked thoughtful for a moment, his smile turned familiar and crooked.

"Might I suggest, 'grandpa'?"

"Oh sweet hell, I am going to need so much therapy," I muttered. "'Grandpa' is fine. I'll come see you again soon. I have more questions about Kavoh . . . and everything else."

Sydney's apparition nodded, and his smile failed for once. The corner of his mouth tucked down an instant before he disappeared.

I tangled my fingers together, eventually replacing the notebook on the shelf and sliding the carving back into place.

My head spun. I had access to all the answers we wanted about the Shadow's origin, but how would Bane react to this ghost of his father? I shuddered, imagining it was my mom who'd done it—left a shallow, irreverent echo of herself. No, I would definitely not tell Bane. It would be a secret between me and my grandpa, for now.

CHAPTER
SEVENTEEN

ANOTHER WEEK PASSED, AND I FELL INTO THE WARM COMFORT of a routine. With a razor-thin amount of time to spare, I focused on my Camden workload . . . and learning to be a superhero. Each night as I'd fight to stay awake at my desk or in Sydney's office, I got distracted noticing the healed scrapes and fading bruises littering my arms and legs, watching my body restore itself faster than ever now that I knew to stay warm. I didn't mention my use of the office to Bane. He'd no doubt have a conniption if he knew I was talking with Sydney's narcissistic technological legacy that lived in the attic.

Each day was an exciting, exhausting whirlwind. My hours were a blur of class and rushing through homework to lay my hands on Max. After, I power napped until sunset and then headed out with the Shadow.

Impressive purple bags developed beneath my eyes. Prioritizing rest was exceedingly difficult when I was constantly buzzed with excitement and eagerness at what waited for me next, between stopping crime and spending time with Max. Amidst the insanity, no matter how hard I worked, my grades wavered barely at an acceptable level. It would have to be enough.

One afternoon, after an exceptionally frustrating calculus exam and a particularly long goodbye kiss with Max under the cover of some ornately pruned campus shrubbery, I swept into the living room and dropped my backpack. I sank into the couch, consumed by my thoughts. Six hidden Tempatches I wore gave off heat that vastly improved the frustration brewing within me. I'd made stupid, simple mistakes on the exam.

I rolled out my shoulders, bullying cracks from my neck, when my phone buzzed.

Pool party at my place this weekend? No beer pong, I promise.

Lips curling, I texted Max back.

Sounds wonderful.

His response was instant.

Do I have to invite anyone else?

I squirmed as I typed back.

No. Just us.

I grinned and leaned further into the couch, debating delaying an essay for a nap. Bane interrupted my reverie when he appeared in the doorway, still dressed from his day at the office, his tie loose and crooked.

"Can you help me with something?"

"Of course." I rose from the couch with a long stretch.

"Are you sleeping alright?" Bane asked as he led the way to the garage.

Unconvincingly, I stifled a yawn. "I'm tired," I admitted.

"No wonder it's hard for you to do any work." That pulled a smile from him.

"I'm learning balance . . . slowly," he said and gestured toward a hideous floral loveseat haphazardly dangling out of the back of the SUV, dripping with loose bungee cords.

"Did you manage this all by yourself?" I asked blandly.

He scratched the back of his head and winced. "I, uh, found it at the end of the neighbor's driveway. It's getting pretty cramped in the Den . . ."

"Fair point."

He went to the car and began throwing off cords and straps. "I can lift it fine, but it's difficult to maneuver alone."

Bolstered by the heat of my Tempatches, it was easy to catch the edge of the couch opposite Bane as he slid it out.

"I'll go backward down the stairs," I offered. "Knowing you, you'll trip and concuss us both in the process."

Bane snorted. "You're not wrong."

As I shifted to hold up my end with one hand and open the portrait door to the Den with the other, Bane remained quiet. An anomaly, for him.

"Are you alright?" I asked finally, my eyes trained on the floor as I carefully moved down a step.

"Yeah, I uh, I was actually going to ask you the same thing. Time's been flying since you got here. How are you handling school and, you know, superpowers?"

I nearly missed a step, but caught myself before I could waver. I couldn't see Bane over the rolled arm of the loveseat except for the top of his wild hair bobbing as he kept his eyes on his own feet.

The innocuous question hit me like a punch to the chest. I wanted to tell him everything. My worries over school, my excitement over Max, and how nearly every moment of the day I spent looking forward to my next outing with the Shadow.

But what would he think of my less-than-perfect grades?

That I was dating the son of his enemy? Would he try to keep me from joining him on his vigilante outings?

A soft crack emanated from where my grip had ticked around the couch's base, and Sam's voice was immediately in my head.

You destroy everything you touch.

"I'm good," I said as we neared the bottom of the stairwell. "Classes are good. The professors are nice, for the most part . . ." I knew what else I needed to tell him. "I—uh, I've been spending a lot of time with Max Keep."

"Oh *really?*" Bane's eyes got wide.

"Yes. He's a good friend. And a good . . . more than friend."

"Oh! That's amazing, but . . . his dad isn't my biggest fan. What does Max think?"

"Max doesn't seem to like his dad that much, either. He's not worried about it."

Bane nodded slowly, confliction contorting his face. Glee and concern were both evident there. "Well . . . Okay then. Does Max make you happy and treat you well?"

It wasn't the response I'd expected. "He does."

"Then I'm happy for you both," he finished, the tension dropping off his face.

Now on flat ground, we traversed the Den easily to set the new loveseat perpendicular to the blue sofa. Vennie grunted a greeting, not looking away from the LUMA where he played a video game. As Bane straightened, a frown tugged at the corner of his mouth, like my answer had been disappointing.

"How are you?" I ventured in a panic, resolving to start getting up earlier to spend more time studying. I'd do anything to keep from letting him down. Getting accepted to Camden made sure I could live on campus in the fall and stick around.

Returning to Sam was unacceptable, and now . . . The thought of having to leave Bane . . . I couldn't bear it.

My uncle rubbed his chin. "I'm good," he said finally.

There was something he wasn't saying, either. Had he finally figured out what Sam knew to be true? Maybe he didn't want me to finish my stay through the end of summer.

"Wanna go out tonight?" I asked hurriedly, using the subtle phrase the entire house adopted to mean fighting crime. At least my uncle was easy to distract.

Bane's responding smile covered a flicker of an emotion I couldn't place, a part of Bane I didn't know, and maybe wouldn't ever, unless my plan worked.

When. *When* my plan worked. I'd show Bane bringing me to Crown City wasn't a mistake.

"Oh good, you're both here," Chezza called as she flaunted down the stairs, somehow near silent in thick heeled boots. She waved a Leo Optics tablet. "I've finished putting our ideas together."

She flicked the tablet and Vennie's game disappeared. She ignored his sound of protest and swiped again, bringing what she saw on her tablet to full size on the LUMA's broad, curved face.

"Woah," I murmured as I beheld what she'd shared. It was a design for my own super suit. As I took in the details, I barely heard the rest of the team talking.

"It can't look just like your suit. It's her suit." Chezza argued, peering at Bane through the LUMA's opaque glass as she admired her and Vennie's handiwork.

"Obviously," Bane conceded, resting his chin on his fist. "I don't think it should look *exactly* like mine, but the technology and style of mine works well for our . . ." He blanked. "Specific needs. If we look like a team, I don't think that would be bad."

I offered Bane a smile.

Vennie snorted. "You're worried she'll look more badass than you."

"No!" he insisted. ". . . Maybe I'm a little bit jealous. The mask is super cool. But will the hood provide enough protection? My helmet keeps me from getting my head bashed in."

"True," Vennie said, "but Mel is more careful with her head than you are with yours. The hood is heavily cushioned. She'll be fine."

Chezza walked me through the rest of the drawing. "We're going to give you a small platform on the shoes, plus another two inches of heel."

She saw the nervousness erupt across my face. "You can handle it. It's not to make your butt look nice, though you should count that as a perk. Your stature is a hint to the outside world of your true identity. We want to throw off observers."

Vennie added, "You're puny. That narrows your possible identities. The shoes add a few inches, and the intimidation factor adds a few more. That will put you in the realm of average adult female height, thus making a bigger pool of possible candidates who can be behind the mask."

"Bane has a small heel on his shoes, too," Chezza said.

"That's right. And I love how it accentuates my figure." Bane cocked a hip for emphasis.

I snorted. "What about the Shadow finding a partner so soon after I show up to live with Bane? The media's bound to catch a glimpse of me soon. Won't people notice the coincidence?"

Vennie nodded. "Absolutely. And there are already whispers that Shadow's got a friend in the online fan club, but Bane's been on the suspected list of Shadow identities before. We'll spread false leads on message boards, point out any pair that makes sense—couples who recently got together, other people who have moved to Crown in the past year. Logan has vouched for Bane being present at parties or events plenty of times the Shadow has been active."

"What does Logan think you actually do when they cover for you?" I asked.

"I'm sure they'd rather not know."

"Remember that time you bled through your dress shirt at the staff holiday party?" Vennie said. "And Logan bailed you out by telling the press it was an injury you got during se—"

Bane shot him a look.

Vennie cleared his throat. "Anyway, the most popular theory right now is that the Shadow is a supreme weirdo holed up in a cave in the mountains somewhere."

"Half true," Chezza muttered.

As Bane scowled, I surveyed the sketches again, trailing a hand over the sleek lines, the entire thing limned in shadows.

"It's glorious," I said.

Chezza elbowed me. "I modeled it after you."

"If you approve the design, Mel," Vennie said, "it's ready for production."

I nodded my assent. Bane swore suddenly.

"Forgot about that, didn't you?" Vennie said. "I can handle the mask in-house, and her brick, but the suit . . ."

"What?" I demanded. "How long does it take you to make a suit?" Technology this complex had to take weeks.

Chezza shook her head. "We just come up with a list of specifications and a general design. We don't produce them."

I turned to Bane, who viciously massaged his forehead.

"Then who does?"

🔥🔥🔥

CLARE'S STUDIO WAS IMMENSELY HECTIC. HER STAFF WHIPPED through the rose-colored rooms while she sat at a high table across from us, looking bored. Her assistant served black coffee for her and tea for us, and she ashed her cigarette into a fancy pearl dish at her elbow. A cerulean dragonfly brooch glittered amidst the folds of a scarf over her otherwise entirely black ensemble.

She didn't speak for the first five minutes we spent in her

presence after Bane had explained our request. Her eyebrows remained lowered, tugging together the wrinkles of her pale face.

Bane squinted and shifted in his seat. "Clare . . ." he began.

"You want me to make her a suit." She took a drag on her cigarette, fluffing her short, straw-colored hair with her free hand.

I straightened, meeting her flashing eyes. "Actually, *I'd* like you to make me a suit." After a second, I thought to add, "Please."

I pulled my tablet from my backpack and brought Chezza's sketches up. Clare swiped through them, scrutinizing.

"They're based on what you've done for my uncle, but adapted to help me. You'll need less material, obviously." I gestured to my short torso, hoping some self-deprecating humor might win Clare to my side.

The corner of her mouth quirked up. It was a start.

"Why do you want this suit?" she asked, and waited.

I thought it over, folding my arms before me. I clenched my hands closed tightly, stifling my nerves.

"I want to help people." I grinned a little. "And I want to survive if someone stabs or shoots me up close."

Clare stared at me for a long time. She pulled the cigarette from her lips and studied it, then swiftly darted her hand downward to snuff it out on the back of my hand.

Bane started, but I touched his arm under the table. He froze.

The smoldering cigarette butt felt like a puff of wind. As gentle as if one of Clare's dragonfly friends had decided to land on me.

Clare held her hand over mine, the embers smoldering against my skin, her mouth a flat line. I grinned wickedly and reached across the table for her steaming cup of coffee.

I gripped it and squeezed, easing a groan from the ceramic

an instant before it exploded in my hand, spewing coffee over the table and her lap. Bane leapt out of the way. Clare saved the tablet instead of her outfit.

"I'll do it," she said, her frown easing an inch further, and she called for a towel.

Four of her staff offered one immediately, and she walked toward the back of the shop. As we stood and she dabbed herself off, I realized she was even shorter than me.

Clare turned and called over her shoulder, "Come watch or don't. It makes no difference to me."

I shrugged and followed her, Bane close behind me.

"She is so strange," I muttered. He nodded in agreement.

CHAPTER
EIGHTEEN

I HUGGED MY GREEN JACKET CLOSE TO MY CHEST AS WE PUSHED into the crowded stadium. "What's the name of this team again? The Ducks?"

Bane laughed. "Close. They're the Crown City Mallards. So, like a duck, but elitist."

A massive banner above us proclaimed the Mallards as the top team in the minor baseball league three years running. A ferocious-looking duck—mallard, whatever—leered down at us from every pillar and window. The marketing team had even given it sharp teeth. A swarm of fans streamed through the gates, decked out in green and gray memorabilia with trademark blue markings on the sleeves. Bane wore an emerald jersey, the name "Gribble" emblazoned across the back.

After a week of nonstop coursework and training, Bane insisted I needed a break. His excitement as we passed over our tickets was infectious. A solid string of average grades on assignments almost had me saying no, but I wanted to spend time with him. Normal time.

"You've never been to a live sporting event before?"

I shook my head, awed by the bejeweled swathe of concourse and sheer number of food options.

Bane pointed. "Priority one: hotdogs."

Our seats were a few rows behind home plate. My hands full of snacks, Bane plopped a brand new Crown City Mallards ball cap on my head. He had opted for a foamy one shaped like the angry mascot's head, complete with a protruding beak. Sitting there, with mustard on my cheek and salt on my fingers, with Bane cheering and commentating . . . It was the happiest I'd been in a long time.

The sun had nearly set by the final inning. I basked in my food coma while Bane shouted jubilant, rallying cries as the Mallards increased their lead over the opposing team from Michigan. Their mascot, which was a camel, for some reason, wandered by giving high fives, and Bane gave his hat to a kid in front of us who had narrowly missed a foul ball that got picked up by his older, taller brother.

As the sun disappeared behind the grandstands, I used my phone to click my Tempatches up a few notches and zipped up my jacket. I settled deeper into the seat, comforted by the thought of Bane's Tempatches doing the opposite work of mine. I watched the pattern of the game and was lulled by the dull roar of the crowd around us. The sky flared purple and gold at its edges.

"Having fun?" Bane asked.

I nodded, smiling up at him.

"The best part is coming up," he said. "They set off fireworks when they win."

"I love a Crown City spectacle," I said, suppressing a yawn. We'd agreed to not go out after the game so I could catch up on sleep.

Cheers floated from the crowd as the opposing team's final hit landed snugly in the glove of a Mallard outfielder. We rose, cheering, as the players jogged to their dugouts, the Mallards leaping around in celebration and pounding each other's backs.

Underneath the cacophony, a deep, hollow boom sounded, like a distant car crash. My head whipped around, but no one else seemed to notice. I glanced up at Bane. He typed on his phone, the lip of his promotional beer cup clenched precariously between his teeth. I giggled at the picture he made when another boom sounded. A twin to the first, but louder.

Bane's head snapped up to survey the field. A few people began to murmur around us. Even the catcher dropped his arms to glance around.

"That was a weird sound, right?" I asked.

A section of the outfield wall exploded.

Before I could think, Bane thrust me down between the rows of seats, shielding my body and tucking his head to his chest as debris rained down.

Bane swore under his breath. "So much for a night off."

He risked lifting his head above the row of seats, and I squirmed to do the same.

The dust settled and screams rose in its wake. The far wall of the stadium was a mess, split apart in the middle to make way for the monstrous creature that strode through. Bane swore and tugged my sleeve, tearing me away from our seats as I tried to parse what I saw.

An eight-foot-tall, blistering red lizard man traipsed onto the field, flanked by two rifle-toting men in ski masks and body armor.

They fired into the air. Bane glanced over his shoulder to assess the pandemonium as everyone in attendance attempted to flee the stadium at once. He darted sideways down a row of seats, stepping over them to traverse faster past the crowd. I followed close behind.

"Is that a . . . ?" I shouted over the mayhem.

"Yep," Bane said, veering toward a utility hallway that the

stampede of fans passed by. He picked up speed and I ran harder to keep up. It was one thing to know they existed, but another to see one in the flesh. Another Extrahuman was here.

"But we can help these people!" I yelled, pumping my arms to stay level with him as we sprinted.

"Not dressed like this, we can't!" He skidded around a corner, nearly tripping over his own feet. The hall ended in a barred gate, the parking lot visible through the metal slats.

He lifted one side of the heavy chain holding it closed, glancing over his shoulder to check we were alone. "Help me with this?"

I complied, and the links split easily between us.

"Very nice." He flashed a grin at me and ducked through the gate.

He spun to face me abruptly, pulling up his hood and making sure my hat was low across my face. "Sunglasses on," he instructed, though it was fully dark by now.

"Where are we going?" I asked as he slipped on his own sunglasses.

"The car. Hurry!" Bane sprinted ahead, and I trailed close behind. We toed the line of how fast a regular person could feasibly run in an instance of crisis, moving quickly without drawing attention. The frantic crowd spilled out the front gates, too terrified to notice us as we sprinted between cars.

We were at the car in a flash. As soon as I slammed my door shut behind me, Bane made one glance through the windows before pressing on the dashboard. A small control panel popped up. He slammed a button, and the inside of the car went dark.

Every window blacked out. Mechanisms whirred around us. Soft blue light glowed to life, and I could see Bane again, his sunglasses and hat off. The sounds of chaos in the parking lot quieted thanks to some sound deafening technology.

"What the hell?" I stammered.

"I told you I bought this car because of you. Let's just say I was hopeful about your Extrahuman potential." Bane jerked a thumb toward the back seat. "You're getting your surprise a little early. Sorry, Mel, I had a grand reveal planned, but this will have to work. Scoot!"

I glanced between the seats. The entire rear of the car had smoothed out and dropped down a foot, leaving a wide space with monitors set against the walls. The seats had folded in on themselves and receded against the walls to serve as benches. A black duffel bag sat square in the middle of the space, waiting for me.

A silver dragonfly was embossed across the front panel.

I scrambled back and crouched before it. My hands shaking, I carefully unzipped the biggest compartment. An emblem, a crimson curling flame, grinned out at me. My heart skipped a beat. Clare had finished my suit.

"I was hoping this would be more momentous," Bane said, "but we're in a rush. Can you hand me mine? It's behind you."

The back of his seat cracked open to reveal the full Shadow suit on a set of hangers. I passed him the pieces and tore my own from the duffel.

I shimmied into the slick gray pants, bolstered with irregular gray scales and fitted perfectly to my proportions. I hitched them up, almost able to stand fully in the back of the car. Pulling on the matching jacket, I felt the veins that would disperse the heat slide comfortably along my arms as Bane changed into his own suit up front. He donned his helmet and started talking hurriedly with Vennie while I pulled on my shoes, a cool, heeled hybrid between a tactical boot and a high-end sneaker.

"Has footage hit the news yet? Yeah, big red reptile creep. What's he doing—" Bane listened for a moment, then called back as I checked my suit's fit, brushing the crimson emblem over my chest with shaking fingers. Bless

Clare, every component closed with a well-lubricated zipper.

"Almost done, Mel?"

"Yeah!" I called, slipping on my gloves.

Bane made to say something else, but I could hear the ghost of Vennie's voice demanding something from within his helmet. "I'm showing her, I'm showing her. Lions, relax."

Bane reached for the glove compartment. The same type of light that scanned our entry to the Den flashed beneath the handle, and it flipped open to reveal a deep, steel-lined hollow. Several passports rested there, alongside a stack of cash and a wicked, angular black mask.

I crouched between the seats.

"Vennie says to pull up your hood so he can hear you," Bane said.

I tugged up the deep hood. Weighted magnets kept it forward and my face tucked into its shadows.

Bane handed me the mask. I cradled it in my hands, staring at the two small holes where my eyes would look out.

"Vennie . . ." I breathed. "It's amazing."

"I know," he said. I heard his rare grin through the speaker hidden in my hood.

Bane closed the compartment and pressed another button on the dash, but I didn't see anything change. "Put that on," he said. "We were hoping to run a few tests at home with your suit before trying it in the field, but it looks like you're going to have a trial by fire."

I turned the mask over and stared at the sleek inside. Hesitantly, I pressed it to my face.

I gasped as the mask came to life. The long edge that ran across my forehead had points that extended back into my hairline. They tightened to hug my face gently, sealing against my skin. The mask covered my nose and cheeks, thicker in places to distort the true planes of my face. Two vicious points crawled down either side of my mouth.

"Like Bane's helmet," Vennie explained, "Your mask seals around your face to protect your identity. Only those of us on the team will be able to remove it. There are hidden buttons along the left side—at the top of your forehead, outside your eye, and near your chin. You have to press and hold all three to make the mask release."

I looked into the rearview mirror. An absolute demon stared back. I grinned.

Bane met my eyes in the mirror before closing his helmet's visor. "Woah. I'm glad you're on my team."

"Ready to run initial diagnostics," Vennie prompted.

Bane stared at me expectantly.

"Oh!" he started. "Press your emblem."

I glanced down at the pointed flame. It fit neatly under my palm. I laid my hand over it and pressed. The slim power brick between my shoulders softly whirred to life. Instantaneous heat roared across my limbs, from the tips of my boots, searing across my chest, even echoing from the inside of my mask.

I couldn't help but sigh, "Oh, that is *toasty*."

"Now we're cooking with sustainable energy sources," Vennie crowed.

Bane laughed and opened his door. I stepped out behind him, feeling like I could move the mountains around Crown City if I wanted. If I had one, this would be the moment my theme song kicked in.

I spun, it looked like we had gotten out of an entirely different car. This one was blue. "Is the... Is the entire car body made of screens?"

"Sure is," Vennie quipped smugly. "License plate, too. Can you two pick up the pace? Police are still a few minutes away. I hacked the stadium cameras, and Redzilla is really tearing it up in there. No casualties that I can see, but there are still some staff in the stands and it looks like the sours with the guns are . . . herding some of the baseball players?"

"Alright." Bane's face shield snapped over his face. "Ready to have your face put on a lunchbox?"

I grinned. "What's the plan?"

"Maybe you've picked up on this: I've never been good at plans."

Luckily, I was.

Now, as the Shadow and the . . . somewhat smaller Shadow, we dashed back into the ballpark like a pair of dark comets.

CHAPTER
NINETEEN

GUNSHOTS ECHOED FROM WITHIN THE STADIUM.

Straggling escapees exclaimed when they saw us. The bottleneck at the main gate had thinned before Bane took us back in that way. We emerged onto the concourse and beheld the destruction.

The Extrahuman had fully torn through the away team's dugout. All that remained was a pile of splinters. The creature strode back and forth across the front of the field, screaming as he tore things apart. Bright red scales covered his bulbous head and shoulders, and a thick, monstrous tail dragged behind him through a split in his jeans, kicking up dust. He wore a sleeveless shirt, baring corded muscles. Vibrant yellow flooded the area around his irises. He huffed and swung his head around, slitted nostrils flaring.

He dug in the decimation, pulling out a gangly bat boy who squirmed in his unforgiving grip. The boy tried to scream, but it choked off as the Extrahuman threw him against a wall.

The explosion had unmoored one of the stadium's massive light poles, toppling to its side, electricity sparking.

The two other sours trapped a trio of players between it and the outfield wall.

"I was really looking forward to the fireworks," Bane sighed. "I'll start on the Extrahuman. Can you get those players out of here?"

I nodded curtly, not trusting my nerves to stay out of my voice.

"Perfect. Vennie, get Roger on line. Let him know we'll have an Extra needing extraction within the hour. Okay. Let's go—WAIT." Bane caught himself, jolting me. He rested his hands on my shoulders and withdrew his visor. "Are you ready? What do you need from me?"

My mind was fuzzy with adrenaline. "External validation, mostly."

Bane snorted and tousled where my hood rested on top of my head. "Let's go get 'em, then. Be careful."

"You too."

Bane looked at me oddly, emotion twisting his mouth.

Unsure of what to say, I took off, flitting around the left side of the field toward the trapped players.

Bane snapped his visor closed and started off a moment after I did. "Hack in and kill the lights, will you?" he asked Vennie. "Maybe our red friend won't be able to see very well in the dark."

The lights cut out immediately, and one of the baseball players yelped. The two sours looked around in confusion. I sprinted toward them as Bane barreled down the steps between rows of seats, heading straight for the Extrahuman, who turned in slow circles.

"Quick Shadow history lesson," Vennie said as I ran. "Of the few Extrahumans we've encountered, none have powers as smooth or successful as you two. We figure Kavoh's devotees have failed to replicate whatever she did with Sydney. The results are these lab experiments with various types of powers, and some have . . . unsightly consequences."

As Vennie explained, I reached the wall where the lights had fallen and leapt onto the pole. I danced along until I was level with the players. A thud sounded behind me, followed by a frustrated roar as Bane engaged the Extrahuman.

I resisted the urge to look as I leapt, landing in front of the first sour. He was incredibly tall, sheathed in dark body armor, his features obscured by a ski mask.

I wrenched the gun from his hands and threw it away. He lunged for me, and I barely vacated where his arms closed in time. Whirling, I kicked him in the back and sent him rolling through the dirt.

A pair of arms, corded muscle tough as rebar, wrapped around me and yanked me off the ground. I wheezed, thrashing, trying to move my pinned arms. He threw me to the ground. The last scrap of breath I had hacked from my lungs.

With a groan, I rolled to my stomach to desperately assess. The first sour regained his footing and lumbered toward the cowering players, brandishing a knife from his belt. The second strode toward me, hefting his rifle.

"Would you like a suggestion?" Vennie whispered in my ear.

"Nope. I got it," I grunted, and heaved to my feet, launching myself at the sour. I pressed in so he didn't have room to aim between us. I ripped the gun from his hands and jabbed him in the temple with it, a trick I'd picked up from Roger. He withered to the field in a heap, clutching his bleeding head.

Wheeling around without a moment to catch my breath, I sprinted toward the first sour, tearing him away from the baseball player he kneeled over. I gripped his arm and swung him around, banging his head against the fallen light pole.

He dropped something to the ground. I kneeled on his back, eliciting a grunt, and examined them. It was a handful of thick zip ties he'd been using on the players. I used them to bind him and his friend, then approached the trapped players, all three of them head and shoulders above me. One of them screamed as I stepped to them through the shadows.

"I'm here to help!" I hissed, and was shocked to find that my voice came out slightly warped, deeper with a scratchy tone to it.

I grasped my throat. "Special features," Vennie quipped in my ear. "The mask has a ton. I went a little overboard. Lenses are built in that can pop down over your eyes and are screens as advanced as Bane's visor. The pieces by your jaw can extend to cover your mouth and act as an air filtration system."

"Cool," I muttered.

I approached a bearded player, snapping the ties around his wrists. "Over the wall," I commanded, giving him a shove. "Then run as fast and far as possible."

He didn't question and faced the wall. I crouched and grabbed his foot, lacing my fingers beneath his cleats. I barely felt the points through my gloves. Unceremoniously, I heaved him up. His hands scrabbled for the top of the wall in the faint light from the surrounding buildings. Meanwhile, the ground shook at the other end of the field—I was tempted to turn my head and see the fight, but I wasn't finished here.

Once I felt his weight leave me as he pulled himself up, I reached for the next player. This was the catcher, and let me push him up as well.

The last one, the screamer, looked doubtful, but wisely said nothing and let me give him a boost. I shoved, and he huffed in surprise as he flipped over the wall onto the walkway.

"The players are free," I said, short of breath as I turned to search for Bane. "The sours are down."

Across the field, my uncle was locked in a fight with the lizard man. Bane pummeled him with a storm of blows. He'd aim a kick, land a punch, then dance away, though it was hard to tell how much effect his attacks had. The Extrahuman swung wildly, energy never lagging, forcing Bane backwards.

"Shadow, what do I do now?" I asked.

"Uh." He ducked under the Extrahuman's flailing tail. "Great question."

"Fucking lions, how have you made it this far?" I growled. Launching myself up, I heaved myself over the wall for a better view.

I sprinted the field's perimeter, closer to the fight. The Extrahuman kept his back to the wall as he and Bane traded punches. The walkway behind the wall closest to the lizard man was blocked by the fallen light pole, its light panel a crumpled mess of broken glass and snarled metal. I scrambled over it, keeping an eye on Bane and his foe.

Bane made a mad leap and dive, clenching his fists together to bring them down hard on Redzilla's head. At the last moment, the creature brought its massive, scaled arms up to block.

Luck? I wondered. But then I saw, as Bane danced back, the creature's eyes flicked. His head stayed pointed away from Bane, as if he couldn't see, but his irises followed my uncle's every move. He could see in the dark just fine, and Bane hadn't noticed.

"Turn the lights back on," I said, trying to stay quiet as I shoved through the mangled lights. They would blind him and give Bane the advantage. By cutting the lights, we'd helped our enemy.

Vennie's line remained silent. He was still contacting Roger.

Bane bent for a moment to catch his breath. The Extrahuman's torso twisted toward him, hinting at his intent to take advantage of the opening. He lifted one massive arm, his bicep bigger than the Shadow's helmet, claws gleaming at the end of his fingers.

So I screamed, *"Turn on the lights!"*

Vennie swore, frantic clicking erupting from his end of the line. "Shadow, move!"

The Extrahuman spun, his wicked yellow eyes narrowing at the sight of me. He hauled up a mangled seat and chucked it at me.

I dodged, flying across the grass. I hauled myself upright as the Extrahuman howled with rage.

An aluminum bat nailed him in the back of the head.

"Hey, Jurassic chump! Someone clearly spared every expense on whatever test tube you came out of . . . because you're very unfortunate looking!"

Redzilla turned on Bane again.

"Solid reference," I gasped.

"Thanks!" His reply died into a surprised yelp. Quicksilver fast, the Extrahuman kicked Bane, sending him sprawling onto his back. Redzilla leapt on him and hauled him into the air. Bane squirmed, limbs flailing as his captor withdrew a massive, clawed hand.

"Lights incoming," Vennie said.

The stadium flashed into brightness once more, including the bulbs in the fallen panel behind me.

My shadow stretched, massive, along the field, casting darkness over the creature that threatened my uncle. The Extrahuman turned, squinting against the sudden light, but didn't drop Bane. I sprinted the short swathe of grass and leapt off the wall, pushing with all my might.

I flew through the air, pulling my legs in tight at the last moment before lashing out, kicking the Extrahuman in the chest with both feet.

He dropped Bane, who scrambled out of the way. Redzilla crashed to the ground. I gripped his shirt, bracing myself to land squarely on his chest. His eyelids fluttered as we landed, and he reached out, claws coming for me. I snapped back my arm and punched him between the eyes. His head fell back, eyes closed before we hit the ground.

Bane jogged over, a hand pressed to his chest. "Are you okay?"

"Are *you*?" I demanded as Bane staggered, left leg wobbling from the Extrahuman's kick. I pulled his arm around my shoulders and let him lean on me.

Bane nodded shakily.

"Police incoming," Vennie said as red and blue lights highlighted the sky from the front of the stadium.

"Convenient timing," Bane muttered as the first officers leaked into the arena. He cupped his free hand around the vents in his helmet. "You're welcome!" he shouted in their direction, the sentiment clashing with his dark, garbled voice.

Bane lolled his helmet against the top of my head, out of breath. "That was amazing. You are amazing."

"Uh," Vennie cleared his throat. "More bad news, you two."

"What, *Date Wars* is cancelled?" I deadpanned.

"No, they were just renewed for season twenty-five, but I think Redzilla was a distraction. A lab in Ferntown got blown open a few minutes ago. Something's being stolen. Two sours dressed similarly to our friends down there are escaping with some machine in an unmarked box truck."

"My sweet *ass*," Bane swore. "Can you track them?"

"Of course."

"Toasty."

It took me a second to realize Bane was talking to me. "Yeah?"

"I need to keep Redzilla out of the police's hands until Roger's people get here." He gave a regretful sigh. "I'm gonna need you to stop that truck."

Damn it. I sagged. So much for a good night's sleep and extra studying.

"You don't have to," Bane said gently.

I shook my head, easing Bane's weight back on both feet and untangling from his arm. "Send me the location."

"On it," Vennie replied.

Lenses snapped down over the holes in my mask, projecting a red lit map over my vision. A slow-moving gold skull blinked twelve blocks away. Without another word, I bolted through the hole in the stadium, my body flush with heat.

Behind me, sparks leapt into the air as the Mallards' firework display started, basking the surrounding area in green and white light.

"What the hell?" Bane asked in my ear.

"I uh, hacked the stadium's pyrotechnics control panel," Vennie said. "I know you guys really wanted to see them."

I let out a wild laugh, and as I raced through Crown City, the booming fireworks kept time with the pounding of my boots and the steady, satisfied thrum of my heart.

CHAPTER
TWENTY

I STARED AT SYDNEY'S HOLOGLASS AI PERSONA OVER THE LIP of my coffee mug, my textbook abandoned over the chair's arm. "My mom was probably like Uncle Bane, right? She was weak in the heat and strong in the cold."

It had occurred to me late the night before as the power in my veins slowly receded without the enhanced heat from my suit.

My grandpa smiled knowingly, his wide lapels crisp. "Almost certainly, if she passed the gene on to you. And your reactions to temperature flipped so that you are just like me." He smiled brightly, his expression the opposite of my own.

"Her powers are why she died," I murmured, ache twinging my insides.

"Hm?" Sydney asked, pale eyebrows drawing together.

I took a shaky breath. "Our house was on fire. She got me out. My powers might have helped a little. But she would have been so weak. That's why she didn't make it out when she should have."

Sydney stared solemnly, his smile fading until his mouth was a tight line.

He sighed, looking to the window. "Loss exacts a terrible

toll, doesn't it? It changes people dramatically . . . Reforges the corners of their soul in iron and diamond."

I let my chest heave, breathing deep to push back the tears.

Sydney continued, solemn. "Loss is what drove Dr. Kavoh on her mad mission for immortality."

I tilted my head. "Did she ever succeed?"

He frowned down at his form, vaguely translucent in the early morning sunshine streaming through the window. "It doesn't appear so . . . if it is any condolence, Melbourne, I can assure you no great parent would question sacrificing their own life for that of their child."

His conviction ran hollow, given what Bane had to say about Sydney's parenting style.

"Why did my mom leave Crown City?" I dared to ask.

Why did she leave you? I didn't need to say that part aloud.

Sydney's image remained so still I wondered if it glitched.

Finally, he spoke, in a single, monotone phrase. "Adelaide left because I was not good to her. I thought the absence of mistreatment constituted good treatment. I gave her an allowance, opportunities, and praise. But I never gave her earnest attention. I didn't take a true interest in her. I never listened to her. I completely missed the mark on what a family is supposed to be. Of course she left. It's a miracle Brisbane ever came back when he left, too."

"Thanks, Grandpa," I said in dismissal, unprepared to digest all he'd admitted. Shifting from my chair carefully so as to not nudge my sling, I stood and stretched as his projection faded.

I trudged to the kitchen, hoping light movement would relieve some of the stiffness pervading every inch of my body. I felt like I had been hit by a truck.

Which I had, after throwing myself at a massive reptilian mutant with the density of several refrigerators, so at least it all made sense.

"Better or worse than the worst hangover you've ever had?" Vennie asked from his spot at the stove scooping scrambled eggs over rice and veggies.

I groaned and loped to my chair as Chezza set the table, waving off my help.

"Are you using Lola's recipe?" she asked her brother.

He nodded absently, and Chezza shifted her attention to me. I lifted my arm obediently, wincing as she checked my shoulder's mobility, then wrapped a gigantic ice pack around it. Even the Tempatches on every other part of my body couldn't do much to cut the discomfort, but my shoulder was in terrible shape.

I closed my eyes just as Bane traipsed into the room, his limp already faded. "There she is, glowing and refreshed off her superhero debut!"

"Unghhhh." I attempted to glower at him, but his grin was infectious as always. My own grin lifted my cheek in response and pain blossomed across my bruised cheekbone.

Bane frowned at the small glacier affixed to my shoulder.

"Stopping a careening vehicle with your body," he mused. "Resourceful and impressive, but alarmingly reckless."

Chezza coughed something that sounded like "genetic."

I chose to focus on the incredible smell of breakfast.

"How do you not have the news on? I bet coverage is everywhere already," Bane scolded.

At the sound of his comment, the screen on the counter clicked on and changed to Bane's preferred news outlet. Like he predicted, the program was in the middle of showing shaky cell phone footage from the night before from a brave fan that had lingered in the stands. The red Extrahuman stomped slowly across the field, screams all around. Bane turned up the volume.

"—the creature's origin and intent are still unclear. Thankfully, injuries were few due to the appearance of Crown City's favorite vigilante, the Shadow, and a second masked figure that some are speculating may be his new sidekick."

My chest grew warm as I appeared on screen, kind of looking like I knew what I was doing.

"Sidekick," Bane huffed. "Absolutely not."

The camera zoomed in as I darted across the field and leapt onto the Extrahuman and toppled him. The video captured the moment I helped Bane up and pulled his arm around my shoulders before cutting back to the anchor.

"Alarmingly, this is the third report of mutants of some kind in Crown City this year, and the first one that has been clearly caught on camera. A private government agency has taken charge of the suspect, but not released further information on its origin. Needless to say, Crown citizens are deeply concerned . . ."

"Besides Redzilla, what other kind of Extrahumans have you seen?" I asked.

Bane muted the TV and rubbed his chin. "One woman had super agility, but her strength was average, and a guy kinda like Redzilla—less malformed though. He was pretty strong but the left side of his body was all lumpy and weird. There are also rumors of almost a giant werewolf- or sasquatch-type monster, but I think that's just a regular Crown City myth."

I shivered at the thought. A giant dog—my worst nightmare. "If Dr. Kavoh had the cover of a gene therapist working on preventing diseases, how are there people who know about her Extrahuman work to continue it?"

"Our best guest is that she shared her human projects with one of her closest colleagues," Vennie said, "or that they figured it out on their own. Either way, they're good at keeping it secret. We can't find a facility they're working out of." He nudged the morning papers my way. "Check *you* out."

Bane peered over my shoulder as I read and gave a low whistle.

The *Chronicle* featured a grainy cell phone photo of me. The caption read that it was provided by one of the baseball players I'd rescued. My small figure was poised before the downed stadium lights, my shadow stretched across the field. A headline bold and wide over top:

Silhouette Appears as Crown's Second Savior

I gaped. Bane flipped through the stack, reciting every front-page headline. "'Silhouette saves the city *and* the Shadow.' 'Crown's Vigilante force now a duo.' 'The Silhouette appears—are we safer than ever?' Mel, this is amazing!"

I sat back, seeing the same photo over and over. Everyone else at the table waited to hear what I thought.

I reached a hand up to touch my cheek, where the mask lined up against my face.

Silhouette.

Daintier than the Shadow. A little more feminine. Just as mysterious and intimidating. Like how my suit made me feel —strong and a bit scary.

"I like it," I admitted, my face warm.

Bane beamed. "Me too, Mel." He raised his orange juice. "To Silhouette! Crown's lucky to have you."

Chezza pointed her lips at a pristine pink box at the end of the table stuffed with pastries. "Clare sent those early this morning."

I plucked the notecard taped to the front.

Inside was a sharply scribbled note—

You make the suit look good, girl.

Sheepish, I stuffed a croissant in my mouth. Bane flipped through one of the papers, pointing to a small feature in the middle.

"This one is my favorite."

The section covered the Mallards game. One corner featured a picture of Bane and me in the stands. Bane stood riotous, his hands cupped around his mouth, shouting to rally the team. I sat at his elbow, leaning away, clearly shocked by his jubilance, a hysterical and unfortunate wide-eyed look on my face. The writer speculated that maybe I hadn't known what I was getting into when I came to visit my long-lost relative in Crown City.

Accurate on so many levels.

Bane dug in a drawer for scissors so he could display it on the fridge.

"Any news on where the Extrahuman came from?" I asked.

"Roger's people have him. His name is Rhett Fannon. He's a local underground cage match fighter. His girlfriend reported that he disappeared a few months ago. There isn't evidence that his display was related to the theft you stopped, but the timing is too coincidental."

"We'll have to do some more investigating." Chezza nodded.

Vennie quipped, "Bane, you should tell her about the downsides to having a fancy superhero name. The fanfiction and all that."

I grimaced as Chezza spit into her cup. Bane blanched.

My phone buzzed, and one glance at the name had me leaping from my seat.

"Later," I said. "I forgot I've got a date."

Today was just going to keep getting better. I needed to maneuver my stiff body into a bikini.

CHAPTER
TWENTY-ONE

I STARED AT MYSELF IN THE LONG MIRROR, HEART POUNDING. There was no way I could hide a single Tempatch beneath this swimsuit.

Max's house was pleasantly warm—the temperature wasn't what caused my subtle shaking. It was the memory of Max from a few minutes prior, the brilliant smile he'd flashed me from the edge of the pool, where he'd stood in a sleeveless shirt and short swim trunks, his toned arms and legs bare. So much of his light brown skin exposed that I found it hard to breathe.

Max's was the only room I knew, so I commandeered his bathroom to change. Chezza had helped me procure a few options. The bikini I'd finally settled on was white with wisps of petal pink in a small pattern all over it. I loved the way it hugged my hips and bared my soft stomach.

I looked amazing.

I grinned at myself, eager to turn some of Max's infamous confidence back on him.

I checked the concealer hiding the bruise across my cheekbone one last time and shook out my shoulder, most of the stiffness gone through my Extrahuman-assisted healing. Tossing my hair over my shoulder, I stepped into Max's room and halted at what I hadn't paid any attention to on my hurried trip in. His bed, the slate gray sheets still rumpled from last night's sleep, or lack of it, considering the headphones and records scattered across his nightstand and the floor. An open notebook laid between the pillows, cramped with Max's handwriting.

My core heated of its own accord. I wanted to dive into that bed significantly more than any pool.

In the quiet of the cavernous room, the click of the French doors opening caused me to nearly jump out of my skin. Max stepped inside from his small private patio, limned in muted light.

He swiped at his clothes with a frown. They were dotted with dark spots.

"It's raining—" he muttered, then caught sight of me. His mouth stopped working for a moment, and his hand fluttered behind him for the door handle. Max regained his composure and cleared his throat. "That swimsuit looks incredible on you."

"I thought so, too," I said. I glanced around him, noting how his eyes traveled up and down, and noted the overcast sky in the yard. "Any sign of it letting up?"

Max actually threaded a hand into his hair. "Not for a while. I should have checked the weather. I'm sorry that our party's . . . ruined."

But I had checked the weather. I knew we'd have to spend our afternoon inside. I walked toward him, my toes stopping just an inch before his own. "I wouldn't say that."

Tentatively, Max laid his hands on my hips. His fingertips against my skin felt incredible. "No?"

I shook my head, sliding my hands up the bare lengths of his arms.

Max stilled. "We could do anything you like. Watch a

movie, go grab something to eat." His mahogany eyes were molten and serious, leaving our next move up to me.

I pretended to consider and took the final infinitesimal step to bring my body flush against his. "I'd like to wait out the weather with you right here. Would you like that, too?"

"God, yes," Max breathed, and crushed his lips to mine.

Max pressed, his strong arms wrapping around my waist. I bowed against him, cupping his face. His lips parted, and his tongue swept against mine, lingering longer and deeper than any of our other times tangled together.

I wanted to feel all of Max, right away. I stepped back, leading him with my hands on his toward the bed. His smile grew. "I should've cleaned," he grumbled. I silenced him with another deep kiss.

As we neared the bed, Max slowed me with a touch. He pulled my arms from his neck and lifted me gingerly, one hand at my back, one behind my knees, and laid me amidst the stormy sea of sheets. He shoved his notebook off the bed and braced his arms on either side of my head, kissing me soft and slow. I pressed my hands to his chest, savoring the heat beneath his shirt, and reached for the hem.

Max pulled back again. "One second," he said, kissing my forehead. He got up, leaving me splayed on the bed, panting, and stepped to his record player. I raised an eyebrow as he deftly flicked through a crate until he found the vinyl he wanted. He laid it on the tray, clicking a button. Each movement highlighted a line of muscle at his neck, his arms, hinting at the hems of his shorts. I fought not to writhe against the satiny sheet in protest of his body away from mine.

Soft jazz music and a croony voice emanated from Max's sprawling sound system. Seeming satisfied, he sauntered back slowly, his eyes shamelessly trailing up and down my body. At the bed's edge, he pulled his shirt over his head and I nearly gasped.

I knew. I *knew* Max's perfection could only extend across

his entire body. But the smooth, subtle muscle, the careful grooming of his chest hair, the telling lines at his waist and tight lines of sheet music tattooed across one side of his chest . . .

"Lions," I murmured.

Max's quiet laugh elicited goosebumps over my entire body as he crawled onto the bed, dragging his body over mine. "Are you alright?"

I gratuitously ran my hands from his waistband up his stomach and chest and back, drawing out shivers from Max in kind. "I'm wonderful," I managed.

Max pointedly stared down the length of my body beneath him, tracing the seam of my bikini. "You really are," he agreed, and started up with the kissing again.

Gently, Max pressed into me, eliciting a soft noise in the back of my throat as I felt his eagerness press against my stomach. The promise of it left stars behind my eyelids, and my breaths echoed, ragged, through the room as Max moved his lips to my jaw, then my neck, then my collarbone, attentive and curious prodding from his tongue at every stop.

Max's hands slipped behind my back to fumble with the ties to my swimsuit. I helped and got the ones around my neck myself. After a moment, Max pulled the fabric away and continued his tour of kisses lower across my body.

As Max's lips met the curve of my breast, I arced from the bed, needing him somehow closer. He released a soft, satisfied laugh and ran his teeth first over one nipple, then the other. I dug my fingers into his back, needing to touch more of him.

Max withdrew a little, and I rose to trace kisses along his neck, sinking my palm down his torso and beneath his waistband. Max's breath caught as my hand closed around him, and he swore, closing his eyes.

Pulling his mouth to mine again, I focused on getting his shorts off.

We were a hectic tangle of hands as we took off our

bottoms, and we paused only so Max could dig in the night-stand for a condom.

"Do you want this as badly as I do?" I asked as I watched him put it on.

He paused, taking my face in his hands seriously. "Are you kidding? Of course I do." He pressed his forehead to mine. "Contrary to what you might think, I don't approach everyone like I approached you that day on campus. You stunned me with your beautiful face, as serious as it was."

I scoffed and bit at his lip. He dodged back and sank his body toward mine, tracing me. I whimpered, and he kissed beside my cheek, then whispered in my ear, "And then I find out you're bold, and brilliant, and possibly the only person who can understand my messed-up life." He looked me full in the face again, and I traced my thumb over his lower lip.

"It doesn't seem so messed up from where I'm sitting."

"Exactly," he said, teasing me now, tracing one hand up my thigh, sliding his fingers between my legs. My breath hitched, and I wrapped my legs around his back, trying to bring him closer, but unless I wanted to reveal my Extrahuman strength, my efforts would need to seem fruitless.

"You'll be a mess with me?" he asked, softness glinting at the back of his self-assured stare. The undertone of his voice surprised me. It was desperation.

"Absolutely," I said, and sealed the promise with a kiss. Max removed his hand, and finally sunk into me. I let go of every thought, especially every worry, and contented myself to drift in this storm with Max for as long as we wanted.

🔥🔥🔥

THE CLOUDS EVENTUALLY DISPERSED, BUT MAX AND I MADE NO move to leave his bed, though we shifted positions plenty. In one of the rare minutes we broke apart and lay on our backs, chests heaving, Max slid a hand into mine. I rolled over, sighing as I sprawled across his chest. Max tilted my chin and his molten eyes found mine. My heart beat out a funny, uneven rhythm. The dim light cast shadows from his unfairly long eyelashes across his cheeks as he looked down at me.

He sighed in response, though this one didn't sound as contented as the many I'd drawn from him over the last few hours.

"Pool party's over?" I asked.

Max closed his eyes and leaned back, dropping my chin. "My dad has a thing tonight, and I should make an appearance."

"What kind of thing?"

"A presentation on the city's security budget."

"Sounds boring," I said, tracing the lines of his chest.

"It will be, but even worse . . ." He hesitated, and an uncharacteristic line of worry creased between his brows.

I took his hand back. "What is it?"

He sighed through his nose. "He received a death threat this morning."

"And he's still going to make an appearance?"

Max smoothed my hair with his free hand. "He receives death threats more often than you'd think. His security team reviews them all to determine risk. They're rarely plausible, but I still worry."

I nodded as he spoke, though my thoughts drifted. Maybe I would see Max again tonight, but he wouldn't be seeing me.

CHAPTER
TWENTY-TWO

Like upstanding citizens of Crown City, Bane and I spent the evening in our Shadow and Silhouette armor, hidden atop Crown's largest outdoor amphitheater, prepared to save Mayor Keep's sorry ass.

It had only taken a few minutes to convince Bane.

"I heard about that. Someone in the mayor's office leaked the threat. It was all over the news this morning. I suppose regardless of his opinions of us, we should at least make a small effort to keep the mayor from getting assassinated," he'd mused.

We arrived at the outdoor venue early and scaled the theater's outer wall where we'd have the best vantage point of the stage. Mayor Keep's arrival came without incident, several members of his security team following him into the space. We perched at either end of the pavilion's gently sloped roof.

Max showed up with a few moments to spare, looking divine. He'd tidied all the mussy undoneness I'd created in his bed, looking immaculate in a maroon suit. Warmth pooled in my stomach at the sight of him, his grin wider than usual.

As the straggling spectators moved to their seats, I stood,

stretching until my spine popped. I crept to Bane. It was impressive how still he could be when he tried.

I plopped down next to him. "Does this seem off to you? I haven't noticed anything."

"Not yet." He reached into his chest pocket and withdrew a crumpled bag of sour candy and offered it to me. Our comms were quiet, as Chezza was staying the night with her partner and Vennie had retired for one of his rare full nights of sleep.

He mused as I took a handful, "Maybe we lucked out, and it was all fluff. The mayor has enough security here, he hardly needs us."

Bane withdrew the bottom half of his visor and popped a handful of candy in his mouth. I stared at the stars, hard to make out this close to all the city lights, half listening for anything unusual.

Since I planned to only see Max more and more, I figured it was past time to come clean. "Uncle Bane . . . You know Max and I are more than friends."

He chewed, waiting patiently.

I braced myself. "You know I won't let that put our identities at risk, right?"

Bane shook his head vehemently. "I trust you, Mel. You deserve to be happy, and Max makes you happy."

"It is nice . . . I didn't plan on dating when I came here, I have other priorities." I grimaced, thinking of the half-written essay waiting for me back at the house that I'd need to finish after this adventure. "Do you have a partner? Someone special?"

Bane's smile faded. "It's been a while. I usually manage to screw it up. I was seeing a great guy last fall, but he moved away."

"I'm sorry."

"Don't be. I'll meet someone, when it's right."

"How well do you know Mayor Keep?" I asked after a

while. An emcee had stepped up to the podium and was reading a short biography of the mayor.

"Our rivalry didn't start romantically, if that's what you're asking." Bane sighed. "Though I did betray him, a long time ago. I haven't been allowed beyond his big bad businessman persona in years. He might be like that all the time, for all I know. Has Max said much about him?"

"He's hinted at things. He makes it sound like his dad is the same as we see. Serious, critical."

Mayor Keep took the stage, as emotive as concrete while roaring applause washed over him.

"He certainly doesn't like how I've resisted throwing Leo Optics's support behind his projects." Bane said. "He thinks we should do a little less charitable giving and a little more funding of his initiatives."

"It makes me wonder how Max turned out so . . . different," I said, biting the head off a sour gummy.

"His mom's a delight," Bane said as he watched the mayor talk.

Bane got quiet. His telltale shifting began, his chest twitching.

"What is it?" I asked, searching the night for a threat I might have missed.

"What was your mom like? I didn't—We weren't . . . She left when I was young."

"Oh," I said. Longing gouged through my chest, the ache of seeing her face in my mind threatening to pull me under into a fit of sobs. I swallowed and breathed deep, searching for the loving warmth that softened the sharp edges of my grief.

Carefully, I dredged up memories of her. "She was always moving, like you," I started. "Always guarded, like you, I realize now. Because she was hiding her powers and trying to take care of me." My voice cracked at the end.

Bane placed a gentle hand on my shoulder, iciness from his glove warring with the heat of my suit. "Thank you."

I sighed shakily and looked up at him. "It felt like she was my only balloon. The only thing helping me stay upright. I didn't know what to do when she was gone."

Bane pressed a hand to his mouth as I continued.

"Sam only ever weighed me down, anyway. I've been holding myself up for so long, so constantly. And sometimes . . . I just didn't. I'd lay in bed or lash out or make a shitty choice . . . I was violently desperate to ever feel any kind of joy again."

Bane stared off. "When my parents died, I at least had Vennie, and he brought in Chezza. And *lions*, I had a salary, a driver's license . . ."

I nodded, waves of hurt wracking through my body. It was better to let them run their course and enjoy some peace when they faded.

"You're a balloon for me," Bane said finally.

I laughed, the sound slightly choked. "Likewise, Uncle Bane."

The moment was shattered by Mayor Keep's booming voice as his speech reached a crescendo. I rolled onto my stomach to watch.

The mayor swept an arm wide. "Without further ado, I'd like to introduce the crowning achievement of this new, comprehensive security program. Crown City's Exemplary Threat Squadron, or as I like to call them, the Gold Guard."

My draw dropped. Six hulking figures in gleaming black armor marched onto the stage in eerie unison. The plates across their chests, stomachs, knees, and shoulders had been plated in gold. Like they *wanted* to be seen coming. They each wore combat helmets emblazoned with a gold crown on the front, thick goggles with lenses slick and dark as oil that reflected the stark stage lights.

Mayor Keep continued, "I've charged this task force with handling the alarming growing threats to our great city—the terrifying mutants who seek to make our streets their own, and the farcical vigilantes who aim to handle them."

Bane's mouth hung open.

"This is really bad, right?" I asked, unable to tear my eyes away from the team of people curated specifically to destroy us.

He snapped his visor closed. "We need to leave. Now."

"In fact," Mayor Keep continued, "the timing of this program's initiation could not be better, as this elite security team discovered a threat to this very event."

The crowd began to murmur, and halted Bane with a touch to his arm. Yellow glinted at the corner of my enhanced vision. I snapped my head around. "There!" I hissed.

Gold markings shone from a darkened corner at the back of the amphitheater. Two more of the Gold Guard stood watch, some sort of rifle aimed at us.

Bane and I scampered backward as eerily quiet shots pierced the night, sounding hollow and electric, and bullets glowing like bright lasers whistled past our heads.

The crowd erupted into panic. Bane and I clambered down the far side of the roof and darted around the building. Mayor Keep's muffled voice boomed through the speakers, urging the crowd to remain calm and stay in their seats. As Bane and I bolted through the surrounding park, I glanced back to see the Gold Guard pounding off the stage, fanning out to pursue us.

The park around the pavilion didn't provide much cover. We dodged the pools of light from the decorative lamps that dotted the area, sprinting toward the cover of the city blocks waiting beyond the park's edge.

"Left!" Bane called.

I turned and sprinted blindly down the first street we reached.

It was eerily quiet, and I realized Bane wasn't with me. I slowed. "Shadow!" I hissed into the night.

A beat of silence, then Bane's voice over the comms line. "Where'd you go?"

"I turned *left*," I hissed.

". . . Did I not?"

"Sweet *fuck*," I gasped, pausing to lean against the railing outside a restaurant closed for the evening.

A strange, lasery bullet zipped past my head and buried itself in a hanging flower basket decorating the restaurant's entrance. The pot exploded, showering me with damp soil and desiccated pink flower heads. I swore and dove behind a trash can.

"Was that another gunshot?" Bane demanded in my ear.

"Sure was," I said tersely, scanning for an escape route. "Did you really forget which way left was?!"

"Apparently. I'll loop around and be right there. Keep moving."

"No shit," I gasped, staying low as I ran down the street, sticking close to the walls. I risked a glance behind me, spotting three of the Gold Guard advancing slowly down the street, helmets swiveling as they searched for me in the darkness.

I put on another burst of speed, too fast to avoid the person emerging from a branch of the Crown City library.

I barreled into her, sending us both over the edge of the library's stone steps and into the carefully trimmed bushes.

"Sweet mother of Hades—what the actual hell?"

It was Gem, her armful of books scattered around us in the mulch.

She shook leaves from her curls and looked into my mask, her eyes going wide. I clapped a gloved hand over her mouth and held a finger to my lips.

I withdrew my hand.

"You're Silhouette, from the news!" she whispered.

I nodded, hesitant to speak despite the voice-altering tech

in my mask. "Stay hidden till I lead the bad guys away from here, alright?"

"Wait—" Gem laid a hand on my arm.

I stared, trying to intimidate her.

"What are your pronouns?" she asked. "I intern at the *Chronicle*. I can let them know."

I grinned in spite of myself. "I use she/her pronouns. Now stay down."

She obediently pressed deeper into the bushes, against the base of the library building, gripping a book and staring at me in thrilled awe.

I tried to maneuver, but the greenery rustled too loud. Steeling my nerve, I sprang from the bushes and bolted up the street. Though my steps were near silent, the sudden burst of foliage alerted the Guards. One shouted and pointed my way. I held off from putting on a burst of speed to assure they followed me away from Gem's hiding spot.

"Almost to you," Bane said in my ear. "How about you lead the way this time?

I grunted my agreement and bolted onto the street. Bane blurred to my side, a swift shadow, darker than the night. I glanced back. The guards converged on the corner, their speed flagging.

I led us beneath the awning of a closed shop, where we could catch our breath in the shadows. Bane tapped the screen on his wrist, placing some sort of external call.

"I'm waking Vennie up," he explained.

I peered onto the street. The Guards had disappeared. I stepped into the road, and Bane followed. "I think we may have lost them . . ."

Headlights flared, and a monstrous, black, armored van striped with gold tore straight for us down the middle of the road. Bane and I dove sideways. We rolled across the asphalt as the strange gunfire rang around us.

Bane threw himself over me, curling his arms over my head. An electric jolt jarred across my side.

"What's going on?" Vennie asked groggily in our ears as Bane pulled back, grit from the street ground into the vents in his helmet.

My breath shuddered. Searing pain slowly demanded my attention. I looked down.

With a groan, Bane's helmet turned toward me. "What?"

My stomach roiled at the sight of the suit's material along my side, warped and torn below my ribs, a dark stream trickling out.

"I've been shot," I said, my mind going blank.

"What," Vennie said.

"Get Chezza," Bane commanded. He leaned toward me, gently surveying my side as the pain grew. "Silhouette got skimmed by whatever firepower those Gold Guards have."

"Calling her in now. Is there blood on the street?"

Bane pulled a vial from a pocket in his suit and dumped it onto the small spatter of blood beneath us. "I just tainted it, so it won't be a problem," he answered Vennie. "Can you run?"

I blinked, realizing he spoke to me. The truck had screeched to a halt a few blocks away. Gold Guards converged on the corner, helmets pointed our way.

Bane swore. He tugged me up and pulled us down the narrow alley behind us. I leaned against the wall, trying not to whimper when I pressed my hand to my wound.

"She'll be home in twenty. She says to pack the wound and seal it. There's gauze in Silhouette's other hip pocket."

Bane nodded, digging in my suit.

"Why isn't there gauze in your pockets?" I asked, panting.

"I took it out to make room for candy," Bane muttered.

I focused on the Guards's terse voices as Bane worked. "They're making a plan," I said, searching the cramped alley's high, unforgiving brick walls. "They're going to come for us."

Bane stayed quiet, carefully pressing a length of Super-seam over my padded wound. I bit back a yelp.

"Full disclosure: I'm a bad field medic," he said tersely. "I need you to think for the both of us. You're better at planning than I am, anyway. How do we get out of this?"

Happy to focus on anything other than my bullet wound, I scanned the alley again, slower. A fire escape's landing beckoned two stories above our heads. I tapped my uncle's shoulder and pointed.

Bane tore off the edge of the Superseam. "Perfect. We'll climb, and we won't pull down the ladder to give them a hand." He squatted, cupping his hands. "Just like the maneuver we practiced," he said evenly.

"We didn't practice!" I hissed. "We talked about it and then watched *Date Wars* instead!"

"Right, but we discussed the basic principle. Come on."

I backed up then took a few jogging steps toward Bane. I pressed one foot into his palms, my side screaming. Synchronized, he lifted as I pushed, and I shot into the air. I kept my body stiff as I reached, clumsily wrapping my arms around the landing's railing. My body slammed against it. I groaned and hauled myself over, my side shrieking in pain, getting my bearings in time to see Bane press his back against the far corner of the alley.

A Guard approached the alley's mouth, rifle raised.

Bane sprinted and leapt directly at the wall, pushing against it when he made contact to garner a few more feet of height with his momentum. He wasn't going to make it, so I threw my arms over the railing, grabbing him.

He rammed into the landing like I had, making the entire rusted frame shudder. A bullet pinged off the armor at his shoulder.

He grunted, but made no other sound, and we climbed.

It was a hellish few minutes as we pulled ourselves up each narrow stairwell, ducking to avoid the scant shots that came our way. Thankfully, the alley was cramped and the higher we got, the more rusted metal was in the way of a clean shot. My ears strained for the sound of Guards pulling down the ladder to pursue us, but it never came.

I was almost comforted, but their sudden quiet unnerved me more.

Finally, I pulled myself onto the roof, Bane close behind me. I hunched over, gasping, as Bane checked the alley for pursuers. I finally let out a low moan at the pain stabbing through my side.

Up this high, the noise from the alley and street beyond was nearly extinguished. I surveyed our surroundings. On either side, our building was the shortest. We were up six stories and its neighbors both doubled that. Behind us, the building extended to the next street, dropping down to a shorter roof. We could leap down and run off that way, as soon as we caught our breath.

Bane followed my stare, as did Vennie through our suit cameras.

"Don't get excited," he said. "I hacked the street cams, and more Guards are pulled up behind the building. That's where they expect you to go."

Bane peeked down into the alley again. "They're not climbing. That doesn't make sense. Are they waiting us out?"

I straightened and clicked up my heat a few notches, hoping it might help with the pain. I picked up a strange sound. A soft click, followed by metallic creaks. A pause. Soft thuds for a few seconds, then another pause, then the sequence repeated. They were familiar, mundane sounds. Ones I had trouble placing since I was not in a mundane situation, dressed in a super suit and resting on the roof of a building, recently shot.

The creaking came again, this time slightly louder.

"What building is this?" I asked.

A few seconds of nothing, then Vennie's voice. "That's the downtown courthouse."

The sound was the door to each stairwell being opened and pairs of shoes sneaking up the stairs.

"It's a government building," I breathed. "They have the keys. We need to move!"

Bane's helmet swiveled, surveying our options. "I say we jump," he said finally.

He pointed toward the opposite side of the building from where we'd come. He poked his head over the edge. "No Guards. They don't expect us to go that way. We can jump down and make a run for it. Come on." He reached a hand back for me.

It was a good plan, really. The best option we had. But there was one problem. He'd just asked me to jump off a building. I forced myself to step toward him. It was clear from his beckoning hand that I wasn't moving as quickly as he'd like.

"Alright, you go first," he said.

Bane wouldn't ask me to jump off the roof if he didn't think I'd survive, but everything fantastical that had happened over the past weeks warred with my lifetime of surviving on logic.

I didn't actively fear heights, but I was mostly human, after all. My steps stuttered. In the reflection of Bane's helmet, I saw my face tinged green with dread around my mask.

"Look, I get it," Bane said hurriedly, resting his hands on my shoulders. I flinched at the contact. "I promise you'll be fine. We'll easily survive this."

"Risk doesn't come into play until seven and a half stories up, at least. Usually," Vennie offered.

Bane grimaced. We both heard the much closer opening of a door. The Guards crept up the final stairwell.

I gritted my teeth. I wanted to jump off this building, I

really did. To leap with abandon like the Shadow did, but I couldn't seem to force my coward feet forward.

Bane withdrew his visor and looked me in the eye. "You can do this," he said, stepping to the building's edge. I followed. Staring down the six stories made it worse.

"Be sure to not lock your knees," Vennie said, "and try not to land face first."

I took an involuntary step back.

"Silhouette, we have to jump *now*." A key sounded in the lock of the roof access door behind us, and Bane lost his cool.

Bane raised his face to the sky and sighed. "I hope this isn't about to be a failed teaching moment."

"What do you mean?" I demanded.

He grabbed my wrist, slammed my max heat button, and shoved me off the roof.

CHAPTER
TWENTY-THREE

BANE CARRIED ME BACK TO THE DEN, WHIPPING THROUGH THE woods at a breakneck speed. It was work to not puke from the pain rocketing through my torso.

Chezza had the med station prepped when we burst into the Den. Bane laid me gently on the table before pacing frantically, throwing off his helmet and tearing at his hair.

"Sorry to ruin your date night," I stammered.

Chezza shook her head and brushed me off. She helped me unzip my jacket and gingerly pushed the material back, baring the gauze packed over my wound. Her gaze appraising, she peeled the patch away. I gave in to the searing agony and shouted at the ceiling. My cries rooted Bane to the spot, horror contorting his face.

Chezza pulled out a pen light and crouched close to my wound. "They must have landed a lucky shot when the car was right next to you, to puncture the material like this. The bullet skimmed you. You're going to be fine," Chezza murmured, grabbing a spray and angling it toward me. "This next bit is the worst part."

"I believe you," I gasped. "Fucking *lions!*" I yelled again as she sprayed.

"I lied," she said. "I need to seal it and that will hurt worse, I'm sorry."

"It's fine." I winced, biting on my sleeve as a tear leaked down my mask.

Bane stopped his frantic pacing and crouched by my head, bringing his face close to mine.

"This is why," he said to himself, breathless. "This is why I'm not good for you. I can't—*won't*—keep you away from situations where you'll be *shot*." His voice cracked on the last word, and he gulped.

"I'll be fine," I insisted, fighting to keep my voice even.

"But I'm supposed to protect you!" Bane's voice was tight.

"From what, exactly?" I growled through my teeth, holding his gaze. "Trav Keep? I handled myself against my dad for a long time and did just fine. I can handle the mayor."

Bane withdrew and changed his line of reasoning. "Being around me will get you hurt, or worse."

"Can we not do this tonight?" Chezza asked. "We all choose to be here, day after day, for good reason."

Bane growled and stormed to the corner. "Don't make it sound like this is some fit I throw."

"It *is* a fit you throw. Way too often," Vennie said, not looking away from the Crown City FC match he had replaying on the LUMA.

"How do you make him to stop ranting?" I asked Chezza in a whisper, her disinfectant spray miraculously numbing the pain, too.

"You haven't been taking notes?" she hissed.

But Bane was already going again. "This is in all the comic books, you know. If you love someone, the villain's going to take them and suspend them over electrified water, or experiment on them, or break their spine, or—"

"*Uncle Bane!*"

He froze and turned to me. I beckoned him over, swallowing a groan at the motion. He crouched by my head again, and I glared my twin gaze into his. "I appreciate the sentiment, but you're not being helpful."

He squeezed my hand and mercifully stayed quiet, his sparse attention focused solely on me, so I continued, "I'm your only niece, and I'm dealing with my first gunshot wound, likely of many, so rather than ranting and feeling guilty— when we're all adults capable of making our own decisions and I *chose* to become Silhouette—can you please help me?"

"First bullet wound," Vennie mused. "We'll have to put that in the scrapbook."

Bane ignored him, staring at me, transfixed. "Yes, yeah. Of course. I'm sorry, Mel. You're going to be fine."

"We established that already," Chezza said flatly, helping me sit up. "I patched her up while you were monologuing."

Bane frowned, sheepish. "Right. So . . . should I make brownies?"

I nodded solemnly, and he sprinted for the stairs.

"You should change out of your suit first," I called.

"*Fuck!*" he shouted, and unzipped his jacket.

🔥🔥🔥

As I rested at Chezza's insistence, the events of the last hour caught up with me. I was cradled in the hoodie I always kept in my cubby, my mask long removed, and tried to distract myself with the movie Vennie had pulled up on the LUMA for me. All I saw in my head, however, was the menacing Gold Guard, their eerie goggles and boots thrumming as they chased us down.

The LUMA blurred before me.

"Are you okay?" Chezza asked. "Do you want something for the pain?"

I swallowed back the tears building in my eyes. "It's not that," I said hoarsely.

Chezza lifted one eyebrow. She wouldn't press me to explain. But I wanted to.

"This has to be my fault," I said finally.

Her dark eyes flicked to me, kind and inquisitive. "How so?"

"The mayor clearly wants the Shadow gone, and I doubled Crown's vigilante problem."

"Oh, Mel, no," she insisted, laying an elegant hand on my shoulder. "You are not responsible for the decisions of terrible men. They'll have you think that you are, but it's all on them."

My mouth twisted doubtfully.

Bane traipsed down the stairs in a clean pair of gym shorts and another of his favorite band T-shirts, this one with the spiraled red and white design that looked like a melted peppermint candy. I swiped the last of the moisture from my eyes and Chezza didn't try to continue our conversation. An oven mitt on each hand, Bane set a tray of brownies carefully on top of Chezza's instrument table. "Go on ahead, but don't distress her," she muttered.

Bane glanced at the LUMA. "Why is that bear in jail?"

"He was framed," I said, trying to sit up.

Bane caught my elbow and helped. Then offered me a steaming brownie, which I accepted gratefully, the oven heat pleasant on my fingertips.

Bane held up a letter. Camden's seal gleamed in the corner. "You got mail today."

"Terrific. Will you open it?" I pleaded, reaching for another brownie.

"It's a reminder about your hearing coming up. I didn't realize it was so soon."

My stomach twisted as I thought of the final exams I hadn't started studying for.

"Is it okay if I come to the hearing?" Bane asked. "I'd like to support you."

"Absolutely." But then I frowned. "Does it say who will be sitting on the panel for my hearing?"

"The dean of academics, one of your professors, and of course, Travis Keep, or most respectable mayor and Chair of the Camden College Board of Trustees."

"There it is."

Bane settled at the end of the blue couch. "I wish they'd let me testify on your behalf. I could vouch for you. I'm a good judge of character."

I swallowed a bite of brownie. "You literally just pushed me off a roof."

He pouted, his hair seeming to deflate. "Your health and well-being are my greatest priority. Of course I pushed you off a roof."

The statement settled, and his crooked smile appeared, drawing out my own. Bane leapt from the couch and brought a blanket to tuck firmly under my feet. "Are you okay?"

"I am. I promise."

Bane rubbed his neck, then spoke. "I know that you knew from the beginning that this . . . superhero . . . thing wouldn't be easy. That helping people is dangerous. That's why more people don't do it. You've received your first major reminder that you're not invincible." He stared into the distance, his eyes hazy. "Mine was a knife wound to the shoulder."

"I'm not upset that I got hurt . . ." I began.

"I wondered. And that's the problem," he said. "I thought I recognized the look on your face the minute you got here. The set of your chin . . . I catch it in my mirror each morning. Being Silhouette is dangerous. Deadly. Rescuing innos is valiant, it's the reason I suit up, too, but it's *always* at the risk of your own life. And I value your life more than anyone else's. Most nights the risk isn't that high, but this new Gold Guard changes things. They're designed to stop us. Maybe even kill us. I want you to think: Do you really want to do this?"

I opened my mouth and he stopped me.

"You don't need to tell me. You need to decide for yourself, and I'll trust you. I make this decision every night. You can too. Just . . . Be prepared to see a lot of bad people make good on their promises."

I turned his words over in my mind, running my fingers through my hair. "I'll think about it. Thanks."

Chezza stepped back, the bags under her eyes more prominent under the fluorescent lights. "You're all set, Mel. You should head up to bed. Rest as much as you can for a few days."

I squeezed her hand as she helped me off the table, willing as much of my gratitude as I could into the contact. She smiled.

Bane shadowed me up the stairs, even though I moved slow, like he was sure I'd fall. "Should I expect this talk about hanging up my Silhouette suit every time I'm injured?" I asked over my shoulder.

Bane snorted ruefully. "Nah. Only once or twice a year. I don't even try with Chezza and Vennie anymore, though they're often in significantly less immediate mortal danger than you for me. Everybody needs somebody. Somewhere along the line of trying to keep everyone safe by connecting with no one, I realized that. So I let you know you've got options and leave it at that."

I chewed my lip as he watched me waddle up the stairs with minimal hissing and wincing. As I got to my door, I heard him say, almost too quiet for my Extrahuman hearing, "The world's a better place with you in it. Especially my world."

I slipped into my room and spent the night unable to focus on homework or sleep, instead thinking about all that Bane had said.

CHAPTER
TWENTY-FOUR

"This philosophy assignment is bullshit," Max complained, waving papers through the air in disgust.

I made a noncommittal sound as we traversed the campus sidewalk, overjoyed that after a week of minimal movement, my wound was mostly healed.

Max rambled in accompaniment to my silence, his indignance too intense for the early morning. Finally, I cut him off.

"I need to study. You're welcome to join me after classes. Preferably in a public place where I won't be so tempted to take off your pants."

Max winked but shook his head, and not a single gold-tinged curl moved out of place. "I can't. I have an event to attend tonight, per the mayor's orders. It's the opening session of the Tech Expo. It'll be boring and stuffy, and I'll be speaking as the voice of a young and inspired generation." He rolled his eyes.

"We're doomed," I said. *At least it'll be less eventful than last weekend*, I added silently.

The mayor's PR team had done a truly impressive job of spinning altercation at the amphitheater, saying that it was a live, controlled demonstration of how quickly the Gold Guard could be deployed. Of course no reports reached the news of how they pursued and subsequently failed to capture Silhouette and the Shadow.

"There has to be something good about this event. Like an appetizer bar or something? Shift your perspective. Find a way to enjoy it."

Max abruptly turned and put his hands on my shoulders, jarring me from my fried mozzarella daydream. "You beautiful genius. Come with me. To the event."

I frowned. "You just finished telling me how awful it will be."

"I did," he said, "but *you* don't have to speak. You can enjoy the snacks and keep me grounded."

I chewed the inside of my cheek, more concerned about missing out on a potential evening as Silhouette, though Chezza had said she'd prefer I hold off another day at least.

"Last year there were gourmet mini corndogs and an espresso bar," Max pressed.

"Fine," I conceded. "But you owe me."

Max's grin flashed. "I'll buy you a dress."

"No."

"I'm serious. As a thank you gift."

"I'm coming as moral support," I said. "Not arm candy."

"I know that. But you're doing something exceedingly nice for me. You probably already have something suitable to wear, and you'd look wonderful in jeans and a sweater. Actually, that's my favorite way to see you—never mind." Max rubbed his face, more flummoxed than I'd ever seen him. He took my hand. "Let me start again. You are perfect. I'm nervous and dreading this function tonight. You've graciously agreed to come, so can I please fund a new outfit as a small token of thanks?"

I blinked a few times as the morning class rush swarmed around us.

"Have you ever been so generous with praise in your whole life?" I said finally. "I should have recorded it."

The tension dropped from Max's face. "Is that a yes?"

"Fine. You could have said that this was about wanting to be nice, rather than thinking I look frumpy. I'd believe you. No need to martyr yourself."

He straightened his collar. "Please let me live it down."

I nodded, checking my bag for my next class's textbook.

"Plus," Max added, holding the door to the business building, "I'm still me. It is a little self-serving. I'd *love* to see you in black."

🔥🔥🔥

AFTER CLASSES, I LAZED ON THE LIVING ROOM COUCH WITH Chezza, trying to study as she watched a crime procedural. I'd let her bully curls into my hair while I memorized equations. "This will go with any dress style," she insisted, "but we can't make an informed decision about lip color until we see it."

"Wouldn't any lip color go with black?" I asked.

Chezza tutted. "In theory, but not every color will be *right*."

The doorbell rang.

Chezza squealed with glee and raced me to the foyer.

I beat her there and threw the door open. Nearly out of breath, I lost the rest as I beheld Max on my front step in a steel gray suit with midnight black lapels and gleaming, pointy shoes.

"You are unreal," I breathed. "Do you even own sweatpants?"

Max raised his perfect brows. "They are French and terribly expensive."

"I'll take that," Chezza said, snaking around me to snatch the garment bag from his arms. She grabbed me and called over her shoulder to Max. "Kitchen is to the left. Procure yourself a beverage. I'm excited to see how good you are at dressing someone other than yourself!"

I risked a glance back at him as we neared the top of the stairs. He had taken a few steps toward the kitchen, but his eyes were on me. He smiled.

I missed a step and jolted into Chezza's back. She barely kept us both upright. "Tangina! You couldn't charm the pants off a rattlesnake." She muttered. I hadn't picked up much Tagalog from the hurried chats between Chezza and Vennie, but I knew she'd just cursed.

I sighed. "Max is the one with a gift for that kind of thing."

She ushered me into my bedroom. "Yeah, but he's only sparkly on the outside. You're sparkly on the inside, too. I've talked with Max a dozen times at different events, and I still hardly know anything beyond that immaculate pretty boy wall he has up. You're earnest. That's why people like you."

A response died in my throat as she unzipped the bag and drew out my dress.

Chezza whistled. "I'm going to talk him into switching to a fashion merchandising major. His taste is wasted in politics."

I slid the silky material through my hands. Then tore off my clothes and pulled it over my head. Chezza zipped the back while I appraised myself in the mirror. The neckline plunged sharp and brief down the middle of my chest, with sheer mesh panels over my shoulders to hold it upright. It hugged my waist and flared out over my hips to swirl just above my knees, a frothy petticoat built in. Max had made good on his promise. It was black.

"We need to be *very* creative with where we put my Tempatches," I said.

Chezza flitted to her room and back, offering two pairs of sleek black pumps.

I reached for the ones with the shorter heels.

Chezza nodded her approval. "Red lip for sure," she added.

Being mindful of our timing, I was ready in a few minutes. As I approached the top of the stairs, voices floated to us. Bane was home from work and talked with Max in the foyer. My shoulders loosened, as they were beginning to relax whenever my uncle was around.

I gripped the banister and took a few steps down. Max looked up, mid-laugh from one of Bane's anecdotes, and froze.

His mouth stayed open and he dropped his glass of seltzer.

Bane snapped his hand out with Shadow speed and grabbed it before it was even past his hip and could crash on the ground. Water sloshed over the side and splashed to the tile, splattering Max's pants. He didn't notice. Bane winked at me and turned to the kitchen.

"You look great, Mel. Try not to fall asleep during the speeches, you two." He clapped Max on the shoulder, startling him back into the moment.

"Tell me again how you got out of this?" I scowled at Bane.

"Logan let me know I was politely uninvited. Apparently no one wants to risk me talking with investors."

I slipped my hand around Max's offered arm as I hit the bottom of the stairs. "Thanks for the dress," I murmured.

"No, thank *you*," he said appreciatively as we left.

A black town car idled expectantly in the driveway.

Max shrugged. "I'm encouraged not to drive myself to special events."

He didn't have to say who decreed that.

He helped me into the back seat. I sidled over so he could scoot in next to me.

He heaved a huge sigh as he shut the door and turned to me. Our legs pressed together, mine feeling particularly bare against the smooth silkiness of his dress pants.

"You look breathtaking," Max said. "If that wasn't obvious by how long it just took me to find words. You know normally I can't shut up."

That startled a laugh from me. "Thank you, Max. Really." I smoothed the fabric over my hips. "You did a great job."

Max took my hand in his, staring down at his palm that dwarfed mine. "It's not a good enough thank you for all you've done for me, but it's a start."

I cocked my head. "What do you mean?"

He traced a design on the back of my hand. "Since the moment we met, you made me want to be more myself. I forgot about some of the good parts of me. You make me feel worth more. I want to return the favor."

I leaned my head on his shoulder so he couldn't see my frown. He couldn't know about all of me.

It was packed inside the sprawling opera house, people dressed like jewels all chatting under massive chandeliers. Grumbling, I snagged something bacon-wrapped off a silver tray, halfway to our seats before I realized Max wasn't with me.

I spun. Max remained by the flung-open double doors that lead into the auditorium, his face sallow. He stood rooted to the spot, stiffer than normal, staring unfocused at the elaborately molded ceiling as he crumpled the evening's program in his hands.

I jogged back, calling his name until he snapped his focus back to me.

"Are you trying to bail already?" I asked.

"What?" he asked, blinking rapidly, a sweat shining along his forehead.

"Are you okay?"

Max's eyes darted around the room like a cornered woodland animal. "Can we step away for a minute?"

His voice was tight and tortured. I nodded, making for the front doors. He grabbed my elbow, his fingers clammy.

"Too many people." He surveyed the room frantically, his usually controlled eyes wild, and ducked down a hallway. His shiny shoes clicked impatiently against the marble floor, my heels echoing as I kept up. Max swore and pushed through a door on our left.

I followed him into the dressing room and closed the door. Max unbuttoned his jacket and collapsed onto a small, tufted sofa.

He pinched his forehead between two fingers, his knuckles bloodless.

"Max, *what* is wrong?" I demanded.

He took in slow, shaky breaths through his nose. He had one leg extended before him on the sofa and the other on the floor. I sat and pushed my way between his knees, setting a hand on his forearm. I waited.

Finally, he opened his eyes, revealing a thin sheen across his gaze. Max was scared. I snagged the handkerchief from his breast pocket and dabbed the sweat from his nose and cheeks.

"That's decorative," he said flatly.

I fixed him with a stare that could have withered the most hardy of houseplants, and he snorted. His shoulders relaxed a little away from his ears.

I catalogued his symptoms, comparing them to times I'd seen them or felt them myself. "You're having a panic attack," I said.

Max scowled and tugged his tie loose. "Apparently." He popped open the top two buttons on his shirt.

"Because of speaking in front of all those people?"

He shook his head and closed his eyes again. "Because of all the pressure." He spat the last word through his gritted teeth.

I waited. A few tremors passed through his shoulders.

"Try to take deep breaths," I said. Miraculously, he listened.

"It's never happened in public before," Max admitted finally, quietly. "Never this bad."

Hesitantly, I took his hand away from his face and placed mine within it. He twined his fingers with mine. His mahogany eyes looked a little less troubled, though bloodshot in the corners.

"Pressure from your dad?" I asked.

"Him, and others like him. I have to be a flawless representative of the Keep family. Poised and polite and charming. Handsome and articulate enough to make the press forget about doing any negative reporting on the Gold Guard."

"Too bad you're ugly," I said.

That startled a laugh from him, and he trailed the fingers of his free hand absently up and down my back where the dress's edge cut low as he talked, sending giddy trills to my toes.

"An absolute shame," he agreed. "So, I guess with tonight, and seeing the cameras and realizing it would be on TV, and broadcast to the entire city . . . I've never had to speak publicly on this scale before. The pressure is too much. I freaked out. Am freaking out."

"How long until we should be back out?" I asked.

He checked his watch. "Ten minutes, probably. I can blame it on a wardrobe malfunction."

I grimaced, thinking of the short hem and low neckline of my dress. I tucked a piece of Max's hair that had fallen forward back into place, even though I liked it better loose. "I'm sorry that you're scared, Max. I wish I could help."

He looked at me seriously. "You do."

I gave a tight smile. "Let me find you a glass of water. Get through your speech, then we can go for tacos."

"I'm supposed to be the one bribing you to make it through the evening," he said.

"You can pay for the tacos, if that will make you feel better. Either way, they'll cure your feelings."

Something changed in Max's face, then. His expression soft, he leaned forward and let go of my hand to cup my cheek. I barely heard him say "thank you" before his mouth was on mine.

The kiss dissolved the room around us. It started sweet, but as it went on, urgency and desperation buzzed from his body to mine.

He squeezed my waist tightly, and I pulled myself closer, nearly on top of him on our little couch. He deepened the kiss further, and my breath hitched. Our mouths moved together frantically. I gripped his collar, heat radiating from the exposed skin of his chest. His cologne consumed my senses. We had somewhere to be, but his lips were so soft and comforting that I didn't want to move. It escalated so quickly, in a delicious, delirious way.

Max broke the kiss to look me up and down, panting. He ran both hands from the backs of my shoulders, down my sides, across my hips. I shivered and kissed him again, from his lips to his jaw, and then I nudged his chin and he tilted his head up so I could kiss his neck.

Ten minutes . . . I could work with ten minutes.

Max's hands slipped beneath the skirt of my dress and squeezed. He found my lips with his again.

"I'm tired of having to be so *perfect* all the time," he growled into my mouth.

I wondered exactly what that had to do with our kissing when the doorknob turned.

I withdrew quickly, but there was no fixing Max, sprawled out beneath me, his shirt and tie askew and red lipstick at the corner of his mouth.

Mayor Keep opened the door.

Mortification flushed every inch of my body while Max, in true Max fashion, acted unbothered.

The mayor ran an unimpressed eye over us, a satisfied set

to his mouth. "Max. I wanted to make sure you made it to your seat on time."

Max offered a lazy smile. "Of course. We'll be out in a minute. Thank you."

"Miss Alloway," Mayor Keep said dismissively as he turned away, with the same tone most people reserved for describing cockroaches. "I wasn't expecting to see you again until your hearing."

Given all the time I'd recently spent among criminals, I knew the subtle tone underneath his statement marked it as a threat. The mayor disappeared through the door without another glance.

My head sunk to my hands before the door clicked closed. For some moronic reason, Max began to laugh. His hands sought mine and tried to pry them from my face. When he couldn't succeed, he quieted.

"Mel," he said seriously.

I dropped my hands and looked up at him, forlorn. "Everyone is going to hear about this."

"I am thrilled to be rumored to be romping with a Leo in a broom closet."

I scowled. "This is a dressing room."

He had the audacity to nestle his face against my neck and murmur, "Yes, but the rumors always turn so much sexier."

I groaned, taking a small comfort in the fact that even though Mayor Keep disliked me, maybe his care for Max would keep him from leaking this to the press.

"You're not worried about this?" I untangled myself from Max, and he stomped to the mirror-lined counter and found a tissue, since apparently Max's hankie wasn't for anything practical. I sat before him and dabbed the lipstick from his face as he did up the buttons on his shirt, resetting back to the perfect young man.

"No. I'm not. For the first time I'm doing what I actually want at one of these things. And I'll still make it to my responsibilities on time, and the endorphins have me feeling much better. Maybe we can continue this after the event, back at my place." His roguish wink flipped my stomach before he said more evenly, touching my cheek, "You saved me tonight."

If kissing people was all it took to diffuse tension, then Bane and I were taking the entirely wrong approach to fighting crime. I rolled my eyes and dabbed the perfect lipstick mark I'd made on his neck, hiding in the shadow of his jaw.

He caught my hand. "Leave that one."

I was tempted to argue, but above his mischievous smirk, Max's eyes were warm and sincere. "Please. Let me have this one mark of rebellion."

"Fine, but it's going to take at least five tacos to make me feel better about this."

He helped me from the sofa. "As many as you like, my dear granite face."

"Shut up and go give your speech."

My phone rang as we started down the hallway.

It was Sam. I denied the call and passed Max off to the moderator that would be introducing him on stage. He kissed me on the cheek and I wished him good luck.

Then my phone rang again. Sam. Calling twice.

That had never happened before.

My stomach plummeted. I turned away from the auditorium, swiped a glass of complementary champagne, and tucked myself into a corner of the lobby.

"Hello?" I asked breathlessly.

"Mel," Sam said, despair an angry ache in his voice. "What did you do?"

"What the hell are you talking about?"

"Thatcher's gone missing."

Thatcher. I hadn't thought about Sam's assistant since I'd run out of his house so many weeks ago. I didn't think I'd ever see her again.

"What do you mean?" I demanded, the champagne and heat stamped on my skin from Max's kisses making me brave.

Sam's voice was edged in a snarl of frustration. "She's been distant since you took off. And now she's gone without a trace. I haven't heard from her in days. All that's changed is that you left, so I'll ask you again: *What did you do?*"

I hissed out a breath and drank the last of my champagne in a single swallow, taking an instant to muster words only possible with Sam hundreds of miles away.

"Did it ever occur to you," I said, shakily and quiet, "that maybe you're such a nightmare that she left of her own accord? That this has nothing to do with me?"

Sam was impressively silent for all of three seconds.

"This has gotten out of hand," he spat. Another frustrated growl, and he hung up.

I stared at my phone blankly, at the blinking timer indicating our short call had ended.

A round of applause brought me back to the moment as the crowd welcomed Max onstage.

Worrying my lip at the cold abyss Sam's voice had left in my stomach, I texted Max an apology that I wasn't feeling well and needed to go home. Pummeling sours with the Shadow was the only thing that would fix this night.

CHAPTER
TWENTY-FIVE

"Did you see last night's episode of *Drag Bonanza*?"

I perked at Gem's question, happy to tear my eyes away from the dull passage of the textbook I'd been staring at for fifteen minutes, taking in nothing.

"Yes," I said. Bane and I had watched it to decompress after busting a particularly nasty car theft. "It was amazing. Who do you want to win?"

Gem tapped her bottom lip with one long, neon-green nail. "I *want* Tacky Cardya to win, but I'd put my money on Juggsy Balone."

"What about Isasoleese? She's my favorite."

Gem considered. "She's hilarious, but she really can't dance. I think that'll be her downfall."

We were cloistered in Gem's room. I was sprawled across her bed with a textbook discarded beside me. I stared blankly at the stack of notes I needed to get through in preparation for my exams, the final hurdle between me and my admittance to Camden.

Gem hadn't brought up her run-in with Silhouette, so hopefully she hadn't made any connection between the warped-voice vigilante and me. We had the house to ourselves

—Gem's parents had taken her younger siblings to a fair in a local park to celebrate yet another made up Crown City holiday.

"Ready for a study break?" Gem asked, turning from her desk where she'd been working on an article for the *Chronicle*.

I rolled to my side with a desperate moan. "*Yes.*"

Gem shoved back from the desk. "Perfect. I'm ordering pizza. Pepperoni and bacon sound good?" She jabbed in an order on her phone and absently chucked a rock at me from the pile on her desk.

Catching it easily, I examined the stone in my palm. It was perfectly smooth and soft purple.

"That's amethyst," Gem explained. "Keep it in your pocket for a while."

I smoothed my fingers over the cool stone.

"Okay," Gem said. "Pizza's incoming. Let's get to the good stuff. How are things with Max?"

My face must have belied something salacious, because Gem squealed.

"Gods, that man is good looking. Tell. Me. Everything."

I smiled in spite of myself, pressing the crystal to my forehead. "Max is, well . . . He's a . . . confident lover." I cringed.

Gem shrieked, sending Honors certificates and A+ papers flying from her desk. "That's amazing! Are you in *love?*"

I hid my face in a textbook. "I don't know. Maybe? Kind of? I just know I want to keep doing what we're doing."

Gem nodded enthusiastically. "Do we know if he has any single friends that aren't idiots?"

As we plotted and debated the merits of Max's small friend circle, the doorbell eventually rang.

I followed Gem to the front door. "What about that girl who lives next door to him? She seems nice."

Gem mulled it over. "She's incredibly pretty, but she hasn't talked much the few times I've met her. Like, is she stuck up or shy? Because I can work with the latter . . ."

Gem trailed off before flinging the door open. "Sweet ambrosia!" she crowed, handing cash to the delivery guy that looked hardly old enough to be able to drive. He offered a wavering smile as Gem shut the door.

Gem opened her mouth to continue our conversation when the doorbell chimed again. "Must've forgotten the garlic sauce," she muttered, and turned to reopen the door.

It was the delivery guy again, but a fierce woman glared over his shoulder. It took me a moment to make sense of the pair they made. Gem dropped the pizza, figuring it out a split second after I did.

The woman held a pistol to the delivery boy's head.

"Evening, ladies," she said, crimson lips curling. "Let's go on an adventure."

CHAPTER
TWENTY-SIX

COLD, CHOKING DREAD WORMED UP MY SPINE AS THE PIZZA boy squirmed in the woman's manicured grip.

Gem twitched.

The woman clicked her tongue in disdain, tossing her long braid. Her hair was nearly as light as mine, though much thicker, and her skin was like perfect porcelain. She pressed her gun to the boy's temple, squeezing a wheeze of desperation from him. "Do anything other than exactly what I say, and I'll kill him. I have backup. Follow me." She caught my eyes, then Gem's. "One inch out of line, and I'll empty his head all over the front lawn."

We tailed her down the driveway, Gem shooting wild, bewildered looks at me. Gem's house was the first in a developing subdivision, the only building for acres. No one was present to witness our abduction among the dusty hills besides a few sleepy backhoes and the occasional crushed sports drink bottle that blew across the street.

Behind a battered sedan with a lit pizza shop's sign on top, a nondescript van idled at the curb. As we approached, three men in dark but otherwise unremarkable clothes stepped out to meet us.

One took charge of the pizza boy, knocking him unconscious, then stuffing the poor kid across his own back seat. Another took my arm and shoved me into the van's middle row of seats while Gem was forced into the back. She hissed in indignation as the woman circled to the driver's seat. I stared the entire time, obedient and morose. I could do something, *should* do something, but my mind was blank.

Gem didn't seem to have the same problem.

"Get your hands off me, you soulless sack of—"

"You can hit her," the woman said evenly.

Gem yelped as a fist cracked across her cheekbone. Though I faced forward, I recognized the sound. In the rearview mirror's reflection, blood drained from my face as Gem slumped over behind me, silent beyond quiet sobs. Still, I didn't act. I didn't have my suit, and they had guns. I only had three Tempatches on, and the batteries were fading this late in the day.

I was frozen. Useless.

I thought I was so grand in running off to Crown City, but nothing had changed. I couldn't help myself, let alone anyone else.

The woman adjusted the mirror so I was forced to look at her eyes, extended with sharp wings of black eyeliner.

"Melbourne."

I blinked in recognition.

She smirked. "Good. I was expecting a little more resistance from you, honestly. It's why we grabbed your friend here." As she spoke, the sour assigned to me slipped a zip tie around my wrists. I could snap them off with little effort, but then what? Fear saturated my every limb, leaving them leaden.

The last sour climbed into the passenger seat as the woman continued. "You're indispensable. Your friend"—she whipped her gun around casually to aim at Gem—"is, on the other hand, quite disposable. So behave. There are lots of creative ways to harm her if you need motivation to do as I say."

The van was quiet with militant adherence. I didn't realize she was waiting for my response until she swung her pistol and cracked me between the eyes with the muzzle. Red light exploded across my vision as I cried out. My bound hands flew upward to block another strike that didn't come. I winced back tears.

An edge crept into the woman's voice. "I will dismantle your friend's hands knuckle by knuckle while you watch. Do you understand?"

Eyes watering, I nodded. She turned back as a sack was slipped over my head, and the van lurched into motion. The sour next to me efficiently patted me down, checking for the phone I didn't have. An electric crunch sounded as the one behind us found Gem's and destroyed it.

In the shady escape provided by the hood, I wrestled my panicked thoughts into orderly lines. There were three sours plus the woman. It was likely they all had guns, and Gem wasn't bulletproof. Neither was I, close up and without my suit. Worst of all, I was the goal of this abduction, with Gem simply a pawn to influence my actions. But why? The flimsy zip ties suggested they weren't aware of my Extrahuman alias. A small relief.

"What do you want?" My voice wavered.

"Relax, wild child," the woman said blandly. "Just a big fat check that your uncle should have no problem writing. Behave and you'll be home by morning."

Ransom. Wow.

She shifted as she drove, and the slight heat from my Tempatches and my held breath beneath the sack helped me hear the subtle ringing of an outbound call.

"Cellina," a gruff voice answered.

The woman answered with a scowl. "No resistance here. Everything's prepared on your end?"

A grunt of assent.

"Good. Tell the doctor we won't need him tonight. See you momentarily. Prep the message."

A light beep indicated she'd hung up.

I ground my teeth. This Cellina and her team were sure I wouldn't put up much of a fight, and that they simply had to babysit until my uncle sent them their money. Were they wrong? I had no superhero suit, no mask to hide my identity if I was brazen with my strength. My few Tempatches radiated soft, steady heat, but I didn't know for how much longer. This late in the evening, the summer sun had long since leeched below the horizon, so I wouldn't receive any extra warmth from the weather. My jacket was also back in Gem's room, along with my phone.

Maybe the Shadow would show up. With enough time, I bet Vennie could find us.

The van pulled to a sudden stop, bumping over a curb. We were hauled out and shuffled across the pavement into a structure. I let my feet drag, tripping over them on purpose. A few awkward steps in, one of my guards swore and tugged off the hood so I could see, just like I hoped he would, though Cellina punched me for good measure.

They'd brought us to a dim warehouse. The high walls were lined with mostly empty shelves. Giant, unmarked barrels towered in tall stacks all over, and the place reeked of rust and acid. Machines I couldn't guess the use for were shoved to the corners. Another sour awaited us, rangier and more unkempt than the others, a starburst-shaped scar splattered across the cheek he barely turned to acknowledge Cellina before swiveling back to watch a battered TV resting on a barrel.

They marched us to a small room, removing Gem's hood and tossing her inside first. I struggled in my captors' grip, turning to look at Cellina, hoping for any bit of information that could help us. But the question that escaped me was one of hopeless desperation. Born of wondering how my luck always turned this far south.

"Why me? You could have nabbed any rich kid in Crown City."

Her dark eyes cut to my face, annoyed. The corner of her mouth twisted up as she sauntered toward me. I swept her up and down, noting her intense lipstick, her dark, formal clothes, and a metallic glint at her jacket's lapel. She looked familiar.

Before I could place her, she grabbed me by the throat.

My gasp died as I choked. Cellina squeezed, her nails digging into my neck, then shoved me into the room.

As I hacked and rolled to a stop, Cellina lounged against the door frame. She pressed a fingertip absently to the spot of shiny black resting over her heart. "Why you? None of those brats' parents wear their emotions on their sleeves like your uncle. Anyone with eyes can see that he'd jump in front of a train for you, doll, and all we want is a little money. *Fast.* There's no time to waste with calling lawyers or moving funds or deciding if their kid is worth it."

Cellina continued, "He'd do anything for you, and we just need him to write out some zeroes and sign that stupid name. Now—" She struck like a viper, her gun flashing. She fired over my shoulder. Gem screamed, the sound cutting off abruptly.

"Be good," Cellina commanded, and slammed the door.

Shallow breaths slicing my throat, I whirled. Gem was slumped over, a bullet hole in the wall inches above where her head had been. I could see the white of her eyes as they rounded in shock.

I'd failed us. I should have handled the situation back on Gem's front lawn, bluffing and attacking before they had a chance to move us. I had every scrap of power and knowledge to save us, but not the courage.

My months in Crown City had changed nothing. I was still

useless on my own. Only made extraordinary by those who deigned to interact with me.

A memory flashed in my mind of another small room, miles away and months in the past. Of another woman with my smile and Bane's hair collapsed on the floor, reaching toward me with desperation. That house had been on fire. An inferno buffeted the walls of the little home office, pounding and howling and demanding to be let in. The ghost of her fingers jabbed into my side. *"Move!"* My mom had commanded, then begged. *"Run, Melbourne!"*

I'd managed to get myself out, but I didn't save her. I hadn't known how. I'd thought she'd be right behind me as I tripped through the hallway, the foyer, dodging towering, hungry flames and a blanket of smoke, wondering how our unplanned nap at either end of her couch had morphed into that nightmare. I remembered diving onto the front lawn as firetrucks peeled around the corner, sirens screaming. I realized my mom wasn't with me the instant after the house collapsed on top of her.

The weight of my grief pinned me to our prison's floor.

Sobs built in my chest. Immense, wracking pangs that finally burst past my attempts to dam them. On my hands and knees against the grimy ground, inhuman groans eased from my chest as my tears finally fell.

It didn't take long for my voice to fail, my suffering quieting to noises raw and small. I heard a scraping and sniffling over my hiccups.

Gem scooted to my side, touching her hands to my shoulder.

"Shh, we're going to be okay," she said.

I looked up into her wild hazel eyes. She believed it.

A tiny flame of furious indignation kindled in my chest.

I pushed to my knees, straightening, lifting my torso from the ground with her help. I wavered, but stayed upright.

Everybody needs somebody, Bane had said. The thought of him inspired an image that knocked me breathless.

At that moment, my uncle was likely learning I'd been abducted. Reading an anonymous message threatening my life if he didn't pay. Cellina was right. He did wear his feelings up front, where anyone could see. The ones he wasn't ashamed of. Like he *wanted* the world to know what I meant to him. The color would drain from his face, decimating his uneven smile on the way down. His expression would match my mom's the last time I saw her, stretched in desperate agony.

And he would blame himself.

I knew because it was what he showed me. What he told me. I knew what I meant to him—he made sure of it. And I kept my heart too blocked off to notice.

I could be both at once. The saved and the savior. Mel and Silhouette, together. Independent and supported, strong and loved, and better because of it. I'd been so determined to avoid it that I hadn't seen it happen—I'd let people in. Chezza, Vennie, Max, Gem . . . and strongest of all, Bane. Even Sydney, with his strange holographic legacy. They were like steel cables shot through my heart, holding me together whether I liked it or not.

And I'd been doing them all a vast disservice by not realizing it.

Pressing a sleeve to my cheek to catch the tears, I leaned against Gem. "How bad are you hurt?" I asked hoarsely. She leaned against me, too.

Fear flooded all but a spark of determination in her wide eyes. She shook her head, her freckled face shiny with drying tears. "I'm scraped up and scared, but mostly super annoyed."

"You're very brave," I said, forcing myself to take deep, shuddering breaths and survey our surroundings. The walls of our tiny holding area reached up eight feet into the air, not enclosed with a ceiling. The tile floor was grimy, and all that shared the room with us were a toilet in one corner and a sink and mirror on the opposite wall. They'd turned a bathroom into an impromptu prison cell.

The warehouse as a whole was nondescript. I didn't have a clue where we were, besides being sure we hadn't been in the van long enough to leave Crown City. Worse, it wasn't climate controlled, and the slight nighttime chill in the air bothered me like slow-seeping poison.

I had noticed only one supremely useful detail on our way through the warehouse, and double checked my theory from the limited view of the space I had in our cell. No security cameras. This made sense; it was safer for our captors if none of their actions were at risk of being recorded, but it was also safer for me.

The hazy outline of a plan formed in my head.

"It won't help if I freak out while you're having a melt-down," Gem said. "I'll panic when you're done. How are you?" She pressed her sleeve against the scrapes Cellina's nails had left on my neck, where blood and tears mingled.

I offered a weak smile. "I'm awful."

Gem choked a laugh and rested her head on my shoulder.

As we sat, our captors' muffled voices drifted from nearby. I quirked my head, trying to discern what they said. Slowly, my hearing sharpened.

I swallowed a dry, delirious laugh. Where our bodies touched, Gem's warmth leaked into me, making me warmer and enhancing my strength and senses.

"Can I borrow your sweater? I'm freezing," I asked.

Without hesitation, Gem shifted to untie it from around her waist. Struggling with her hands bound, she draped the long, luxurious red cardigan around my shoulders.

"Thank you," I said quietly.

Outside our cell, a chime sounded from the TV. Cellina hushed her cronies. "This is it," she said tightly. I heard the voice of a familiar news anchor.

"Breaking news coming from the Crown City Police

Department. Minutes ago, the screen over the entrance to Leo Optics was hacked, and a message presented to CIO Brisbane Leo, claiming his niece, Melbourne Alloway, has been kidnapped. The currently unidentified kidnappers are demanding a ransom of . . ."

My throat dried up at the amount, and the method. They'd told him publicly.

"We've been unable to reach Brisbane Leo, but a source at the company informed us that he wasn't in the building when the message was relayed. Leo Optics staff are all working overtime this week in accordance with the Crown City Tech Expo—"

"Adding insult to injury," Cellina purred. They were shedding light that once again my uncle wasn't where he was supposed to be. This attack on Bane was personal. But why?

"They sent him the message," I murmured quietly, only loud enough for Gem to hear.

She looked up at me. "Your uncle's gonna haul ass over here, right?"

I grimaced. "He's not very good at plans," I said, tracing a Tempatch's outline on my thigh through my jeans with a fingertip, not sure how long its gentle heat would last. How long until the Shadow found us?

"They're just whining," a voice grunted from right outside our cell, closer than the others. Though the bathroom had no windows, they were keeping an eye on us somehow. With my slowly building heat, I heard light footsteps walking away.

"Let me know if they get feisty," Cellina said, her voice fading. She must have come to check on us.

Our guard snorted. "Doesn't seem likely."

I scowled.

Gem felt me tense. She nudged me. "Don't worry. Your uncle will show up."

"I know," I said. "But I'm tired of waiting."

I'd been absently calculating a mental list of factors in our favor, and I focused my thoughts on them entirely. There were no cameras, not too many sours, and I had the element of surprise. Most important, they underestimated me . . . and I underestimated Gem. I shifted to stare into her face.

Gem was about to think I'd lost my mind.

I cleared my throat. "Can you *believe* that exam in Advanced Soap Carving Principles?"

Gem stiffened as I echoed her sentiment from the night we met, when she'd needed my help.

"I don't know how I'm going to pass that stupid class," I continued.

I reached over and took her hands in mine. With them tucked between us, I shifted to grab the zip tie binding her wrists. I tugged on it, and she glanced down. I pulled, and the tie snapped, dropping the few inches to the floor. Her dark brows shot together at my show of strength.

"I need your help, because that test will be *unbelievable*," I said. "I need your help with it like when we met up last week. Out front of the library. Remember?"

Recognition dawned across Gem's hazel eyes, her mouth dropping open.

With a rueful grin, I shoved to my feet. Gem shifted to tuck her knees beneath her chin, watching me as she kept her hands together like they were still bound and hid the broken zip tie beneath her shoe. "I'll help you," she said finally. "With the test. *Tell me what you need.*"

I nodded, giving her a meaningful look. "Ugh, it reeks in here. My uncle better come soon." I began to pace, the picture of a frustrated, petulant brat, I hoped.

I walked back and forth, subtle warmth building. I heaved in a deep breath, holding the air before working my stomach muscles like a bellows to shove them out, nursing the small spark of heat in my core. Gem watched me diligently. Painfully slow, my hearing sharpened further.

I paced, and I breathed, and I *listened.*

"Police are on the scene at a warehouse in Edgetown," the broadcast continued. I could barely make out the whine of sirens in the distance.

"What now?" one of the sours asked.

"We wait for further instruction," Cellina replied. There was an agitated scrape of her running her hand over her braid.

I was sure one of the sours watched us, and the rest were distracted a few yards away by the TV.

"Are you sure they won't breach?"

"I doubt it. They know we'll shoot the girls if they do."

"Will we?"

"Gladly," said another voice. It was the scarred sour who had greeted us at the warehouse.

"Easy," Cellina chided. "The client wouldn't like that."

"Who cares? He doesn't call the shots. He thinks we're for-hire thugs anyway. For whenever he has dirty work."

I didn't like the edge in that one's tone. He was unpredictable. We needed to get out of here. Gem cocked her head. She had seemed to realize I was listening, somehow.

I faced the door and eyed the locks I could see through the crack. Five thick bolts. It might take time to break them, and I needed the element of surprise. I had to incapacitate the sours before they got to Gem. And not look much stronger than an average human as I did it.

Our captors could not suspect I was anything other than ordinary. Our escape had to seem hectic and lucky—blamable on adrenaline and desperation.

Emulating that wouldn't be a problem at all.

I scanned our prison again, searching for any option that would make me a few degrees warmer.

I stepped up to the sink and turned the left tap. "It's so gross in here," I muttered, and stuck my hands under the warm spray.

I stared at myself in the mirror, allowing the water to heat as much as it could. I examined my reflection. My hair was flat as usual, and I had smudges under my eyes. Stress and terror lined my face.

Steam rose, fogging the mirror that didn't look quite right. The plain, silvery frame seemed brand new compared to our otherwise grimy prison. So did the row of light bulbs above it. The entire thing was set into the wall, not hung on or screwed into it. A thin border of torn drywall traced the frame.

A faint screech sounded as my hearing enhanced and strength flooded me. It sounded like a chair or stool being settled into. Someone huffed a sigh . . . right in front of me.

The water streamed over my hands. I would only have a minute or two to nullify them all. I was pretty sure I knew what to do. Bane would say it was enough.

The sirens grew louder. Cellina sighed and cocked her pistol. "Start the car."

She was going to act. I needed to, too.

I snapped the zip tie binding my wrists, hiding them under the hot water.

"Get behind the toilet," I said. Gem shifted to follow my instruction. I imagined the sour I was now certain sat on the other side of the two-way mirror tilting his head, baffled by my comment.

With a growl, I hauled back and punched both fists through the glass.

CHAPTER
TWENTY-SEVEN

GEM DIDN'T SCREAM WHEN THE GLASS EXPLODED OUTWARD, OR when I reached through the frame with bloody hands to grab the sour that sat observing us.

I hauled the man through the ruined mirror and punched him between the eyes.

I kicked his gun out of reach and threaded my arms through the sleeves of Gem's sweater. It was bright red and hung to my knees. Pulling its long sleeves over my hands, I gripped the jagged remnants of the mirror's frame.

Ignoring the glass that bit into my palms, I climbed onto the sink and wormed myself through. Outside was a hastily constructed plywood observation room, shielding me momentarily from the other sours, their voices just starting to rise in question over the racket.

I squared my feet as two sours crowded the doorway, massive fists clenched before them. Acting fast, I grabbed the first's arm and shoved him into his friend. I rapped the first on the temple and leapt for the next, ducking beneath his arms. Hurling myself onto his back, I wrapped my arms around his neck, searching for a pressure point. He tore at my arms for a moment before I found the sweet spots along his neck and he wilted.

Behind them, Cellina and the scarred, rangy one stepped into view. Looking furious and incredulous, respectively.

"I must be dreaming," he said with a laugh.

Cellina's hand flew for the holster at her hip.

I dove and spun, kicking her in the thigh. She howled and dropped, then scrambled for my ankles, her nails clawing my skin. The sting had my blood roaring. I dodged back, right into the arms of the rangy sour, who grabbed me by the shoulders and tried to throw me to the floor.

I barely kept my balance and swung wildly, letting my lack of finesse lull him, the sweater whirling around me. He bobbed, dodging my punches and landing several of his own to my chest, my arms, my stomach. More pain blossomed, my Tempatches flooding my wounds with heat and fighting the pain. With a snarl, I released a little Extrahuman strength and clocked him across his scarred cheek, sending him staggering backwards.

He touched where I'd struck him, confusion on his face. His arm twitched, betraying he'd reach for the pistol stowed in his shoulder holster, mere inches from his hand.

I tackled him before he could reach it. He swore profusely as we rolled across the oil-stained floor. With a snarl, he jabbed his elbow into my face, sending stars rocketing across my vision. One scarred hand wrapped around my throat. His other grappled for his gun. As I choked and my sight went dark around the edges, I brought my knee up between his legs as hard as I could.

He roared and his grip loosened, and that's when I grabbed his gun and chucked it away.

His bloodshot glare followed the gun's trajectory. I took advantage of his distraction and whipped my head forward to bash my forehead into his.

Blinding sparkles dotted my vision as pain rocketed through my skull. His eyelids fluttered.

I shoved him off me and rolled to my stomach with a groan, searching for other danger. Cellina had regained her footing and pulled her gun, but wasn't coming for me. Instead, she limped for the bathroom door. For Gem.

She frantically withdrew the first lock, then the next as I struggled to my feet.

I sprinted, panic pushing me to reckless, inhuman speed.

Cellina unhitched the final lock, pulling the door open an inch.

I slammed her head forward against the door, crumpling her into a heap. I grabbed her by the jacket and hauled her out of the way. Her lapel tore in my grip.

My kick threw open the door. Gem stood there, feet planted squarely, wielding the toilet tank's lid like a club.

I waved my hands. "It's me! It's just me!"

Gem waited, not dropping her weapon, as she took in Cellina in a pile at my feet. An echoing voice blared through the warehouse. The police had arrived and were calling for a negotiator.

"We gotta go," I said hoarsely.

She nodded and dropped the lid with a crash.

I tugged her along and we sprinted for the door the sours had dragged us through earlier.

We burst into the night, temporarily blinded by a helicopter's floodlights and red and blue lights from cop cars. A small fleet of guns pointed our way. Our hands shot into the air.

I could barely make sense of the scene before us, because directly in front of me, hair torn forward, shirt rumpled and wearing mismatched dress shoes, was my uncle. He was in the grips of three officers who'd clearly been assigned to restrain him.

The Shadow had never been on his way . . . because Bane believed I could save us.

A choking noise escaped my throat. I stepped toward him without thinking.

"Not until it's secure!" a police lieutenant roared.

Bane shoved the officers aside and threw himself at me. We collided, our arms wrapping around each other, and collapsed to the ground in a heap.

Over my own gasps of relief, Bane repeated my name over and over, his head a comforting weight against the side of my own.

Gem's mom broke through next, having a harder time shaking the cops than Bane.

"God dammit!" the lieutenant yelled, "They are not clear!" He gestured for half his unit to sweep the warehouse. Another handful of officers encircled us. Meanwhile, ambulances loomed and paramedics were headed our way.

Bane hyperventilated, frantically touching my face, my shoulders, then back to strangling me in a hug. He eventually managed a few more words: "Are you hurt?"

My bloody hands twitched, wrapped around his neck. I couldn't speak. Still warm, I pulled back in his grip. He finally held still long enough for me to get a good look at his face. He had the puffy, pinkish look of someone who had been crying for a while.

"What the hell happened in there?" the lieutenant asked, looking from me to Gem.

Bane wrapped an arm around my shoulders and helped me up. "They need medical attention."

Gem's mom nodded in agreement, setting her jaw.

The lieutenant rolled his eyes and ordered his officers aside. "This whole operation is a soup sandwich. I'll have someone talk with you as you're treated." Through the radio, we could hear his unit reporting the warehouse as empty except for a few unconscious bodies. We walked toward an ambulance, Gem and I insisting vehemently that in spite of our appearance, we did not need stretchers.

"Mom," Gem said, "does Dad know I'm okay? You should call him."

She glanced at Bane. Clearly they'd bonded a little over their shared worrying.

"I'll stay right here with them, Mrs. Jellis."

She nodded and stepped away. Bane eyed the approaching paramedics.

The lieutenant beckoned over an officer and stayed resolutely at our side. "We need to know what happened, you two. How did you escape?"

I swallowed. I hadn't thought this far. "We—Uh . . ." I stammered.

"It was Silhouette!" Gem burst out. I tripped, my eyes wide. Luckily, Bane steadied me and the officer fixed his gaze on Gem. She hopped to perch on the lip of the ambulance, nodding confidently. She patted the space next to her, and I sat beside her, numb and confused. Gem moved her hand absently, drawing the same line up and back along the ambulance's interior wall. Touching, I realized, the faint line of my shadow in the dim light. Tracing my silhouette.

"The Silhouette saved us," she said. "It all happened so fast. She busted us out of the room they were holding us in, took out the bad guys, and disappeared."

Bane stammered, an excuse forming on his lips. Gem patted his arm, as if she wasn't the one bleeding from a head wound. "I bet the Shadow's with her. They couldn't have gone far." The lieutenant swore and began shouting into his radio, ignoring us to command his officers to search for the vigilantes. The police all but forgot about us as they scrambled. As Bane and I gaped, Gem tossed her hair and turned her cosmic gaze to a handsome, approaching EMS. "Are you who I can talk to about getting some ice for my head? I think I'm going to need every concussion test you know."

As Bane slowly grinned, I nudged Gem's shoulder. "You're a regular superhero."

She grinned back. "Work hard, Mel, and I might consider taking on a sidekick."

I snorted, shaking my head as a pen light was flashed in my eyes and a blood pressure cuff slipped over my arm. At the sight of my torn-up hands, the EMT went digging for more gauze. Bane sat beside me, keeping his space so I wouldn't feel the coolness from his Tempatches. I spoke so quietly that only his Extrahuman hearing could pick it up.

"It's not like you to be somewhere someone tells you to be."

Bane patted my knee, "You needed your family tonight, more than you needed the Shadow."

I nodded absently, pulling the emergency blanket tighter around me.

"So . . ." Bane said after a while, "Silhouette saved you."

The corner of my mouth quirked up at the same time his did. "Yep."

"I knew she would," he said, and kissed the top of my head.

CHAPTER
TWENTY-EIGHT

As the clock ticked closer to the start of the hour, I put every ounce of effort I had into keeping my face even. Six minutes remained until my academic hearing for formal acceptance into Camden College, and Bane was late.

Across the dark-paneled meeting room, Mayor Keep sat at a wide table, alongside the dean of academics and one of my professors from the summer program. The mayor's dark eyes flicked up, noting I was alone. He laughed to himself and returned to scrolling on his phone, looking for all the world like a cat that had gotten the canary.

Until Max sauntered in, smug as a shark that intended to devour us all.

Mayor Keep went right back to scowling.

"What are you doing here?" I asked.

Max brushed raindrops from his coat. "Supporting you, obviously."

"I told you I didn't want an audience," I said flatly. My nerves were bad enough.

Max grinned. "I'm not an audience. I'm Max Keep."

"And unable to follow directions. The best way to help me would have been to listen."

He frowned just like his father and changed the subject. "Where's Bane?"

I closed my eyes and breathed deep. "Unclear."

Max traced a finger along the still bright cut on my cheek. "Are you okay?"

I'd given him our cover story the night of our abduction, when his frantic calls after the news coverage wouldn't cease. We'd barely had time together since while I frantically completed my exams. "I'm as fine as I can be," I said, scanning the room. I eyed the panelists. Professor Gray-Phoenix flipped through the folder before him. Mayor Keep did not.

"Yeah, right," Max scoffed. "It would have been easier to let Bane pay the ransom. I'm sure he has insurance that would cover the loss." He nudged my shoulder. "Where the hell is he? You can't do this without him."

I finally looked at him again. "I *can't?*"

Max floundered. "Um . . . You *could*, I guess, but his influence is vital—"

"You should find a seat," I said through gritted teeth. He pressed a quick kiss to my unresponsive mouth. He took one of the chairs against the wall, staring daggers at his dad.

The mayor ignored him.

Three minutes left. I smoothed the white collar that poked up from under my sweater.

The door burst open in a flurry, and Bane swept in. He looked around wildly till he spotted me, then briskly stepped to my side, concern etched across his face.

I gave him a small smile. He smoothed his tension away, running both hands through his disheveled hair. When he gave me a hug, my vision snagged a tiny spray of blood on his sleeve.

"Necessary delay," he said, stormy eyes searching mine.

I searched back. "I trust you."

His crooked smile appeared, and he joined me in leaning against the wall at the back of the room.

"You've got this, Mel," he said.

The dean cleared her throat, and I stepped up to the table facing the panel. Bane took a seat at my side.

The dean lifted her glasses and scanned the paper before her. "Melbourne Alloway, we're here discussing your full admittance into Camden College, based on your academic and professional performance during your probationary period. We'll start with your grades." She handed a sheet of paper to her peers. "Which are . . . acceptable."

Professor Gray-Phoenix nodded.

Bane grinned triumphantly, a little too early. He squirmed in his seat. I wanted to kick him.

The dean ran her finger down the agenda. "As for extracurriculars, which we highly encourage here at Camden as a part of a cohesive student experience . . . Have you attended the summer informational sessions for any organizations here on campus?"

"No," I said evenly. "I've been focused on my school work."

Mayor Keep leaned forward. "I don't expect you to cite time commitment as an excuse. What we should be most concerned with is how she spends her evenings. The tabloids will show that you've certainly made time to participate in Camden's social scene."

Anger heated my face. I wished for a hood to disappear into.

The dean ignored his remark, though she did make a note on her pad. "We do understand, Melbourne, that you've had an intense transition in coming to Crown City, though we did hope to see a stronger initial showing from you academically."

Bane cleared his throat. "Mel's been exceedingly patient, and tolerant of my busy schedule and forgetfulness. I'm lucky to have Mel agree to be in my life, just as Crown City is lucky to have her within our mountains, and Camden on her campus." He grinned at me like I was the most amazing thing he'd ever seen.

Mayor Keep laughed. "I'm not sure you're the best judge of that, given your own record at Camden, Mr. Leo."

Bane maintained his peaceful smile. I wondered if he, like I did, vividly imagined strangling the mayor.

The dean sighed. "As heartwarming as that is, your input is not needed or appreciated for this hearing, Mr. Leo." She shot the mayor a look, too. Then returned to me. "You provided a letter of recommendation to support your case, right, Melbourne?"

I nodded as she opened her folder.

"Let's see . . ."

The mayor cut her off. "I think you'll find that a recommendation from my son is a conflict of interest, unfortunately, given their *closeness*—"

"Excuse me," I said. "The letter isn't from Max."

Mayor Keep sat back, his eyes narrow, as the dean skimmed the letter. "From student Jennifer Jellis. Sophomore. Honors program. Presidential Scholarship. Chair of multiple student organizations. She tutors you?"

"That's right," I said. The dean read, twirling the chain on her glasses.

"So you've scraped by in your classes. You haven't joined any clubs," Mayor Keep said, sounding bored. "What *have* you been doing with your time in my city?"

Max shifted with indignation somewhere behind me.

Then I toyed with my collar, letting the light catch on the stolen pin I'd fixed there.

"Oh, you know. Studying. Researching. Learning. I'm not fast at schoolwork but I always figure it out eventually."

The Mayor really looked at me for once, and his eyes widened when he saw the pin glinting at my collar. Shiny black metal shaped like an asterisk, some of the spokes longer than the others.

I'd torn it off Cellina's jacket, and like I suspected, Mayor Keep recognized it. Just like I recognized Cellina from his office on the day I first met him. He had arranged my kidnapping, I was sure of it. To embarrass Bane and scare me out of Crown City, no doubt.

He sat back.

Professor Gray-Phoenix broke the silence. "It's a miracle you're able to stay awake in your classes at all, if that's the case. Speaking of—" He plopped a newspaper on the table. "Why wasn't this hearing delayed? She was *kidnapped* a few days ago, for goodness' sake. I know you two watch the news." He glowered at those on either side of him. He levered an open palm toward me. "She's been recently traumatized, and she's still here, explaining to us why she should be admitted. For me, this was decided when we saw her grades. They're admirable considering the circumstances and I imagine Mel's performance will only improve when she's not constantly under threat of being kicked out." He closed his folder. "Her display of work ethic alone tells me she's a credit to this institution, and we'd be lucky to have her."

Bane pumped a fist. I barely concealed my cringe. The professor hid a laugh, poorly, behind his hand.

The dean scowled at Bane, who at least looked sheepish. She turned her stare to me again, impatience tightening her eyes.

"All fair points from our trustee representative, and also Professor Gray-Phoenix. Why do you want to be enrolled in Camden College, Melbourne?"

I stared at my hands, feeling Bane's concerned stare sweep over me. I laid a hand over a hidden Tempatch under my sleeve, steeling myself. The truth was good, but these people didn't deserve it. I'd tell them anyway, so I could stay here, with Bane.

"A little over a year ago, I decided that college might be the right move for me. My mom—" My throat caught on the word. "She was thrilled. She never went to college, and was so excited for me. We started researching, and brochures started arriving in the mail from all over. This summer . . . we were supposed to take a road trip all across the country to visit campuses and see which might be the best fit."

Bane held out his hand under the table, and I took it. "But then she died before we could go. Attending college helps me feel close to her. To honor her and the dream of mine she believed in so much."

The dean's mouth was cut into a deep frown. "Thank you for sharing that, Melbourne. If you don't mind stepping outside, we'll confer."

🔥🔥🔥

IN THE HALLWAY BEYOND, I WAVED MAX OFF AS HE SILENCED the barrage of calls coming into his cell.

"Go on. You should be at the Tech Expo."

He sighed. "There's no way they won't admit you."

"I know," I said, patting his cheek. "Do you want to be here when your dad comes out and have to explain why you're running late?"

Max blanched, and left.

Bane took his place, having just got off the phone with Logan assuring all was well with Leo Optics's role at the Expo.

As we waited, I eyed the manatee statue and patted it for good luck, reflecting on how much had changed since Max had first walked me through these halls weeks ago.

"You knocked it out of the park," he said. Behind his wondering grin, I saw he was curious.

I squared my shoulders and met his stormy gaze. "When I chose to come to Crown City, all I wanted was to be normal. Ordinary. With an ordinary life of my own. By myself." I swallowed, my voice suddenly hoarse. "And now I don't want that at all," I finished quietly.

Bane swallowed, the look in his eyes triumphant. "I'm honored to be your family," he said, his voice choked. "Everything I have—my resources, all my affection, it's yours."

I smiled, feeling tears well and finally not having the urge to hold them back.

The double doors opened and the panel filed out. The dean approached us.

"Congratulations, Melbourne. You've been admitted to Camden College."

Warm relief flooded my system. I wanted to nap for a year.

Bane whooped how I wanted to, soliciting another scowl from the dean. She ignored him. "Professor Gray-Phoenix has your paperwork. Be sure to turn that in to the registrar so we can get you settled for the fall semester. Welcome to Camden."

She shook my hand and walked off. Mayor Keep was quick to take her place, a vein bulging in his temple. He stepped past me and right up to Bane.

"Face it, Leo. You got lucky today."

Bane faked a thoughtful look, his uneven smile wide. "You know, I don't think luck had anything to do with Mel's success."

The mayor sneered at me, his eyes catching on the asterisk pin at my collar, and stalked off. Bane dropped an arm around my shoulders, looking at me with concern.

The professor approached us next, frowning at the mayor's receding back. "I apologize for that spectacle. The intention of these hearings is good, but it's gotten muddled in recent years. I'm fighting for some changes to the process. In the meantime"—he shook my hand, then Bane's—"I'm in the economics department, Melbourne. I saw in your file you want to join our ranks. I look forward to having you in the fall." He handed me a stack of papers and walked off with a small wave.

"He seems great," Bane mused. "Would you like to celebrate over a gratuitous brunch?" I didn't hear him as I fixated on the first sheet in my pile of paperwork.

"Uncle Bane."

"Hm?" He waited, resting his chin on his fist.

"Now I can move onto campus in the fall! We can still spend time together . . ."

Bane's brow furrowed. "Wait, what are you talking about?"

My heart plummeted to somewhere beneath my stomach. "Do you mind if I stay in Crown City? I know your invitation was for the summer, so if I could stay a little longer until the dorms open. Maybe they have an early move in . . ."

"Mel," Bane said, exasperated. "Lions, how do I continue to be the world's biggest idiot? I invited you to visit over the summer so you wouldn't be overwhelmed or freaked out by my enthusiasm. I want you to stay at the house with us forever. I've always wanted that. Well, as long as you want to."

"I'd love that," I stammered finally, and ripped the on-campus housing form in half. "In that case . . . I have an idea for another document we could sign instead."

🔥🔥🔥

I LIKE ICE CREAM, BUT EATING IT IN SUCH A WAY THAT wouldn't make me feel faint was tough. As Bane and I traipsed across the sidewalk, I layered napkins between my hands and the cone, eating fast enough to ensure none dripped on me. The addition of hot fudge helped immensely, too.

This was the perfect day. Bane at my side, the sun in my face.

Until a nightmare stepped in my way.

At first, the figure, massive and dark against the afternoon sun, looked like your typical sour, but he was much, much worse.

My father leaned into my face, pale eyes wide, breathing hard.

I halted, frozen. Samson Alloway was here, in Crown City. In my safe space. My home. Bane stepped half in front of me, an inarticulate snarl bursting through his teeth.

Sam was taller, and not unfit, but Bane's eyes promised violence. Sam hesitated.

"It's okay," I said, my voice hoarse. I cleared my throat as Bane stepped away but still hovered closed behind me. "What do you want?"

"This joke has gone on long enough," Sam spat. "Great job, Mel. You proved your point."

I narrowed my eyes, hardly feeling the ice cream that dripped down my wrist and puddled on the pavement.

Sam's eyes turned glacier bleak. "Now you can stop imposing on Brisbane, here. Just. Come. Home." He reached for me.

I danced back, avoiding him easily with my enhanced reflexes. His eyes widened.

"You were never my home," I said, my voice low.

Sam gaped. "Everything I've done was to protect you."

"I'm sure there were other ways," Bane growled, his voice deathly quiet.

Sam managed a single syllable of his next garbage argument, but I cut him off. "I'm not coming back," I said. "Not ever. You can do all you want. Stalk me, harass me, call me names, but I'm not going to let you have a single scrap of impact on my life anymore, and I'm never going to share a roof with you ever again."

Sam snapped his mouth shut. He stepped closer, arm extended, like he planned to grab me. I jerked toward him, fast enough that he flinched. "Go ahead and try to make me. Good luck."

Sam hesitated, his face turning crimson. His hand began to shake, but he dropped it.

The tightness in my chest loosened a fraction. "Now," I growled, "get out of our city."

With a final glare, I brushed past him and didn't look back.

After a few seconds, Bane's footsteps caught up with mine, but not before I heard him call back to Sam. "You heard her. Get out."

CHAPTER
TWENTY-NINE

THE NEXT DAY, I SLEPT IN UNTIL SUNLIGHT BLARED THROUGH my windows and insisted I got up. I stared at the ceiling and breathed deep until my shaking stopped and I remember that Sam was gone—Vennie had hacked flight information out of Crown City to be sure—and that I would be staying in the Leo house with my new family for as long as I wanted. It took a while, but finally, exhausted, I forced myself out of bed and trudged down the stairs and pulled up short.

The foyer was uncharacteristically cramped.

A twenty-foot-tall spruce tree dominated the floor next to the staircase, trimmed in twinkling lights and glass ornaments. A stuffed lion with cotton ball angel wings sat crooked at the very top, and a sea of gifts sprawled underneath, all wrapped in metallic paper.

Someone had hauled out the couch and armchairs from the living room to sit before the tree. A stack of bright envelopes with my name on them rested on the couch's arm. I tore one open. It was a seventh birthday card with several bills stuffed into the center and signed by Bane.

I stared, dumbfounded.

Chezza walked in, twirling her hair in one hand, a picture

frame in the other. "Oh good," she said brightly. "Mel's up!" she called over her shoulder.

Bane steamrolled into the room with Vennie close behind.

"Happy birthday and Christmas! Wait—do you celebrate Christmas?" Bane said.

I blinked rapidly, wishing for a cup of coffee. "Not in June, usually. And my birthday isn't for another two months."

Bane set a graduation cap in Upstate City High's trademark red over my bedhead. "I didn't want to wait any longer. We've been planning for weeks already. Today is a celebration of your admission to Camden College, as well as every holiday and major event in your life that I've missed. Congratulations on your high school graduation, by the way."

"It's also in honor of your name change," Chezza said as she set the photo she carried on the front table. It showed Bane and I the day before, in his lawyer's office when I changed my last name to Leo. While I was old enough to not need a legal guardian, I was thrilled to share Bane's last name —to be more officially a family. Chezza frowned at Bane's splotchy complexion in the photo. "You are the ugliest crier, Bane, I swear . . ."

"Lions," I breathed.

Vennie grinned smugly. "Wait till you see the kitchen."

I bolted through the doorway and gaped at the absurdly gigantic spread flooding the counter and kitchen table.

Bane followed and rubbed the back of his head sheepishly. "This is just brunch. Dinner will be Thanksgiving."

Vennie stepped around me and reached for the champagne. "I don't know if you, like, *do* Easter, but I got excited. So, four dozen eggs are hidden all over the backyard... Whenever you're ready."

I sat down hard in a kitchen chair, at a loss for words.

"And, uh, also . . ." Bane continued, shifting his weight.

I raised my eyebrows. "*Also?*"

"I'm throwing a New Year's Eve party tonight."

"People are coming *here*?"

Bane nodded.

"You realize I have celebrated New Year's Eve before?"

"But not Leo style."

Chezza, ever the saint, handed me a steaming mug of coffee.

I finally found words. ". . . It's Sunday." I said lamely.

"Psh," Bane huffed, flapping my protest away with his hand. "Camden's summer program is over. It's officially summer break! Come on, grab a croissant. You have presents to open."

We spent the morning sprawled across the couches, chucking wrapping paper at each other and laughing over mimosas. I stuffed myself with two massive cinnamon rolls and Bane watched like a proud parent as I opened each present. The gifts were all thoughtful and useful, and my favorite was a poster signed by all the women who starred in my favorite spy movie. In addition to the presents, there was a giant sheet cake with a hundred candles. I nearly crushed the red-wrapped shoebox under the tree when I discovered it was full of cartoon valentines from Max and Gem. Definitely overkill, but Bane was enjoying himself. Some of Max's remarks were so explicit that they shocked the tears of gratitude right off my face. By the afternoon, I couldn't articulate my thanks well enough, but the three of them shook me off anyway. They were just happy I was around.

🔥🔥🔥

SEVERAL HOURS, TWO POWER NAPS, AND AN ENTIRE TURKEY dinner later, Gem examined her reflection in the Den's wall of mirrors. She smoothed her sea-foam sequin dress and turned, the hem swishing across our practice mats.

"Your secret hideout is epic. Is this too much for a house party?"

I cocked my head, plucking the vegan leather skirt and jet black, skin-tight sweater Chezza had suggested for me, which matched the onyx earrings that Bane had insisted he would have gotten me for my sixteenth Christmas.

"Not a Leo house party," I said.

"I'm going to need Clare's entire inventory in a size sixteen if everything she has looks this good." Gem sauntered over to Vennie. When she leaned against his station, he didn't seem to mind. "This is the first time I'm seeing anyone besides my family since our little adventure. Remind me of our cover story. Are we sticking with my Silhouette rescue idea?"

Vennie nodded. "That was a stroke of genius, really. And I planted thorough digital evidence that the Shadow was across town busting a robbery. No one should suspect Mel or Bane as their identities for a while."

I turned my back on the mirrors and joined them. "You're sure the kidnappers don't suspect there was something . . . *extra* about my strength?"

Vennie shook his head. "That woman—What was her name, Cellina? She must have done something to the three sours you knocked out. Police questioned them, but they don't remember anything from the forty-eight hours prior to your escape. They can't identify who hired them. Just that they got instructions on where to show up and the promise of a big payday."

"What about Cellina and the scary-looking one?"

"From what I can find hacking the Keep Corp HR files, Cellina no longer works for the mayor's office. She was a temp, and the rest of her squad were all thugs for hire. Maybe Mayor Keep had her on the payroll for tasks he didn't want to dirty his hands with. I managed to get a glimpse of them from a security camera behind the warehouse where they were keeping you."

He pulled up a grainy video clip on the LUMA and cranked the fuzzy audio. In the corner, I could make out

Cellina helping her scarred crony to a nondescript black sedan. While Cellina slammed into the driver's seat looking murderous, the man shouted into a satellite phone. "Leo must have her enrolled in some Krav Maga self-defense bullshit!"

I smirked, but then it faded. "They know the Silhouette didn't save us."

"Not technically," Bane careened down the stairs with a leftover turkey sandwich and a slice of cake in his bare hands. He continued, "They don't know what exactly happened in that bathroom cell. Logan is doing the best they can to keep the media coverage to a minimum. Plus, what are they gonna do? Tell the cops? With your detailed witness accounts of what they look like, they can't go near the authorities. We'll keep an eye out for them in the Crown City crime circles. See if we can't run them out of town. All told, you both did great work."

"Thank you," Gem said with a dramatic curtsy. "Where can I get one of those sandwiches?"

Bane pointed up the stairwell and muttered something intelligible around a mouthful.

Gem patted his arm and picked her way up the stairs, floral combat boots peeking out beneath her glittering hem.

I looked sideways at my uncle. "You don't mind that I told Gem our secret?"

Bane swallowed his massive bite. "If you trust Gem, I trust Gem. You did the absolute best you could under the circumstances. That's all we can ever aim to do."

I chewed my lip. "When you showed up to my hearing yesterday . . . Whose blood was that on your sleeve?"

"I've been a little stir crazy since your abduction. After you went to bed that night, I went out chasing leads." Bane shifted from foot to foot. "I didn't learn anything that night, but one came in in the morning, and I wanted to see if there was anything to it."

"Was there?"

"Eh." He rubbed his chin. "Not related to your kidnapping. No one seems to know anything about that. But this was one of Sprinkles's lackeys. I put on my helmet and caught him finishing a bender at one of the seedier pubs along the lakeshore. He didn't know anything about your kidnapping, but he was antsy. Said all the Crown criminals are because of a new crew that made themselves known in the city."

I frowned, and Bane continued. "If Sprinkles's guys are worried about someone new coming into town, I think we should be, too."

We studied the live feed on the LUMA. It displayed the usually empty great room at the back of the house through a camera Vennie had installed.

Through the feed, we watched Gem wrangle the group of my summer program classmates that Bane had invited. LeRoy handled the rented speaker system with reverence, while Chezza flitted around in heels even higher than normal, pink hair flashing as she strung gold ribbons across doorways leading to the rest of the house, marking them as off limits.

Max was making people light-headed left and right in expertly tailored jeans and a blazer with rhinestone lightning bolts on the shoulders. No doubt he counted on being my midnight kiss.

"You're probably right, but we shouldn't bail on our own party. It would torpedo the Leo family's reputation."

Bane snorted and slung an arm around my shoulders. "And we just got it so sparkly. Fine. Let's go be gracious hosts."

"*Then* Silhouette and the Shadow can do some investigating."

♦♦♦

Balancing a glass of whiskey in one hand, I approached Max from behind and snaked my free arm beneath his jacket and around his waist.

He jolted, and upon realizing it was me, melted down to give me a long kiss. If he kept it up, I'd be light-headed without the alcohol's help.

Someone catcalled at us over the blaring music, and Max pulled back. I gripped his shirt in protest, pouting.

"I need a drink!" he mouthed, the flashing lights tinting us different fluorescent colors. We weaved to the long table we'd set up as a bar where Vennie was holding court, showing off his trick of being able to uncap a beer bottle with his bicep alone. He'd promised us only an hour of being social before he'd disappear back to his virtual life.

I handed Max a glass of champagne and pulled him into a small alcove near one of the tall back windows. We looked out on the wild, dark property, silvered by the moon.

At least, I did. Max was looking at me; I realized when he traced his hand gently over my hair and under my chin.

"How did your presentation at the Expo go yesterday?" I asked. "Did you sufficiently impress all the Silicon Valley gurus who flocked here? Convinced them Crown could give them a run for their piles of money?"

Pursing his lips, Max ran his thumb over mine. "It went off without a hitch, if you'd believe it. When I felt anxious, I thought about you and me in that dressing room. It was the perfect distraction."

I scoffed. "Happy to be of service. I wish I'd been there to see it."

"I wouldn't have been any fun after. Some CEOs from military supply empires swarmed me and took me to dinner. They wanted to hear all about what we plan to do with the Gold Guard project."

I froze, my hand clawing against his chest. "What?"

Max's eyes narrowed as his prideful eyes smiled. "I'm surprised my dad let me field their questions, considering I'm just consulting on the project, but our lab guys aren't terrific at maintaining eye contact and not stammering anyway."

"I—" I made an effort to reform my crumbled smile. "I didn't realize you worked on the Gold Guard."

Max full-on beamed. "Oh, yeah. My dad even worked it out so I'm getting credit at Camden for it. I sit in on all the planning meetings. Who do you think designed their armor? Pretty impressive, right? They'll have the Shadow and that girl —what do they call her, the Shadowette?—in no time."

I shoved my glass into his hand so I wouldn't break it.

"I have to use the bathroom," I muttered, and I bolted, barricading myself in the bathroom of the spare room across the hall from mine where no one would think to look. I braced my hands on either side of the sink, flooded the basin with hot water to splash my face, and focused on turning my expression into an impassive mask that would last the rest of the party.

CHAPTER
THIRTY

A FEW HOURS LATER, AFTER ALL THE STRAGGLERS HAD BEEN sent home in cabs Bane had paid double to drive out to Leo house, we flew across Crown City together as Silhouette and the Shadow. Our earpieces were eerily silent. Both Vennie and Chezza had retired to their beds after the raucous midnight countdown.

Bane followed as I swerved through the city that I knew better every day. After a sprint along the riverfront, I turned and led us deeper downtown, toward Leo Optics. The five towers loomed, glistening reflections of the city's lights as we got closer. Sticking to the shadows, Bane followed as I climbed to the top of an old cathedral turned concert venue that sat directly across the street from Leo Optics. We stood on the roof, surveying the crowd below.

I took in the lit city around us. It was hard to discern the lights from the stars. Honking horns echoed up to us, joined by shouts of people walking from bars to restaurants to taxis and back. People were out and excited after the Tech Expo's keynote address.

Bane propped his chin thoughtfully on his fist, his visor withdrawn.

We were quiet for a long while. Eventually, he broke the silence.

"What did you think when you got my letter?"

I mused. "Before I read it, I hoped it was a secret inheritance."

He guffawed, and we lapsed into silence again.

"I didn't want to admit it for a long time," I said finally, "but your letter made me hopeful. Not for the money or for college. But for a family, which is what I wanted more than anything."

He wrapped an arm around my shoulders.

"No number of gifts can tell you what you've done for me, Mel."

I looked up at him from under my hood, eyebrows raised beneath my mask.

"I was in the kitchen a few weeks ago, refilling my coffee while I was in the middle of catching up on Leo Optics emails. I walked past the living room, and you were napping on the couch . . ." He squeezed my shoulder. "I have *never* felt more content and peaceful than that afternoon. Just knowing you were around in the house, safe and happy, and that I helped with that. I never thought I'd have that feeling of family ever again, either."

I nodded over the lump in my throat, before whispering, "You look a lot like her . . . My mom. You act like her, too. She was calmer—" I choked a laugh. "But you two love the same."

Bane's breath caught. "Thank you," he whispered back.

I tucked my forehead so that it rested against his emblem, which shone faintly in the late-night mist. I remained silent and still for a moment longer. "Max hates the Shadow, and Silhouette by extension."

"Oh, no. I'm so sorry, Toasty," he said. "Is there anything I can do?"

I shook my head in response. "I think I have to break up with him," I said finally, though the thought sliced my heart in half.

He sighed and wrapped his other arm around me, too. "You don't *have* to do anything. But you'd be making a stand for what's right for you, and that's not easy to do. I'm proud of you . . . And maybe he'll come around with time. You never know."

We stayed in pleasant silence on top of that building for a while, observing the city while Leo Optics' massive screen flashed highlights from the Expo.

Our city, I thought, and allowed a smile.

A bulletin flashed across the screen and it shifted to show live coverage.

"Coming to you live from Keep Corp's event venue, we are *thrilled* to announce the last of the Expo's surprises!" The announcer said, "The youngest of one of Crown City's familial scientific legacies is returning home to make a difference for our community."

Bane cocked his head. I straightened, too.

I gasped as a familiar face overtook the screen. Wild hair that was purple instead of black, bright eyes flashing. My heart stopped beating as that stern face stared out at us, identical to an old headline I'd stared at plenty in the past weeks.

The announcer continued, "Doctor Kaylen Kavoh is bringing her groundbreaking work in plant genetics back to Crown City with a new lab, set to be built on the site of her grandmother, Doctor Eleanor Kavoh's, old human genetics lab. Eleanor made many seminal additions to Crown's science scene over three decades ago . . ."

My pulse ratcheted to pound in my ears. The woman on screen was regal and stunningly beautiful. She didn't look much older than me, but . . .

It was . . . not impossible, but infinitely horrifying.

The reporter asked Dr. Kavoh her plans for Crown City.

Her lips, painted the same dark purple as her hair, remained a thin line. "I'm excited to discover what's possible right now. It's still early to plan in too much detail, but who knows? World domination, maybe?"

The reporter laughed good-naturedly.

"I don't like that at all," Bane said.

I grabbed his arm, squeezing with all my superhuman strength. His helmet jerked my way in alarm. "We need to get back to the house, *now*."

"Okay," he said without question.

As we sprinted, I replayed the woman's image in my mind, over and over, making sure I couldn't be wrong.

I nearly jumped out of my skin as we waited for the garage elevator to descend into the Den. Bane removed his helmet, his eyes scanning me worriedly as I ran up to the LUMA and began writing a search sequence across the screen. My chest squeezed tighter and tighter as articles and images populated.

"What is it, Mel?" Bane asked cautiously, coming up behind me.

I pulled open a screen grab from the Tech Expo coverage we'd just watched, and the pixelated photo I'd first seen in Sydney's office a few weeks prior.

Bane gasped. "What the actual—"

I spoke over him. "I don't think that's her granddaughter. That's Eleanor Kavoh. The same one. The one that made Grandpa Extrahuman."

The similarities were eerie, but not obvious if you didn't care to look. Eleanor Kavoh had few pictures on the internet from her life, and from what I could find, Kaylen only had a few more.

But as two people who'd seen plenty of the impossible in our own lives, we knew she was the same.

Bane was shocked into one of his rare silences. He joined me at the LUMA and expanded the sparse website devoted to Kaylen Kavoh and the botany lab she was developing in Crown City. "This is bad. This is so very bad," he muttered. "And I'd bet every lion statue in this house that she's where the new Extrahumans are coming from."

"Should we wake up Chezza and Vennie?"

Bane clicked over to one of the few tabs on the website and chewed his lip. "No. We rest tonight, and we sleep in, so we can start looking into Kavoh in earnest tomorrow."

I peeled my eyes from the screen to look at him. "We can take her," I insisted.

Bane jolted back to the present, shaking his head wildly, his mussed hair flying around his head in a hectic halo.

"I don't want you anywhere near her," he said in an icy tone he hadn't even used on my own father. He conceded, though, and tapped the page he'd pulled up on the LUMA. He mused as we took it in. It was a staff directory for Kavoh Labs, and he pointed to a photo listed directly under Kavoh's.

It was a grainy headshot depicting a striking young man, not much older than me, his pale face defined by hollow cheekbones and an electric blue glare behind thin-rimmed glasses. His mouth was a nearly nonexistent tight line between his sharp cheekbones, like he was uncomfortable having his image captured. Waves of dark hair were half-heartedly tousled away from his forehead, the ends curled behind his ears. He was handsome, in a haunted kind of way. I shivered.

"I'll look into Kavoh," Bane said. "And you can keep tabs on *him*. Her second in command might be easier to get information on."

Next to the picture was a name: Dr. Ian Dove — Head Lab Assistant

I tilted my head to the side, mind wandering as I stared into the opaque glow the LUMA gave his electric eyes.

I grinned, the wicked slice reflecting back at me in the screen. "Happy to."

◊◊◊

TO FIND OUT AS SOON AS THE NEXT INSTALLMENT OF MEL'S story is available, sign up for the newsletter at delaneyandrews.com

ACKNOWLEDGMENTS

Mel's story would not be possible without my amazing parents, Jan and Flip Andrews. Thank you for always encouraging me, and being "proud but not surprised" whenever I come home with news of my newest endeavors. Thanks to you and the best siblings anyone could ask for for always listening when I go on and on about my writing and countless other topics. Mackenzie, Griffin, and Grayce, I love you all so much.

Endless thanks to the many brilliant teachers I've had, especially Renee Juhl, Beth Myers, and Mar'ce Merrell. You are astounding educators and amazing friends.

Thank you to the publishing pros who generously gave their time and expertise when I was just starting out on my publishing journey. Looking at you, Danielle Prielipp and Heather Silvio!

A crew of generous and thorough alpha and beta readers helped this story and believed in Mel in her early iterations. Thank you Mackenzie, Lily, Leeann, Nichole, Caitlin, Claire, Colton, and Katelyn. Also, Brenna, thanks for screaming on the internet with me and for being the one person who won't let Bane get away with his bullshit. Karen and Alexia, thank you for providing insight on some of the characters in this book that don't share the same lived experience as my own. I can't extend enough praise and gratitude to the entire team at Salt and Sage Books, especially Lydia and Rochelle, my absolute dream editors, and Erin, for your formatting prowess that surely saved me hours of crying at my keyboard.

Thank you, Zack, my love, for reading, always believing in me, talking me down, and helping me figure out the mulligan in this book. You're my perfect partner and I'm endlessly grateful to have found you. I love you and our little family.

There's no way I could thank everyone who's had a positive impact on my writing, and though words are my expertise, I'm at a loss to express how much your support means to me. So, to everyone who's been excited for me and never forgotten I called myself a writer, thank you. Lastly, to my readers. It's lovely to meet you. Welcome, and I hope you find a little bit of home in Crown City.

ABOUT THE AUTHOR

Delaney Andrews petitioned her parents to not throw her a fourteenth birthday party, and instead buy her a prolific fantasy authors' entire bibliography. They accepted with slight trepidation, and Delaney is now creating her own catalog of books she hopes a youngster will someday want more than a birthday party. She graduated from Adrian College and lives in metro Detroit with her family. She hates surprises and loves minor league athletic team mascots. You can be friends with her online at delaneyandrews.com and @dj_rhetoric.

twitter.com/dj_rhetoric

instagram.com/dj_rhetoric

tiktok.com/@dj_rhetoric

CPSIA information can be obtained
at www.ICGtesting.com
Printed in the USA
LVHW010010270122
709359LV00006B/167